The Pharaoh's Cat

And Other Stories

Lisanne Norman

PAPER
PHOENIX
PRESS

Pennsville, NJ

PUBLISHED BY
Paper Phoenix Press
A division of eSpec Books
PO Box 242
Pennsville, NJ 08070
www.especbooks.com

Copyright © 2024 Lisanne Norman

ISBN : 978-1-956463-09-5
ISBN (eBook): 978-1-956463-08-8

Cover Images obtained through www.shutterstock.com
Bastet or Bast ancient Egyptian goddess sphynx cat in gothic style hand drawn vector illustration © Croisy
Section Break: calligraphic elements and page decoration © Anja Kaiser

Cover Design: Mike and Danielle McPhail, McP Digital Graphics
Interior Design: Danielle McPhail, McP Digital Graphics

Dedication

For Lynn Andrews and all lovers of fantasy

Original Publications

"The Jewel and the Demon" *Battle Magic*, DAW Books Inc., 1998.

"The Wild Hunt" *Merlin*, DAW Books Inc. Pub., 1999.

"To Catch a Thief" *Spell Fantastic*, DAW Books Inc., 2000.

"Warrior in the Mist" *Historical Hauntings*, DAW Books Inc., 2001.

"Paintbox" *The Mutant Files*, DAW Books Inc., 2001.

"Pharaoh's Cat" *Magic Tails*, DAW Books Inc., 2005.

"Is This Real Enough?" *Fantasy Gone Wrong*, DAW Books Inc., 2006.

CONTENTS

Pharaoh's Cat

IT HAD BEEN A LONG TWO DAYS, DISTINGUISHABLE ONLY FROM THE ONES before by two migraines yesterday and an incipient one now — and the blank page in front of me on the monitor screen.

Out of the corner of my right eye, I caught sight of a svelte, black shape leaping up onto the back of the easy chair that sat beside my desk.

"You shouldn't be up there," I said automatically, assuming it was Shadow.

Svelte? Not even the most doting of cat owners could call my Siamese/Burmese cross that — try big, burly, or, in the vet's words, not mine, a black panther, the veritable Beast of Bodmin Moor.

"Is that any way to greet an old friend?" a plaintive voice asked as I glanced round to see my visitor settle himself on his haunches.

"Tal?" I asked incredulously, swinging my chair round to face him.

"The one and only," he said, stretching out in the luxurious way only a cat can along the narrow chair back. "I see nothing much has changed in the last twelve years."

"Uh." I glanced around the room. "Actually, a lot has," I said, looking back at him. "You, for one."

"I meant the blank page," he said, ears flicking as his tail tip gently rose and fell in faint annoyance.

"And I meant you're... not really here, are you? How could you be?" I muttered to myself, turning back to my screen. "You passed on twelve years ago." Damned migraines, I hated 'em, but the visual disturbances and the odd hallucinations they gave me weren't usually this vivid, nor did they speak.

"Why don't you say it like it is?" he purred, stretching his paws out toward me. "I'm dead, pushing up roses and bluebells on the other side of this window. Nice choice of flowers, by the way, but did those double-glazing cowboys have to squash them when they put the new windows in?"

"You're not here. It's the headache. I can't see you," I muttered to myself like a mantra, reaching for the tobacco tin and lighter on my desk.

From the side of my eye, as I rolled a cigarette, I watched him inch himself forward, paw at a time, just the way he used to do when he was...

"I am always here with you," he said as his damp nose touched the back of my hand and made me jump.

"Geeze, Tal! Don't do that!" I said, clutching for the cigarette before it rolled off my lap onto the floor. "You haven't changed, have you?" I asked, grabbing my lighter and lighting my smoke to steady my nerves. "You never did like me doing anything that didn't involve stroking you."

He wrinkled his nose, whiskers twitching as he pulled his head back a little. "Good job I was disturbed. I always gave you your best ideas, didn't I?"

Swiveling around again, I stared at him. We'd gone through a lot together, he and I, several disastrous relationships and a move of five hundred miles.

"And most of that first book of yours," he added, blinking at me.

"You were the inspiration for it," I agreed gently. *Ah, what the hell,* I thought, reaching out to scritch the sides of his head. If he was a hallucination, he was a damned good one, and right now a dose of Tal was what I needed. I wasn't too grand to have a conversation with him!

"Yes, it is good to see you again," I said, relieved to find the head that reached up to meet me was warm and soft. I don't know what I'd expected, but very much alive was fine by me. "What brings you here now?"

"Your need for a story, obviously," he said, head butting against my hand as he tried to angle the scritches where he wanted them. "The left ear," he purred urgently, cocking his head on that side. "Just behind it... a little more to the right... Now a whisker to the left... Ah!" He dissolved, going so limp he began to slide off the chair back.

In a flurry of black limbs, he scrabbled his way back onto his perch and sat there staring at me accusingly as if it was my fault.

I smothered a chuckle as he sniffed and lifted a front paw, licking it in a very dignified manner.

"So what's the topic of this story you're trying to write?" he asked, wiping his paw across his whiskers. "Must be something about us felines again or I wouldn't have been drawn back to you."

"It is," I said, stubbing the cigarette out in my ashtray. "I'm trying to write a fairy tale."

"Ah, now, that I can help you with," he said, settling down again now that his dignity had been re-established. "I know a lot of good tales. Many's the time I used to sneak out and listen to the storyteller down in the bazaar."

"What bazaar?" I interrupted. "We've never been near one!"

He lifted his nose slightly, putting on the superior air that he'd always been so good at using. "You and I haven't, but there were other lives before the one we shared. Eight to be precise. Now do you want my help or not?"

"Carry on," I said, reaching for my coffee mug. "I'm all ears."

He sniffed, whiskers twitching as he delicately crossed his front paws and rested his chin on them.

"It was 1335 BC in eighteenth-dynasty Egypt and a time of great turbulence. When the heretic Pharaoh Akhenaten had died, he'd left his young daughter Ankhesenamun and her nine-year-old husband as his heirs. Their regent was Ankhesenamun's grandfather Aya, an old man who'd been vizier to Akhenaten. He'd wielded great power while Tutankhamun was only a boy, but now, the young king was eighteen and wanted to rule in his own right, and that didn't suit Aya. One morning, Queen Ankhesenamun was awakened by the wailing of her servants to be told that her husband was feared dead. She rushed to his chamber to find Tutankhamun lying in bed unconscious, a thin trickle of blood coming from his nose and one ear."

Although I knew the popular history of the fabled boy king, I hadn't heard this.

"Don't stop," I said. "You've got me interested."

Have you ever seen a cat smile? I swear they can. Such a self-satisfied look was on Tal's face now.

"The young pharaoh hovered between life and death for two months. Nothing the priests or surgeons could do helped. The queen was distraught. Finally, Tutankhamun died without ever regaining consciousness."

"What had happened to him?"

"No one could, or would, say. When Pharaoh dies, Egypt is without a king until the period of mourning is over. The whole country came to a standstill. The men were forbidden to shave and the women unable to put their hair up. Her grandfather, as the only male relative, naturally took over all the funeral arrangements. Ankhesenamun, too distraught to care, was content to leave him once more in charge. Then, on the evening before the funeral, she went to her grandfather's apartment in the palace to speak to him. Hearing voices, rather than disturb him, she waited outside. But what she heard brought fear into her heart."

Tears coursing unchecked down her cheeks, Ankhesenamun fled through the shadowy palace corridors with no idea of where she was going so long as it took her far from her grandparents' apartments. The strap of one flimsy sandal broke, almost tripping her. Sobbing, she stopped her flight only long enough to pick it up and remove the other; they must never know she'd been near their rooms, that she'd heard them plotting.

Catching the sound of marching feet, she ducked into a darkened doorway, pressing her hand over her mouth — terrified, but it was only the guard changing for the night. Something as natural as that, which scant minutes ago would never have bothered her, now had her hiding like a thief in her own palace. The few lamps that graced the corridors in this time of mourning wavered and guttered briefly as she stood there shaking like a leaf, trying to still her labored breathing in case the guards came her way.

Gradually the tramping of the heavily-soled feet began to fade into the distance and she was able to breathe again. Her enforced stop had brought her to her senses, made her realize she couldn't just keep running. She had to go somewhere, but where? Where in Thebes could she be safe now that she knew the breadth of the treachery her grandfather planned? Stifling a sob, she thought of her husband's mummified body lying alone in the Hall of Purification in the temple complex at nearby Karnak. Then it came to her — her husband's temple! All services to the gods had ceased because of his death. No one would be in the small sanctuary he'd built next to the palace.

Looking around, she tried to get her bearings. From the wall decorations, she realized she'd headed instinctively back toward the royal apartments. Sandals in one hand, she ran. This time, keeping to the shadows, she headed for the hall of pillars that opened out into the main courtyard gardens.

The jewel-bright colors of the lavish murals decorating the white walls and pillars glowed gently in the dim light reflected from the few lamps that were still alight. Darting between the forest of columns, she made her way quickly to the doorway. Though the moon was hidden behind clouds, a quick glance told her the garden was empty. Cautiously, she stepped out into the cool night air, shivering slightly as her bare feet touched the damp grass. Pressing herself against the outer wall of the palace, she inched her way around the perimeter to the gateway. Hearing the laughter of the guards on duty there, she stopped just short, her body huddled against the wall, her ears straining to hear what they were saying.

"Stop scratching your face! Tomorrow, after the funeral, you can get that beard shaved off at the barber's," chuckled one.

"Aye, and so I shall. The wife won't let me near her — says I feel like a sanding sheet!"

More laughter from the first one, and some comments that made her face flush hot with embarrassment even in the darkness.

"D'you think the general's going to move against the regent?" asked the second speaker once his companion's laughter had died down.

"If he does, he'll have to move tomorrow evening," said the first, lowering his voice. "You know the regent — doesn't like to lose anything he considers his."

"True enough. The way Aya acted even before the king's death, you'd have thought he was Pharaoh, not regent. That one's got too many airs and graces! Wouldn't put it past that wily old dog to try marrying the little queen himself, even though he's her grandfather."

"Not if the general can help it!" laughed the first. "At least with him she'd have a man capable of giving her sons, not a dried-up ancient past his best!"

Hot tears scalded her face again as she tried to press herself even flatter against the wall. Was there no pity in this world? Would no one let her mourn her husband in peace? First her grandfather, now the general of her armies wanted her in marriage!

"I think the regent'll get her," said the second, his voice sounding more distant. The tone dropped even further. "The way Pharaoh died, it wasn't natural. No one goes to bed and doesn't wake up like he did. I heard from one of the servants his cheek was bruised, and there was blood on his face. I've seen head wounds like that after battles, haven't you? Sounds to me like someone visited him in the night, and I don't mean the queen."

Silence, followed by the scraping of shod feet and the creaking of leather armor.

"I'd be careful where you repeat that story if I were you," muttered the first. "The general wasn't in Thebes at the time."

"I'm not talking about the general, I meant the regent, Aya. It was a damned shame, I say. He was only a boy. Had the makings of a good king. Looked real promising, especially after that criminal we had last time."

"You're saying too much, just watch your tongue lest you lose that head of yours! Then you won't need no barber! Time we checked the causeway."

The footsteps moved off slowly, leaving her standing there in shock. Was this what the common folk believed happened? There had been a bruise on his cheek, but her grandfather had said it was only because her husband had hit his face on the bed when the illness had struck him down. Could he have been... murdered... by her grandfather, just to get the throne? Though he'd tried to hide it, he hadn't been pleased when Tutankhamun had told him he wanted to rule alone. Many little incidents now came to mind, like the times her grandfather had answered the foreign nobles visiting their court before her husband could.

Could the man she'd trusted to protect her and her husband have betrayed them so completely? Suddenly light-headed, she slumped against the wall with a moan of fear. Would she be next?

"Did you hear that?" demanded one of the guards, his voice just audible.

She shrank further from the gateway into the deep shadows, forcing the thoughts aside.

"Hear what?" asked the other sharply.

"Forget it. Probably just the wind."

Rubbing her hand across her eyes, after a minute or two she peered around the gate into the causeway. The two guards, dwarfed by the huge, seated statues of the goddess Sekhmet, were now halfway along the statue-lined avenue. If she stayed behind them, they couldn't see her until they turned around, then all she needed to do was hide in the shadows till they passed.

"Goddess Mut, Queen of Heaven, protector of Pharaoh, protect me now," she muttered before slowly easing herself through the open gateway and disappearing behind the first statue.

When the guards drew closer to her on their way back to the gate, she clutched the back of the statue, heart-pounding surely loudly enough for them to hear.

"Sekhmet, be my shield," she whispered to herself, holding her breath until they'd passed her and the immediate danger was over.

She remained where she was, face pressed against the cool stone. Memories of hearing her grandfather telling his wife how he intended to become the new pharaoh by marrying her immediately after the funeral chased thoughts of him sneaking into Tutankhamun's chamber to murder him. She pushed herself away and turned toward the sanctuary. It was so close now. She ran, her feet barely touching the cobbles, not stopping till she'd entered the outer courtyard.

It was dark and quiet, just as she'd expected. Hesitantly, she walked through the doorway into the inner court. Fear of a different sort now filled her as she slowly approached the first hall.

Once again, few lamps had been left lit. In the dim, flickering light, the temple looked and felt eerie. Her steps got slower and she had to force herself to walk onward to the even more dimly illuminated inner room. Beyond that was the sealed shrine where the gods lived in their wooden caskets. The scent of orange and cedar incense filled the air, reminding her of the festivals at Karnak she and her husband Tutankhamun had presided over. Her eyes began to fill with tears which she rapidly blinked away as, her footsteps growing ever more hesitant, she approached the shadowed doorway.

She stopped, shocked to see someone in the inner sanctuary! The double doors, supposed to be closed with a seal of clay that could be broken only by the head priest or Pharaoh himself, stood open wide. Light began to glow from the shrine room, spilling out suddenly into the chamber she was in, blinding her with its intensity.

Blinking in the radiance, terrified, she clutched the door frame. Something drew her onward against her will even though her heart was filled with dread.

"Welcome, child." said a low, feminine voice.

Relief flooded through her as a woman suddenly appeared in the doorway. It was only one of the priestesses!

"What troubles you, Queen Ankhesenamun? Why did you call me?" the woman asked.

Puzzled, Ankhesenamun stepped closer, unable to see the face of the priestess because of the intensity of the light.

"I didn't call you," Ankhesenamun said, then stopped as the priestess's head turned slightly and her features became visible—only to blur briefly into those of the lioness Sekhmet before returning to those of a woman.

"I heard your prayers when you were on the causeway," the priestess said. "Why have you need of my protection, Queen of Kemet?"

She whimpered, taking a step backward in terror.

"You have nothing to fear, Ankhesenamun," the woman smiled, holding out her hand. "You need my help else you wouldn't have called on me. Which have you need of—Sekhmet the Avenger, or Bast the Protector?"

"Protection," she stammered, falling to her knees. "My husband is dead... my grandfather Aya wishes to marry me as his first wife... and my servants believe he has killed my husband. If I don't marry Aya, then the general of my armies will take me so he can become Pharaoh!"

Ankhesenamun watched as Mut—for it could be no other than the Mother since this was her shrine—frowned, her features blurring again into those of stern Sekhmet.

"If Aya did kill your husband, this is a serious crime that cannot go unpunished. As Protector and Defender of Pharaoh, I must avenge him. The Rule of Ma'at must be served or Kemet cannot prosper."

"No, Mother! I want only protection for myself," Ankhesenamun wept, her hand reaching instinctively for the goddess's. "I've no wish to be Queen. The husband I loved is dead. Please, let me join your temple, retire from the court and its plots. I don't want to marry my grandfather or the general—I fear for my life!"

The stern face softened as the goddess took Ankhesenamun's hand and drew her to her feet.

"My poor child, you have no choice but to marry one of them. Only through Kemet's queens can the throne be inherited by a pharaoh."

Her broken sandals falling to the floor, Ankhesenamun tried to stem the tears with her free hand.

"There may yet be a way, if you have faith in me," said Mut thoughtfully. "It's not without danger," she warned, her hand gently squeezing the young queen's.

"What must I do?"

"As queen, you're the incarnation of Isis and have a role to play tomorrow in the mortuary rituals for your husband's resurrection so his soul, which is wandering loose now, can return to his body."

Guilt flooded through her. In her fears for her safety, she'd forgotten her final responsibilities to her husband.

"Hush, child. Your fears were natural in the circumstances. Take this and wear it openly," she said, handing Ankhesenamun a small, winged scarab talisman on a chain of gold. "It will show that you are under my protection. Submit to the wedding ceremony, then call on me in the form of Sekhmet-Bast."

Ankhesenamun took the talisman. "But how will..."

"Have faith." Mut smiled, letting her hand go and bending down to retrieve the fallen sandals. "I will make you one of my own, a cat of stone, to be placed in this temple. Statue by day but alive on the nights of the full moon, you will be free of both the regent Aya and the general."

Bewildered, she took the sandals Mut held out to her.

"If your faith is strong, child, your husband will be resurrected—and you will find each other again. Then, my spell will end and you will be reunited to live the rest of your lives in peace. Now put on your sandals and return to your palace. You are under my protection; none will see you or come near you to do you harm as you return. Should they try, I *will* be there."

Mut changed and showed herself in her full glory as Sekhmet the Sorceress, the Wrathful, the Destroyer of Evil.

"Be not afraid, child," she said as Ankhesenamun shrank back. "Only he who killed your husband need fear me. His reign will be short and he will not prosper."

When she risked looking at the goddess again, once more the gentle Mut stood before her.

"Thank you, Mother," she whispered, slipping on her now-restored sandals and getting slowly to her feet. She bowed deeply, fixing the talisman around her neck, then turned and walked from the sanctuary.

The next day passed as if she were in a dream. At the funeral, as Ankhesenamun had expected, Aya wore the leopard skin of the heir and performed the most holy ceremony of Opening-the-Mouth for her husband, designating himself as the heir and future pharaoh.

Once the funeral feast was over, he took her aside to speak to her.

"Egypt needs a king, a mature Pharaoh at her head, Ankhesenamun. You will marry me today."

When she said nothing, he smiled at her, and she shivered to see the naked desire on his face. "You've no need to worry, child. You'll not lose your standing in the court. Have I ever failed you in my years as regent? I'll name you first of my wives, the Great Royal Wife. You'll rule by my side."

She drew herself to her full height. "I rule in my own right, Grandfather," she said formally, trying not to show the revulsion she felt. "I don't accept the need for me to marry you, but if it must be, I will do it for the good of Kemet."

"Don't give me that attitude, girl," he snapped, frowning. "It's thanks to me that you and your young husband kept the throne at all after that criminal, your father, died! There were many who thought they could take it from a mere boy of nine, but not me." He grasped her by the wrist. "Tutankhamun's dead now. Do you really think I'm going to step aside this time? Kemet needs heirs — my heirs — and you'll give them to me."

Up to this moment, she'd hoped against hope she'd been wrong and that her grandfather was an honorable man. That hope had just died.

"Bring your priest, Grandfather," she said quietly. "I've said I'll marry you for the good of our land."

Aya smiled and released her. "You're beginning to see sense," he said, gesturing to one of the servants.

Because technically the court was still in mourning, the ceremony was simple and witnessed only by those few present at the funeral feast.

As Aya leaned toward her to claim his first kiss as her husband, she moved away from him. It was now or never.

"Sekhmet-Bast, give me the strength to do what I must," she said, clutching the amulet with a shaking hand.

A coldness spread throughout her limbs. Cries of shock and terror rang in her ears as the world around her shrank and everyone recoiled away from her. Then her vision faded, as did her hearing, and she knew nothing more.

Her senses awakened one by one. First was hearing, then sight. She felt stiff, and began to stretch languorously, stopping in surprise when she saw the paws of a cat where her arms should have been. The weight of the amulet around her neck reminded her of Mut's promise.

Taking a few moments to examine her new body, she found it pleasing. Then she turned her attention to her surroundings. The room was almost in darkness, yet she could see very clearly. She wasn't in the temple as she'd expected, but in the palace, in the throne room. Surprised, she jumped down from the pedestal on which she sat and padded round to see what changes had taken place.

The room had been redecorated with scenes of Aya's coronation, and there she was, in the place of his First Wife, beside him. Angrily she paced in front of the mural. How dare he put her in the scene when she hadn't been there!

Her rage burned hot and fierce. Raising herself on her haunches, she raked the wall furiously and repeatedly with her claws until she'd obliterated as much of the paintings of herself and Aya as she could reach. Then she padded over to the royal throne and, making sure her claws first punctured its skin of gold, she shredded that. Aya might now be Pharaoh, but she would remind him of her presence.

A grumbling in her belly finally distracted her and she realized she was hungry. Her last meal had been some of the leg of the sacrificial calf at her husband's funeral. Since that had been at least a month ago, it was no wonder she was famished. But where would she find food at night in the palace? Sitting down behind the throne, she began to plan her next moves and was startled to find herself automatically beginning the lick her paws and claws clean of the traces of paint, wood, and gold.

Jumping up, she skittered off toward the doorway and out into the corridor. Her nose, now far more sensitive, caught the whiff of something that smelled deliciously edible. With no more thought than her overwhelming hunger, she began to follow the smell and soon found herself in the courtyard and at the doorway to the kitchens.

The noise of low chattering and the banging of pots and dishes sounded from inside. Sticking her nose round the corner she saw several servants busily clearing up the remains of the night's meal and washing the dishes. Sniffing again, she knew the wonderful aroma came from here. Pangs of hunger gripped her and once again, her belly rumbled. Venturing further in, she tried to locate the source of the smell. It came from a table, the one at the back of the room, furthest from the cooking fires and oven.

Salivating with hunger, she sized up where the servants were and, belly low to the floor, began to creep around the edge of the room. A few steps, then she'd freeze, then a few more.

"Aiiee! A cat!" The woman's shriek almost deafened her.

Plastering herself to the floor, ears flattened against her skull, she stared in equal terror at the servant.

"Where?" demanded a young male voice as she heard his bare feet running in her direction. "Where is it?"

Instincts she didn't know she possessed kicked in as she propelled herself forward under the table and darted for the other side of the room.

"A cat? You're afraid of a cat?" an older male voice laughed.

"It's the Queen, come back to punish us!" wailed the woman, her voice rising in pitch. "Mut save us from her!"

Ankhesenamun cowered there, backing into the corner as she listened to what they were saying.

"Be silent, Meryt," ordered the older man, his voice growing closer. "You'll have the guard in here if you carry on like that. It's only a cat."

"We don't have a cat here, and you know the story of what happened to the Queen..." began the youth.

"Nakht, if you got nothing sensible to say, then keep it to yourself! A cat's a blessing to any house, they keep the vermin away. Where did you see her?"

The voice came closer and suddenly the man's face bobbed into view as he bent down to look along the floor.

"I see it! Over in the corner," he said, grinning. "Go cut the tail and a bit of flesh off that fish on the table up there, Nakht. Put it on a plate and bring it here. Likely that's what drew her in here in the first place."

Meryt began to wail again, and the older man's head disappeared along with his legs as he went over to her. The sound of a sharp slap followed and the wailing abruptly stopped.

"And stay quiet," he ordered. "I don't want you frightening her away!"

Nakht's feet hurried over to where the delicious food smell was coming from, and her attention momentarily diverted by the suddenly increased aroma, she failed to notice that the older man had crept closer. A whiff of his stale sweat made her look back then cower, hissing and spitting, even closer into the corner.

"Here's the fish, Khnum," said the youth, passing the plate down to him.

"Now fetch her a small bowl of water," he said, waving it enticingly. "Here, *miut*," he said gently. "You must be hungry."

She was, but she wasn't stupid enough to let him get close to her yet.

"Block that doorway, Meryt," he said, sighing and putting the plate down. "I don't want her to escape."

Nakht came back and a bowl of water joined the plate on the floor. Hunger pangs were making her feel ill now and that fish — *Ugh,* another part of her mind was saying, Raw *fish!* – smelled so good.

Both men backed off to the other side of the room, joining the woman. Slowly Ankhesenamun relaxed enough to creep forward a few paces, neck stretched out, sniffing. Oh, it smelled so good! Pace by pace she grew closer until she finally reached the dish. Swallowing her pride, she took a delicate nibble, keeping her eyes on the servants. It was as good as any feast dish she'd tasted. In no time at all it was finished, and she was lapping the water to quench her thirst.

"Good girl, good little *miut*," said Khnum, edging closer again.

Looking warily up, she saw he had another dish in his hand.

"Like some more, girl?" he asked, getting down onto his hands and knees and sliding the bowl toward her. "Try this."

She waited for him to push it closer to her but both he and the bowl stayed where they were. Obviously, he wanted her to go to him. Cautiously she came closer, skittering back when one of the others knocked something over on the table where they stood.

"Will you two stand still!" he said over his shoulder to them. "I want her to trust me! We could do with a cat around here, there are too many rats getting into the storeroom."

He sounded friendly, and he could be a permanent source of food for her. Even though she'd only be a cat for three days each month, she'd need to eat if tonight was any gauge.

Trusting the goddess to be as good as her word on the matter of her safety as she had been so far, Ankhesenamun crept closer to investigate the new bowl of meat scraps. Before long, Khnum was stroking her as she tucked into food that appealed more to the human inside her.

"We'll call you Miut, shall we, girl?" he said, scritching her behind the ears.

She stopped eating with surprise as she felt her body begin to vibrate.

A nervous laugh came from Nakht as he ventured closer. "She's purring. Sounds like she likes her name."

"You can't call her 'cat'," objected Meryt from her place by the door.

Purring. *Why should that surprise her?* she thought as she finished off the scraps of roasted duck.

"She likes it," said Khnum, reaching out to pick her up.

Ankhesenamun voiced a protest, surprising herself at the mew that came out. It made Khnum laugh.

"I wouldn't laugh," Nakht said, grabbing the older man's arm. "Look at the talisman she's got around her neck!"

"I told you it was the Queen! The stone cat had one round its neck too!" Meryt wailed, clutching the rag she held to her face in fear.

"Be quiet, woman!" said Khnum, settling Ankhesenamun against his chest with one arm and using his free hand to examine her amulet. "It's a talisman from Mut right enough," he said, letting the winged scarab fall back gently against her fur. "If it is the Queen, even more reason we take care of her." He turned to look at Nakht and Meryt. "You'll say nothing of this, hear me?" he said quietly. "She's got the Mother's protection, it's not for us to interfere. We'll feed her, hide her if necessary. Let the gods see to their own business."

"But what about Pharaoh?" Nakht asked.

Khnum gave him a long look. "You want to argue with Sekhmet?"

"How'd they know Sekhmet was involved?" I asked Tal.

"Who else could turn a person into a cat?" he asked disdainfully.

"Fair enough. What happened when Aya saw that the paintings of him in his throne room had been scratched by a cat they didn't have?"

"Aya was furious. He had the palace searched and all the staff questioned, but Khnum, Nakht, and Meryt said nothing about the cat they called Miut. Of course, they couldn't find her because at dawn's first light she had became a stone statue on her plinth."

"Did she actually go back to the throne room, or was she magically transported there at dawn?"

Tal stretched his forelimbs and frowned at me. "You're rushing me," he said sternly. "She was magically transported there. When the search proved fruitless, Aya called in the workmen to repair the paintings and the throne, but it was a task that took more than one day. You can imagine how he felt when the next day dawned showing all the work had been undone again during the night."

I chuckled, imagining the queen sharpening her claws on the wall and the throne. A small revenge, maybe, but one calculated to drive Pharaoh mad with rage.

"Why didn't he just destroy the statue?"

"He didn't dare because it wore the amulet of Mut, remember?" said Tal. "When the fourth day dawned and there was no damage to the wall or to the throne, Aya began to relax. However, that day, the priests from the temple of Amun came to speak to him about the matter. All of Thebes was talking about how Pharaoh's stone cat came to life and shredded not only his royal throne but the painting of his coronation. This threatened the stability of his reign, the priests said. They began to ask him awkward questions."

"I'll bet they did! Was that the revenge Sekhmet had in mind all along?"

"Possibly," he said. "Aya reassured them, and they finally left. That night, however, when everyone was asleep, he took the statue to the small temple of Mut and placed it in a niche there, telling the priests that he was giving it to them as an offering to the goddess. They had to accept it because it had the talisman of Mut round its neck."

"So what did Ankhesenamun do when the next full moon came? Did she manage to get into the kitchens and get fed? Did she go back to the throne room?"

"Good job patience goes with being a cat," sniffed Tal archly. "By the time Ankhesenamun had visited the throne room for the third time, Aya decided enough was enough and moved his court and his capital to the city of Memphis."

"So what happened to Ankhesenamun? Aya would have closed down the palace in Thebes."

"Not completely. He left a skeleton staff there, including the kitchen servants, so Ankhesenamun was still able to eat there for the next few years. Needless to say, she did scratch the mural again but it was never repaired. Time passed, and when the palace was finally closed, Khnum came to the temple on the first night of the full moon to take her to his own home and feed her there even though by now the priests were aware of her and left food out too. When Khnum died, she mourned him, but as she'd already put in a good word for him with Mut, she knew his afterlife was assured."

"So how does this story end?" I asked. "Does she find her prince again?"

"Pharaoh," he corrected me. "Whose tale is this? Let me tell it my way! Gradually the temple fell into disuse, and even the townsfolk who lived nearby began to forget the story of how a queen had become a pharaoh's stone cat. Ankhesenamun now had to wander further afield to find her food but her amulet still served her well, until one night nearly fifty years later. A new pharaoh was about to be crowned, one called Ramesses II."

As soon as she woke, Ankhesenamun jumped down from her niche and picked her way out through the rubble of her temple until she was where the outer courtyards had been. Turning around, she saw that in the intervening days even more of the building had been taken apart to be reused elsewhere, likely to finish off the mortuary temple for King Seti, Ramesses's father. The outer walls had long since gone, as had the earthly presences of the gods Amun, Mut, and Khonsu from their inner shrine.

On the wind, she could smell the scents of rich food and hear the voices of happiness and laughter. The late Pharaoh Seti had obviously been buried and the time of mourning was now over. Following the noises and the smells, she headed into the narrow streets, keeping always to the deepest shadows. She'd witnessed many funerals—all pharaohs came to Thebes to make their final journey to the West and their tombs in the Valley of the Kings. Though food would be plentiful for many days now, as was the custom, the city would also be full of all the court officials come from Memphis, including the soon-to-be-crowned new pharaoh. That meant she had to be doubly careful since, after the long period of national mourning, the people were ready to celebrate to the full on the free beer donated by their next ruler.

She was in the sector she knew best, that closest to the temple complex of Karnak, the main home to the gods to whom her small temple had been dedicated. There was an inn there where sympathetic drudges would often feed her scraps, and a small bowl of milk if she was very lucky.

Staying close to the walls, she kept her eyes on the groups of singing and dancing revelers. Snatches of songs floated after one such group of young men, obviously from the court by the richness of their clothes and jewelry, and she smiled to herself, remembering Khnum and the others from the palace kitchens. On feast days they had always sung as they worked. Compared with her necessary trips into the city now, those days seemed uncomplicated and almost happy. She tried not to think that before many hours had passed, some of these young men would be reeling drunk and likely to come to blows with each other, and the life of a cat, even one wearing Mut's talisman, would mean little to them.

Hurrying now, she wound her way past the shops, newly opened after the seventy days of mourning, their goods spilling out into the street. Shopkeepers stood in brightly lit doorways, calling to the revelers, enticing them to come and inspect their wares. All was noise and bustle, the air filled with the scents of the perfumed courtiers and the sweat of the common people, all overlaid by the smell of roasting meats.

The inn was just ahead, and hunger had gripped her belly in a tight fist of pain—it was the first night of the full moon and she was starving. Thankfully the inn was just ahead, because the smell of food was more than she could resist. Outside the entrance, several men of various ages stood arguing. She stopped, crouching against the wall watching them as their discussion grew more heated. Creeping closer, she tried to make out what was happening.

"You got no right coming down here and acting the Memphis lordlings over us!" one burly commoner said angrily. "Where are you when we need help from the court? At Memphis, that's where! We're only good enough for you when you come here at festival times!"

"Let's go elsewhere, Merire," said one of the young nobles. "It isn't worth the trouble."

"That's it, go back to the palace!" jeered the commoner's companion. "Drink your own beer and leave us ours, that's right, isn't it, Didia?"

"We're not looking for trouble," said Merire in a reasonable tone. "We just want to buy a meal, that's all."

Ankhesenamun froze. His voice... there was something about it that drew her a few steps closer.

"The court's still too somber after the funeral," said the third courtier. "We wanted to get out and relax, where's the harm in that?"

"Where's the harm?" demanded Didia belligerently, reaching out to push Merire further into the street by prodding his chest. "I'll tell you where the harm is! You people with your fancy clothes," he said, his look raking the young man up and down, taking in his fine pleated linen kilt and the beadwork collar he wore. "You come down here and make for our women, talking sweet to them, taking them off to your lodgings until you go back to Memphis. Then you just throw them aside like used toys!"

"Like used toys," his companion agreed, crowding Merire. "Leave our women alone."

"I assure you, we're not interested in your women," began Merire.

"And I said leave!" bellowed Didia, reaching again to push him.

Merire caught his hand, forcing it back against the wrist, making the man cry out in pain.

"And I said we're not looking for trouble, or your women," said Merire softly as his friends stepped forward to back him up. "Now step out of the way unless you want to make an issue of this. I'm sure the city guards would be interested." He let Didia go, standing with his body held ready for trouble.

The second commoner stepped back hurriedly, realizing the three young men were all well-muscled and not soft-living courtiers.

"Maybe we were a little hasty," said Didia sullenly, rubbing his wrist as he slouched aside.

"You were," said Merire, stepping past him and into the inn, followed by his two friends.

Silent as a shadow, Ankhesenamun followed them in, hiding under a table as she watched the owner catch sight of his noble customers and rush to greet them. They were shown to a small alcove and seated at the best table in the inn.

While they ordered, she darted through the forests of legs to their table and crouched beneath it for a moment before carefully sniffing at each of them in turn. Once again, there was something about the scent of the one called Merire that was vaguely familiar. It drew her to him.

"That could have been nasty back there," said one of his companions. "We should have just left it, Merire."

"You worry too much, Hori," said Merire. "We've every right to come into the town and eat here if we wish. I can see his point, though," he conceded. "He isn't to know that we aren't looking for entertainment with local women."

"Speak for yourself!" laughed the other one. "Personally, if I see a comely young girl..."

"You'll leave her alone, Simontu," said Merire sternly. "What you do in Memphis is one thing, but coming here and womanizing when we know we're leaving in a few days is not right."

"Your beer, sirs," said a female voice she recognized.

She heard the thump as the three cups were placed on the table. "I see you've found an admirer already."

"Excuse me?" said Merire, obviously confused.

"Miut's found you," she said. "She's under your table. Shall I bring her food here with yours?"

A head bobbed down to look at her. Startled, her back automatically arched and her fur began to bristle.

"A cat!" he exclaimed, reaching a hand toward her.

"Our Miut isn't just any cat," the girl said. "She's protected by Mut."

Ankhesenamun relaxed her stance, recognizing him. She stretched her neck forward to sniff his fingers.

"So I see," said Merire, letting her sniff. "Yes, bring her some food."

"Don't encourage it," said Simontu. "These city cats, bags of bones the lot of them. You never know where they've been."

"This one looks quite respectable," said Merire, growing bold enough to stroke her head. "And she's wearing an amulet, an expensive one from the looks of it."

Ankhesenamun ventured closer. Every sense she had was saying she could trust this man.

Another head bobbed down to look at her.

"She certainly looks well-fed," said Hopi. "If she eats here, then the food must be good!"

Merire chuckled. Ankhesenamun moved closer still, butting his hand with her head as she began to purr.

"How do you know she's a female?" he asked.

"All cats are," said Hopi easily, sitting up. "Pick her up, let's have a look at the amulet she's wearing."

Merire reached down with his other hand and scooped her up. The surprise of it made her mew and struggle at first but as he held her close and told Simontu to move up on the bench, she grew still. There was something about this man that she liked, she decided as he set her down on the end of the bench beside him.

"So you're Miut, are you?" he asked, scratching her under her chin.

She purred happily, lifting her head so he could reach her throat more easily.

"Mut's talisman," said Hopi, leaning across the table. "No commoner could afford a piece of jewelry as expensive as that."

"She might be a temple cat," Merire said, bending forward for a closer look. "We're not far from the main one at Karnak."

The whole amulet was shorter than the length of his thumb with the scarab itself made of a beautifully carved lapis lazuli set in gold, with a solar disc of red carnelian at its head. The minute feathers on the upward curving wings were formed of inlays of turquoise, lapis, and red carnelian separated by thin strips of gold. Falcon's legs, separated by the bird's spread tail feathers, gripped the sacred *shen* symbols of eternity. It was a talisman fit to grace the throat of any pharaoh, or his queen.

"It's *kheper*—a symbol of transformation," he said thoughtfully as he continued to tickle Miut under the chin. "Such a talisman ensures the protection of the wearer and is a spell to make her heart receptive to a divine judgement."

"If she was a temple cat, they'd feed her," said Simontu, leaning back against the wall behind him. "More likely she belongs to some minor Theban noble and is just slumming it down here."

"I doubt that," said Merire, caressing her head as she butted his hand again. "You're a real mystery cat, eh, Miut?"

The serving girl came back with their meals and bowls of food and water for her.

"I see you've made friends," she grinned, putting the bowls on the bench beside Ankhesenamun.

"Yes. Do you know where's she from?"

"I don't rightly know for sure. Local talk has it she lives in the ruins of the temple where the old palace was in the days of Tutankhamun."

Startled, Ankhesenamun looked up at Merire just as he looked down at her. Their eyes locked only briefly but it was long enough to send a surge of joy through her heart. It was her husband, born once more into the world of the living!

"How did she come by the amulet?" he asked.

"I don't know. My father would have it that she's a queen turned into a stone cat by Mut when Aya became Pharaoh after Tutankhamun died," she laughed. "Full of strange tales, my father is."

"Can you ask your father to come and tell us the story?" he asked.

"I'll ask," she said, glancing around the room, "but you may have to wait until we're less busy."

"We'll wait," Merire assured her.

Simontu groaned. "Merire, you're not going to keep us sitting here all evening just to hear some tale about a magical cat, are you?"

"I'd like to hear it too," said Hopi.

"I *have* to hear the story," said Merire, a strange look crossing his face as he looked back at Miut. "I don't know why, but it's important to me."

Ankhesenamun's heart began to beat faster. He knew she was important to him! As she ate, she began to pray to Mut that he'd remember who he was and recognize her.

"I know you're interested in entering the priesthood but isn't this carrying it a bit too far?" said Simontu. "We're supposed to be celebrating tonight!"

Merire gave her head a last scritch then turned to eat his meal. "If you don't want to stay, you can go back without me," he said. "I don't mind."

"Not after what happened outside," said Simontu. "We stay together."

As they ate, Ankhesenamun studied Merire's face. Now she knew what to look for, she could see the resemblance to her late husband. This new face he bore was as handsome as his last one had been. Dark hair, worn shoulder-length, framed an oval face. The nose was slim, and like her husband, his almond-shaped eyes were outlined in dark paint. His full lips spread in a smile as he noticed her studying him.

He bent his head toward her. "Like what you see, Miut?" he whispered, a faint chuckle underscoring his words.

Indeed she did, and she mewed her appreciation.

Laughing, he sat up and continued eating.

The owner of the inn came over not long after they'd finished and Ankhesenamun, ears pricked wide, sat and listened to the story as eagerly as Merire and Hopi. The innkeeper knew all the main facts, but he did embroider the tale, saying she had been the avenging spirit of Sekhmet as well as Queen Ankhesenamun taking revenge on her grandfather Aya for killing her husband, King Tutankhamun. He didn't, however, know the final part of the story, that she was waiting only for her lost love to be reborn so they could be reunited.

When the innkeeper had gone, Simontu laughed. "You two were really taken in by his story, weren't you?"

"How would you explain the amulet?" asked Hopi.

"Some child probably found it in the palace ruins and put it around her neck."

"A child would more likely give it to their mother to sell," said Merire thoughtfully, moving the empty bowls onto the table to give Miut more room. "And the story would explain why no one has tried to steal it from her."

Simontu shrugged. "I don't care one way or the other," he said.

"What a terrible fate, though," said Hopi, shaking his head. "To be condemned to a life as a stone cat except for the nights of the full moon."

"Better than marrying your grandfather," said Merire, picking Miut up. "There's something about the story that rings true. Are we ready to leave?"

"You're not taking her back, are you?" asked Simontu, exasperated.

Merire hesitated. He'd automatically picked her up because he knew he couldn't leave her behind. "Yes," he said unequivocally.

"Cats are worshiped in the north, Simontu," said Hopi as they all rose. "Either as Sekhmet or Bast."

"Well keep her away from me! She's probably covered in fleas. And don't blame me if you wake up and find her straddling your chest, fangs bared as she did to Aya in the story!" said Simontu.

That's not true! I only scratched the wall and the throne! she thought frantically. What if he believed the story and left her behind? Her blood ran cold as something else occurred to her. How could she possibly tell him who she was? When dawn came, would she become stone again? How *was* Mut's spell to be broken? She let out a wail of anguish as she realized she had no way to tell Merire anything.

"Sounds like she's not too happy to be leaving," said Hopi as they stepped out into the night.

Head turned to answer his friend, Merire didn't see Didia and the flash of his knife as it sliced toward him, but Ankhesenamun did.

How dare he threaten the life of her beloved, she thought as, throwing caution to the wind, she kicked back against Merire's chest and launched herself at Didia's face, turning in mid-leap into a spitting ball of feral rage.

Instantly alerted to their danger, the three friends turned to face their attacker. Didia's knife clattered to the ground as he screamed in pain, desperately trying to dislodge the cat that was savaging his throat and face.

A circle of jostling, curious passers-by was already beginning to gather. Merire hesitated, torn between rescuing the cat and making sure Didia didn't harm any of them.

"Get the knife," he said to Hopi, making a dive for Didia just as the man tore Miut loose and flung her aside.

Still screeching, Didia was holding his hands over his face and backing away, blood pouring from between his fingers. Merire grabbed the wounded man by the arm, looking around to make sure no one else was waiting to attack them.

"Fetch the guard," he ordered the nearest man. "He tried to stab us. Hopi, where's Miut?" he asked anxiously, knowing that Didia was no threat to them now.

"She's hurt, Merire," said Hopi from behind him. "When he threw her off, she hit the wall."

Dread filled him as he glanced over his shoulder to where the cat lay crumpled on the ground at the foot of the wall.

"It's only a cat, Merire," said Simontu.

"It's a cat that just saved my life!" he said angrily, thrusting Didia at him and running over to Hopi.

Oblivious to everything else, he knelt in the dirt beside her small, crumpled body. She was still alive, but her breathing was ragged and a thin trickle of blood from her mouth was pooling onto the ground beside her.

Ankhesenamun lay there panting. The pain was so great it filled her completely. She couldn't understand why this had happened. Wasn't she protected by Mut? The goddess had said no harm could come to her, and despite many brushes with trouble, she'd been safe, until now. To be so close to her love and then for this to happen! Then a calmness settled over her. He was still alive and that was what mattered most. She had seen him again, been held in his arms, and if that was all the goddess could give her, it was enough. Her senses dimmed and darkness claimed her.

"I think she's dead," said Hopi quietly.

"She can't be!" said Merire, tears springing to his eyes as his hand gently stroked her head. "I won't let her die!"

"There's nothing we can do for her," Hopi said regretfully. "It was a brave thing she did, risking her life to save yours."

"I can take her to the Karnak temple," he said, reaching forward to pick her up. "There's a physician there. She wears Mut's amulet—they'll have to help her! King Seti believed them to be manifestations of the goddess!"

"The guard's here," said Simontu, his shadow falling over them. "I'm sorry she's dying, Merire," he began.

"You tell them what happened," said Hopi, giving him Didia's knife. "I'm going with Merire to the temple."

Cradling her carefully in his arms, Merire pushed the curious townsfolk aside and ran like one possessed, not knowing why the small form whose life was slowly ebbing away was so important to him, just knowing that it was.

At the temple, now that the funeral was over, the elaborate preparations for Ramesses's coronation were underway. The priests were none too pleased to be disturbed by a couple of distraught young men, one of them bloodstained and carrying an unconscious cat. Then they saw the amulet and recognized Merire as the son of a prominent court noble and suddenly, Merire and his friend had the attention they needed.

"There's little I can do for her," admitted the physician after examining her. "She's gravely injured."

"What about the goddess? Mut gave her the amulet, surely she can cure her?" Merire demanded.

"But the sanctuary is sealed," objected the physician. "It can't be opened until morning, and then only by the head priest."

"Then get him! Cats are sacred to Sekhmet as well as Mut! Pharaoh Seti believed they were divine! She saved my life, I can't let her die!" he said angrily, carefully picking up her limp and unconscious body.

Sighing, the physician gestured to one of the acolytes who rushed off to find him.

It took several minutes, but at last, the head priest of Amun arrived. "This is most irregular, " he began.

"Look at the amulet," said Merire, pointing to the bloodstained winged *kheper* still round Miut's neck. "Isn't that enough to tell you she's beloved by Mut?"

The priest paled and turned on the physician. "Why wasn't I told of this?" he demanded.

"Is it important?" asked the physician, puzzled. "Agreed it's an expensive winged scarab but..."

"That amulet is unique," said the priest as he ushered Merire out into the corridor. "Especially when worn by no ordinary cat! Don't you know the story of Ankhesenamun, Tutankhamun's Queen?"

"Wait here, Hopi," ordered Merire as they left the room.

Merire held her close as he and the acolyte hurried after the priest through successively smaller and darker chambers until they reached the innermost sanctuary of Karnak. He suddenly knew without doubt that Miut was more than she seemed, that the tale of the Pharaoh's stone cat was indeed true, and this was Queen Ankhesenamun.

"Mut, please don't take her from me," he whispered, holding her close as the priest broke the clay seal on the cord fastening the double doors leading to the inner shrines of Amun, Mut, and their son Khonsu.

The head priest flung the doors wide, and by the light of the sanctuary's single lamp, Merire watched him hurry over to the wooden shrine housing the image of the goddess Mut. As the priest bowed his head and began intoning a hymn to the goddess, he was filled with a sense of foreknowledge He recognized the room, and the images of the gods and goddesses!

His common sense told him it was impossible. This was the holy of holies in the temple, no one but Pharaoh or the head priest was allowed to enter here. The knowledge was little comfort as he stepped hesitantly into the room. Suddenly light-headed, the walls seemed to swirl around him — he was the one intoning the hymn as he reverently washed the statues in water from the sacred lake, he was drying them, then anointing them with sweet-smelling oils.

The room seemed to lurch once more, and he was back, listening to the priest.

"Hail to thee, Sekhmet-Bast-Rê, Mother of the gods, Bearer of Wings, Mistress of the Two Crowns..."

Merire could feel the small heart beating against his bare chest beginning to slow. "Don't give up!" he whispered frantically, bending down to touch his lips to the small, furred head. "Please, Ankhesenamun, you must live!" For a brief moment, wisps of half-remembered memories tugged at his conscious mind.

"Great one of magic in the Boat of Millions, Holy one…" intoned the priest.

Her heartbeat faltered, then strengthened, but the rhythm was different. Now it matched the beat of his own heart. Even as he wondered about this, Merire felt Miut become heavier in his arms. Her breathing slowed till it also matched his. Surprised, he adjusted her in his arms, watching her as she grew heavier yet. Suddenly her form seemed to blur and lengthen. He blinked, then let out a cry of shock as he found himself no longer holding a cat, but a young woman—one of extreme beauty.

The priest faltered in his prayer and looked around, then fell to his knees before the image of Mut.

"Praise to thee, oh daughter of Rê, Mother in the horizon of heaven!" the priest said fervently. "Thy justice has been done!"

Ankhesenamun stirred, moaning softly as she opened her eyes.

They all heard the gentle voice that filled the chamber. "Did I not tell you that your faith would be rewarded, child?"

"It is you," Merire whispered, looking down at a face he now remembered well, a face of delicate features framed by a fall of rich, dark hair. Her deep brown eyes gazed lovingly back at him.

"Are you still hurt?" he asked anxiously, feeling such joy fill his heart that he wondered it didn't burst.

"I'm well, now we're together again," she smiled, reaching a delicate hand up to touch his face in wonder. Her eyes filled with tears. "I missed you so much," she whispered.

"I remember very little," he confessed, turning his head to kiss her hand. "Only our love for each other."

"That's as it should be. Thanks to Mut, we have a new life together now," she said, her hand curling around his neck and drawing his head down to kiss him.

The priest scrambled to his feet and slipped out of the sanctuary. Outside they could hear him sending the acolyte for a robe for her.

Reluctantly Merire broke the kiss to look over to the statue of Mut. "Thank you, Mut," he said. "I had intended to enter the priesthood before this, but for the gift of my love returned to me, I will serve you."

"You returned the true faith to Kemet, Merire-Tutankhamun. Ma'at has been served well. Balance and order have finally been restored," whispered the Goddess.

Dipping his head in homage to the Goddess, he turned to carry Ankhesenamun out of the shrine room. "What shall I call you?" he asked gently. "I need to know what name to tell the priest if we're to be married again."

"I'll keep the name Miut," she said with the ghost of a smile. "I've grown rather fond of it and it has served me well."

Merire laughed and hugged her close. "Miut, my own little cat," he teased, touching his lips to her forehead.

"That's a great story, Tal," I said, as I finished typing. Getting no answer, I glanced over to the chair back. It was empty.

"Tal?" I called softly, looking around the room. Where was he? Then I noticed daylight showing through the curtains. I began to wonder if I had been hallucinating after all, but when I looked more closely at the chair, on the velvet cushion on which he'd been sitting, he'd left the imprint of his body—and the story I've just written.

Under Her Skin

(previously The Jewel and the Demon)

"BE STILL, IMP!" MOUSE HISSED AT HER TINY COMPANION. "I TOLD YOU, I can deal with the dogs."

Ahead of them lay their goal, the treasure room of Harra the merchant. She knew its encircling corridor was protected by large hounds, one of which lay opposite them, guarding the only entrance.

Mouse reached for the tiny silver whistle suspended on a cord around her neck. She'd won it some time ago in a dice game from a fellow thief and it had become a treasured and useful possession. Putting it to her lips, she blew gently. Though she could hear nothing, the small demon accompanying her clapped his hands to his ears and grimaced in pain.

The dog lifted its head and pricked its ears, looking around. Pushing the demon back, Mouse flattened herself against the wall. She repeated the whistle—one short, sharp blow. The hound growled softly and, getting to its feet, padded toward them. Releasing the whistle, she transferred several small spherical glass phials to her right hand. The dog had finally gotten a whiff of her scent and its growl rose in pitch, becoming menacing.

The gods help me if Tallan's magic doesn't work, she thought.

Taking a deep breath, Mouse stepped out of their cover and flung one of the phials at the animal's feet. The glass shattered, releasing a small cloud of white vapor. As she watched, the dog slowed to a halt, skidding on the wooden floor before collapsing in a boneless heap.

"Wait!" she said as the demon made to rush forward. "We only got one. There's more."

They could hear the rapid click of claws on wood as two more dogs rounded the corner, bounding toward them. It took all her courage to wait until the slavering beasts were nearly upon them before throwing a second and third phial. Seconds later, they lay as senseless as the first.

"Now! Now! While they sleep," the demon exclaimed, hopping from hoof to hoof.

She nodded. The dogs had frightened her more than she cared to admit. Forcing herself to relax a little, she stepped warily past the beasts. Silently they covered the intervening distance to the great double doors. A sturdy hasp, held closed by a simple but efficient padlock, covered the locks.

Mouse spent a few moments examining the padlock before digging into one of her capacious pockets and extracting a padlock pick. Carefully, she inserted the wire in the keyhole, twiddling it round and about until she felt it give. Grasping the loop with her free hand, she pulled it open and laid it carefully on the floor away from the door.

"No time for tidy," the demon hissed urgently. "Hurry, hurry!"

"Untidy could kill us if we have to leave quickly," Mouse replied more calmly than she felt as she stroked her hand over the now-exposed locks.

There were three of them, and her sixth sense was telling her they must be opened in the right sequence otherwise alarms would go off in the guard room.

"You hurry," the demon twittered. "Not want you caught. I be safe, but not you."

Mouse glanced down at him. Pretty he wasn't. With his wrinkled brown face and tiny horns poking through his thatch of dark curls he looked like a prematurely aged child of three. He stamped an insistent hoof. "Hurry!"

She sighed, turning back to the door. "I need quiet to work, imp. Give me peace."

Once again, she ran her hands over the door, trying to sense the order of the enchantment on the locks. She was no magic user to know how these things worked, but now and then, she was able to divine something of their nature. Her luck had made it possible for her to earn her living after her mother had died rather than end up in one of the city bars or brothels.

"Middle one first," she muttered to herself, taking a smaller lock pic out of her pocket and inserting her piece of wire again. This time she placed her ear to the door, listening for the tiny clicks that told her when she'd tripped each tumbler.

Patiently she worked away until she'd freed the first lock without triggering the alarm.

"Now the top one."

As she worked, the demon shifted impatiently from hoof to hoof, knowing it shouldn't break her concentration. "Dogs wake soon," it muttered fretfully.

"Last one," she said, aware of the building tension. "Not long now. Almost there." She continued working, sweat beginning to break out on her forehead. Her hands were trembling now with the effort of trying to keep them steady. She stopped to wipe slick palms on her pants legs. Gods, but she was tired already! By the time this was over, she'd have more than earned her high fee. She banished the thought and bent down to resume her work.

The last tumbler tripped and she turned an exultant face to her companion. "We're through!"

"Open door. Must hurry," he said, urging her forward with his hands.

Gently Mouse grasped the ring handle and turning it, eased the door open just enough for them to squeeze through. Hugging the wall, she snatched at the demon, grabbing it by its naked shoulder as it prepared to dash forward. Its skin felt hot and slightly uneven, like that of a reptile or an exotic fruit.

"No!" she hissed. "We look around first!"

"You want light?" asked the demon, squirming out from under her hand. "I give." A soft glow began to fill the room.

"Keep it low!" Mouse exclaimed. "We don't know what the inner defenses are yet."

The glow obediently slowed, building until there was only enough light to see the whole room. Immediately, their eyes were drawn to the glass case atop the pedestal standing in the center. In it was a gemstone, but a gem unlike any she'd seen before. Now that there was light in the room, colors coruscated through it, sending their rainbow hues glancing off the ceiling in tiny patches of brilliance.

"The Living Jewel," Mouse whispered.

"Yes. Jewel for Master Kolin," said the demon.

"What's your wizard want the jewel for?" she asked, unable to take her eyes off its beauty.

"Not know," he said. "Just say he want it."

"Huh." Mouse tore her gaze away and examined the rest of the room. The walls were lined with display cabinets containing items of rarity or beauty from other lands. There were even some that must have come from the offworld aliens, but none of them compared with the Living Jewel.

"I can see why the merchant doesn't want to part with it," she murmured.

"He refuse to sell it to Master. Say it an item of pride. Reminds him of getting best of enemy," offered the demon in an unusual burst of conversation.

Mouse glanced down at him in surprise, but it was the floor that caught her attention. Her heart began to race as she stooped to examine it more closely, realizing now that since they'd entered the room, she'd been subliminally aware of the warmth underfoot.

The tiles had a faint tracery pattern on them that broadened out as it led to the pedestal at the center of the room. At the base of the plinth, like a spider in the heart of its web, there was a patch of shadow, a darkness. She blinked and looked back at the crimson lines.

Cutiously she passed her hand over the pattern, aware as she did so of the variations in temperature between it and the tiles.

"Increase the light a little," she ordered the demon, turning her attention to the shadow again.

As the room brightened, gradually the shadow began to disperse till she could plainly see the shape of a reptile curled around the plinth.

"Darken!" she hissed in fear. "It's a firedrake! These lines on the floor, they're part of its body! If we step on them, we'll waken it."

"I fix with sleep enhancement spell," said the demon. "We lucky you kept light low. Light wakes it too."

He began to mutter in some guttural outlandish language, making several complicated passes in the air with his hands. Mouse began to feel queasy and looked away.

"Is safe now," he assured her a few moments later.

"We still keep off the lines," warned Mouse, listening to her intuition again. "Do you sense any more protections? I don't."

"I say safe," he repeated, tugging at her hand, trying to draw her into the room. "Must hurry now. Dogs wake soon for sure."

Exasperated, she shook him off, motioning him to quiet.

Carefully they picked their way across the network of lines until they stood beside the pedestal. Mouse looked anxiously at the slumbering firedrake.

"Are you sure it'll stay asleep?" she asked, mistrustful of the efficacy of magic spells when they were supposed to be working for her benefit.

"Sure," nodded the demon confidently. "Can't make things sleep but can enhance it. You get jewel now."

Mouse placed her hands carefully on either side of the glass case and lifted it off, passing it down to the demon. She hesitated a moment before reaching forward to lift the jewel reverently off its bed of velvet. Turning it in her hand, she gazed in wonder at the ephemeral flickering hues. One moment it was clear, then the next, every color of the rainbow seemed to glitter within it. At her side, the demon shifted impatiently.

"A moment, imp," she murmured, lost in its beauty. Suddenly, pain lanced through her hand and up her arm to her spine. Arching her back in agony, she let out a soul-wrenching scream as she tried to fling the jewel away from her. It was stuck to her hand. She couldn't let go of it as it seared and burned its way into her very flesh.

She fell to the floor writhing in agony, cradling her hand against her chest, whimpering, the pain now too intense to even cry out. The demon echoed her cry as she twisted sideways, kicking the firedrake with her foot.

The imp danced around her, for the first time unsure what to do. This was bad. Things were not going according to plan. Then he heard the guards' footsteps pounding toward the treasure room.

"Lady!" he shrieked, the sound galvanizing him into action. "Lady, you get up! Guards come! You be dead if they catch you." He grabbed her by the arm. "Up! You get up!" he shouted urgently, tugging at her.

It seemed to work, for her struggles subsided and she went limp. Behind them, the firedrake stirred, its wings making a papery sound as it stretched them.

"Up! Up! Firedrake wake!" He was beside himself with terror.

Mouse struggled to her feet; her eyes still glazed with pain. "What...?" she slurred.

"Use sword. You must fight good now," the demon said, letting go of her to pull free the sword that hung on her left hip. He thrust it into her unresisting hands. "Fight guards!" He pushed her round in the direction of the door.

"Guards?" she asked as five of them rushed into the room. She could barely see them, so fogged by pain was her vision. How she managed to close her aching hand around the sword hilt she never knew.

Instincts took over and she raised her blade, just managing to deflect the blow of the leading man. Her body knew what to do even if her conscious mind had not quite caught up. She whirled to one side, taking the man out with a chest blow as he raised his sword for a second swipe at her.

The firedrake, thoroughly roused now, reared up and belched flame at her back, but she was no longer there, having skipped to one side to avoid the rush of the other four soldiers. Standing them off briefly, she kept her sword at guard and tried to edge round toward the door. Then she leapt forward, taking out the second man with a deftly turned block that cut him deeply under his sword arm. The third locked blades with her, pushing her back then knocking the sword out of her hands with the sheer force of his next blow. Dazed, she stood there for a moment, her hands limp at her sides. Knowing he had her now, the guard advanced more slowly. Behind them, the firedrake screeched its anger and sent another gout of flame licking at her legs. Mouse wailed at the fresh pain, and flinging her hands up to protect herself, whirled around. She felt a tremendous rush like a tidal wave building inside her — then the room turned dark.

Her wrist was grabbed by a small, clawed hand. "We go," the demon said, pulling her forward. "Take sword. Leave now, before more guards come."

Mouse's senses returned with a rush and, taking the sword that the demon was thrusting back into her hands, she raced for the doorway. The brightness of the corridor made her eyes water and blink, and she slowed down. The demon would have none of it and urged her on again. Trusting him, she ran where he led. Within moments, they were back in the little room where they had forced their entry so short a time ago.

Mouse leapt onto the window ledge, reaching down to haul the demon up after her. They scrambled out and jumped down onto the low roof of the stables, leaping from there to land on the dusty ground below. Then they were racing across the yard to the outer wall, praying their rope still waited for them. Up and over they went as all hell let loose behind them. Swiftly they ran down the street, slowing only when they left the affluent area of the city to enter the market quarter. Finally, Mouse felt safe enough to stop and sheath her sword.

No one was abroad at this hour of night. All the drunks were either long since in their beds or lying in back alleys with their throats and their purses cut. Mouse and her companion skulked in the shadows, heading deeper into the labyrinth of the quarter where only those who were known to be dangerous could safely stray.

Agony stabbed through her head, bringing her to a standstill. She gave a strangled cry and, clutching her head, fell heavily to her knees.

"What happens, lady? What happens?"

Mouse was barely aware of the demon's distressed cry. Strange alien thoughts began to flow compellingly through her mind.

Submit to me. Let me take control. I have the knowledge to make you great. Together we could rule this kingdom. You could be rich, powerful. No ambition would be beyond our achievement. Don't fear this Kolin, we can take him on easily.

"No," she moaned, swaying from side to side where she knelt in the gutter. "Get out of my head! I don't want power!"

But riches. Yes, riches, the voice purred. *I can give you all that — and more.*

"No!" She fought back mentally, pushing against the thoughts, willing them to stop. "Leave me, leave me alone!"

The demon watched Mouse with a glimmering of understanding as she carried on her one-way conversation. He hadn't told her that the reason they'd been able to escape was that from somewhere she'd called up enough Mage-power to blast the last three guards and the firedrake into a smoldering pile of ashes. No, he hadn't told her that — yet.

It seemed as if the jewel had found a home for which it was not intended. The girl must carry mage-blood in her veins like Wizard Kolin, or she could never have made use of the magic. She'd need all her inborn mage instincts if she was going to control the jewel. As for his master, the only way he could now claim his prize was by killing her, unless she managed to kill Kolin first.

Now there was a thought. Kolin was no easy master, always demanding the impossible. Perhaps the girl would make a kinder mistress, if he, Zaylar, could help her. But the nature of his binding to Kolin prevented that. He sighed. There would be no release for him. He could only sit back and await the outcome, changing one master for another when his was finally defeated. And defeated he would be, one day. Magical duels seemed to be all these Jalnian mages lived and died for.

He turned his attention again to Mouse, realizing that she'd finally released her head and was slowly beginning to sit up.

"Lady, you all right?" he asked anxiously.

Mouse got unsteadily to her feet, running her hands through her damp hair and pushing it back from her face. "I think so."

She looked at the palms of her hands, comparing one to the other before scrubbing her right one with her left. There was no difference — no lump, no burned flesh. Nothing.

"The jewel, did I dream it, or did it really disappear into my hand?"

The demon nodded vigorously. "Is what it does. Lives within the mage-born. Who win?" he asked, peering closely at her face.

"I did, I think," she replied. Mage-born? *She* was mage-born?

"Then *you* use jewel, it not use you. You mastered it."

Was that satisfaction she heard in his voice? "Is this why Kolin wanted the jewel?"

"Yes. It make him a stronger wizard. Now you a wizard too." He cocked his head to one side and looked expectantly at her.

"Me, little friend? Not me," she laughed shakily. She found herself suddenly aware of his hopes for freedom. Frightened, she looked away and the sensation was gone.

"Yes, you. We go to Master Kolin. He find you if you don't. He have to kill you to get jewel now, so you must kill him first."

"Me? Kill Kolin? Who's kidding who, imp?" She began walking in the opposite direction.

"Where you going?" Zaylar demanded, scampering to keep up.

"Not to Kolin, that's for sure!"

"Got to! He come after you!" protested the demon, dancing backward in an effort to keep ahead of her. "No place you can hide from a mage!"

"Why should he? I've taken no money from him yet. It isn't his."

"He think so! Won't stop till he's got jewel," the demon insisted, stopping and holding its arms out to bar her way. "Only chance you got is to fight him!"

She ground to a halt in front of him. "You're serious, aren't you? He really will come after me, won't he? Gods, what a mess! Whatever I do, I stand one hell of a good chance of dying!"

"Fighting Kolin is best. Jewel will help you."

"How?"

"Ask it. It protects you now. Maybe it do it anyway, without you asking." He shrugged. "It knows what you know. Maybe it want you to live, think you easier to control than wizard like Kolin."

"Wonderful! What I know about magical duels could be written on a pin head," she muttered, resting her hand on the pommel of her sword.

Zaylar hesitated. She really didn't have a clue about what was happening to her. An opportunity as good as this wouldn't come again in a hundred years. He couldn't afford to pass it up. Technically, he couldn't help, but then he'd never been a great one for technicalities. That's what had gotten him into trouble in the King's Court in the first place. Giving her some advice wasn't really helping her, was it? Advice? Had he called it advice? He would only be talking aloud. If she heard him and got an idea, it wasn't his fault, was it?

He looked down at the ground, scraping one hoof idly in the dust. "If I was a thief, wouldn't use magic," he said. "Thief skills be what I know. I'd use them."

"Thief skills? In a magical duel?" She looked at him incredulously.

He tapped his hoof impatiently, drawing her attention to the ground seconds before a small gout of flame erupted from the center of his scratchings.

"Thief skills," she said again as the demon let out a high-pitched scream. Leaping back, he chittered in pain, hopping about on one hoof as he massaged the other.

"Wasn't helping!" he shrieked to the night sky. "Was not!"

Kolin greeted them in his study. He was a somber man, dressed in robes of deep blue as befitted his dark calling. This hadn't bothered Mouse when she took the job. She'd been no threat to him then, but now his garb sent a chill through to her bones.

"So, you've returned. You have my jewel?"

"Of a surety, wizard," she replied.

Kolin lifted the draw-string pouch that lay on the desk beside him. "Then give it to me and you will be paid," he said.

"Ah, I have this slight problem," said Mouse, keeping her eyes focused on the pouch rather than him.

Kolin frowned. "You said you have the jewel. Where's the problem? Zaylar, does she lie to me?" he demanded.

"No, Master. She has jewel," the demon answered from the doorway.

"Then give it to me," thundered Kolin, putting the pouch down and extending his hand peremptorily. His eyes narrowed suddenly.

"You *have* it, don't you?" He sat back in his seat. "How can a scrawny girl, and a thief to boot, have mage-blood?" he mused aloud. "Were either of your parents mages, girl?"

Mouse shrugged, meeting his gaze this time. "Not that I know of. My father didn't stay around to find out my mother was pregnant. She always said she got me from a passing fortune teller."

"Only the mage-born can carry the Living Jewel," said Kolin. "Without doubt, you're one of us." He frowned again. "Your father broke the law in allowing you to live, but no matter. It is an inconvenience, nothing more." He gestured briefly and a bolt of energy flashed toward Mouse.

Automatically she ducked, lifting her arm and fending it to one side as if it were merely a blow from a raised fist. It sparked and flared against the door, sending the demon chittering for cover.

As shock flooded through her, Mouse felt the jewel stirring within her mind.

Let me fight this battle for you, came the silken thought.

"No," said Mouse, knowing instinctively that if she opened her mind to the jewel, then win or lose this battle with Kolin, *she* would cease to exist. A sound like the wisp of a sigh, then from deep within, she felt a power begin to build, slowly at first, then spiraling upward until it filled her whole being.

You need a shield, came the faint thought, *like the armsmen use.*

She couldn't help it. No sooner than it had been suggested than she could see it in her mind's eye. It was none too soon. Kolin struck again and her shield was suddenly suffused with blue fire. It took all her courage to stand her ground.

"So, the jewel helps you," hissed Kolin. "But it's too little and too late to save you!"

Ignoring his words, she looked for a gap in Kolin's defenses. As he concentrated on gathering his magical energies, she struck. With one hand, she flung her remaining two phials at his desk while reaching swiftly behind her neck for the knife that nestled there. In one fluid move, she'd pulled it out and thrown it into the heart of the sleep spell cloud.

She saw it strike home, taking with it a bolt of raw energy a hundred times more powerful than anything Kolin had used. As the cloud dissipated, she saw him reeling under the impact, hands clutching the knife that now sprouted from the base of his throat.

Lines of thin blue lightning spiderwebbed from the blade across his body. A silent scream was pinned to his face, and for several moments, his petrified form remained transfixed before he suddenly collapsed into a fine rain of ash.

Shocked, Mouse let her arm fall by her side and stared at the empty seat.

"Where'd he go?" she demanded of the demon, her voice high-pitched with shock.

The demon crawled out from under a sideboard. "Dead. He dead now. You kill him, Mistress."

"Dead?" she repeated. "He can't be dead. He's gone, magicked himself away somewhere."

"He's dead. You're Mistress now. All this — the house, everything — yours. And me, Zaylar," he said, nodding vigorously.

"I don't want any of this!" Mouse exclaimed. "Neither his house nor you! I'm an honest thief, not a wizard."

The demon shook its head. "No, you're a wizard now. You're mage-born, you got jewel. Can't change that."

Mouse looked for another chair — she didn't fancy the one so hurriedly vacated by its previous owner — and sat down heavily.

"I don't want to be a wizard," she said again.

"Have to be. Power there, jewel there. Lucky this time, jewel helped you. Must learn to control it before it controls you," the demon insisted, concern on its face.

Mouse looked up. "Why should you worry?" she asked. "You're a demon, you don't care about us Jalnians."

"I care because you the Mistress now. We make a deal, eh?"

"What deal?" Mouse asked suspiciously.

"I want be free so no one ever bind me again. You can fix it. I help you."

"What do I get out of it?" she asked, her interest aroused despite herself.

"I live long, long time. Is nothing I stay with you. I teach you, keep jewel from taking you over while learn magic. Then you use this learning, make me an amulet so never bound by Jalnians again. Is deal, yes?"

Mouse arched her eyebrows quizzically. "So you've got delusions of power in your world. Why can't you make this amulet yourself?"

"Demons can't make amulet, need wizard. You can. Safe for you."

Mouse thought for a moment. Power games she could understand. If the demon was motivated in that direction, then she could be fairly sure he'd keep his word—at least until she'd made the amulet. She sighed and leaned forward to pick up Kolin's purse.

"Seems like I've got no choice. You've got yourself a deal, Zaylar."

The demon grinned and began cavorting about the room, whooping for all the world like a joyful child. Watching him, Mouse couldn't help smiling. As she once more suppressed the jewel's faint whisper deep within her mind, she cursed herself for breaking her own rules and getting involved with a wizard in the first place. She had a horrible conviction she was going to regret it for a long time.

Is This Real Enough?

AZIEL STOOD, HANDS ON HIPS, LOOKING AT THE PAIR OF CHARRED SHOES twenty yards away. "That's it?" he demanded, a faint plume of smoke curling upward from each nostril. "That's the best those damned mages have? Last night's supper put up more of a fight!"

"It's only been ten years, Master," whined the small, hunched figure at his side. "Not even a generation since the last one tried to bind you. Needs time till one emerges as leader among them."

"Leader?" snorted Aziel. "That wasn't a leader! Lately they send thieves and adventurers through the veil to steal and spy on us," he said in disgust, stepping over the chalk circle that surrounded them and walking toward the smaller one in the middle of the cavern floor. "He didn't even know my name! Standards are falling when this is the best that Sondherst can send against me!"

"He got the circles right, Master." The servant limped hastily past him, anxious to reach the distant markings first. "See, two lines with the runes written between them," he said frantically, trying to improve his master's temper. Lurching down onto his haunches, Twilby pointed to where the inner chalk ring had been scuffed open and one still-smoldering shoe lay on its side.

"And broke it when he saw me begin to materialize my true form," Aziel snapped. "What kind of mage is that? He summoned me, yet he didn't even know my name or my form!" Stopping beside Twilby, he peered down at the arcane symbols. He needed to know which summoning spell the mage had used, for that was the key to returning to his own world. The glow cast by the horn lantern the late mage had brought with him illuminated the writing just enough for him to read it. Frowning, he studied the chalk symbols, but the writing was erratic and smudged, especially where the circle had been broken. A glint of metal caught his eye briefly; he dismissed it, knowing it was only the molten remains of the amulet the mage had brought with him in the hope of binding him to it.

After a moment or two, he became aware that Twilby had stopped poking nervously at the shoe and was now flicking it around with an outstretched claw-tip so the vacant top was facing him.

He aimed a kick at his minion, his boot connecting hard with the other's loincloth-covered rump. Twilby shrieked in pain and went sprawling on his side, the charred shoe forgotten as he clutched at his rear end, massaging the stump of a tail that protruded from his grubby rags.

"Sometimes you disgust even me." Aziel snarled. "You'd eat anything, wouldn't you? You're vermin, not fit to be allowed out of the yard!" It had been his ill fortune to be chastising one of his lesser drudges when he'd been summoned to this realm.

"Only looking, Master," Twilby whimpered, wiping his streaming eyes on his forearm as he scrambled further from his master. "Looking isn't eating. Sondherst flesh is tasty. Don't get it often. Usually, you give me leftovers."

"That isn't leftovers," Aziel said, sending the offending shoe into a dark corner with another swipe of his foot. "It's carrion! Have you forgotten where we are? The other side of the damned dimensional veil, that's where! He may have had companions with him."

Twilby stopped whining and peered fearfully around the dim cavern before scuttling hurriedly back to Aziel's side.

"Companions? Like me, Master? What we do?" he whispered, pawing at the Dragon lord's robe.

With a snort of distaste, Aziel aimed another kick at his minion, then flicked his clothing aside and, lifting his other hand, held it before him. A faint golden glow began to materialize in his palm. As it solidified, it rose, forming a small ball of light that intensified, pushing the shadows back to the farthest reaches of the chamber.

The hollowed-out cavern was natural, and not as large as Aziel had first thought—the roof was a mere thirty feet above him. Scanning the walls, he saw the carved steps almost immediately.

Leaving the globe of light hanging in midair, he strode over toward them. "Follow me," he ordered. "And not a sound!"

He took the stairs three at a time, glad that the late mage's inept summoning hadn't forced him to complete the change from the humanoid form he'd assumed earlier in the day. In a cavern this size, his natural shape would have been, to say the least, inconvenient. Thankfully, no matter what his outward form, he lost none of his abilities. Enhanced senses and his innate awareness of and ability to use magic were all that stood between his kind and the predatory Sondherstian mages' desire for power.

The steps spiraled steeply to his left. Ahead he could see a crack of light, like that at the bottom of an ill-fitting door. Slowing down, he took the remaining steps one at a time, head turning this way then that as he checked the air for any other scents. All that lingered was the stale odor of the mage he'd vaporized. Placing his back to the rock face, he reached for the latch on the rough wooden door, lifting it gently before easing the portal open.

Lit only by flickering candles, the interior of the room was dim and slightly hazy, the air redolent with the stink of stale sweat and cheap tallow. He wrinkled his nose with distaste. The smell was offensive to one as discerning as him. Pushing the door wider, he eased himself cautiously inside.

The room was unoccupied. Small and cramped, as well as noisome, only one door led out of it. On his left, a small window, hidden behind a rickety shutter, was the cause of the guttering candles. In front of him stood a table, scratched and dull with age, its surface cluttered with books and papers. Behind it, a chair, its padding so threadbare the original color was no longer discernible. As he stepped further into the room and looked behind him, he saw a similarly ancient sofa bearing a thin, rumpled rug and almost thinner pillow. These comprised the mage's meager furnishings.

Almost empty bookshelves lined the remainder of the room save for where a grate of cold ashes stood, its fire a distant memory. Only half a dozen ancient, tattered books remained. They were stacked haphazardly against each other, except for the one on the desk. Sniffing again, he detected the aroma of magic from it. It would have to wait. Despite the lack of other scents, he needed to know that he was safe first.

"Curious," Aziel murmured as he walked silently across the stained wooden floor to the exit door. Living in such obvious poverty was unusual for a mage, and a hedge-wizard wouldn't have the power or knowledge, let alone the skills, to summon a draconic demon lord, even if he possessed a grimoire such as the one on the desk. But what would a hedge-wizard, or a mage, be doing living in a dank cave backing onto a mountain cavern? Hedge-wizards were itinerants, earning their living by traveling from village to village, performing what amounted to tricks. Very few had the ability to use real magic, and then only because they were the illegitimate and unacknowledged sons of real mages.

Putting his ear to the door, Aziel listened, sniffed, then opened it cautiously. A dark and empty corridor stretched ahead for some fifteen feet, ending this time at a stout door, obviously the main entrance.

"Twilby, go check out the rest of this place," he ordered, losing interest and shutting the door. "There's another couple of rooms off the corridor out there." Whatever the history of its late occupant, he was in no danger now. The mage, if mage he had been, had obviously lived alone.

Returning to the desk, he slid behind it, lowering his muscular frame into the ancient chair, remembering before he did so to adjust his weight. Pulling the book closer, he studied the open pages.

"Is dangerous, Master," whined Twilby from where he still hesitated in the doorway from the cavern. "Cannot defend myself if anyone there! Change me, Master. Make me more than I am."

Aziel looked up at the pathetic figure of the drudge. "You want to be more than you are?" he asked softly, his rugged features creasing in thought, as his piercing red eyes scanned the deformed scrawny frame. "Be very careful what you ask for, Twilby. I may just give you it." The drudge's petulant voice was beginning to grate.

"Afraid, Master. Not strong like you. Not able to change self into form better for intimidating others."

Aziel raised his hand, pointing at Twilby. He muttered a short phrase in his own guttural language. A faint glow surrounded the servant before his body appeared to stretch before suddenly shrinking.

Twilby's mouth opened in a soundless shriek of terror and pain as a mass of sharp hairy bristles forced themselves through the surface of his skin, growing longer and longer before finally softening and lying flat against his now elongated back. The stubby tail lengthened, acquiring a life of its own as it whipped from side to side in panic. His features, not comely to begin with, were forced outward into a muzzle as long whiskers sprouted from either side of his tiny nose.

The transformation complete, the rat collapsed squealing to the ground, sides heaving in terror as it gasped for breath.

Indifferent to the other's suffering, Aziel turned his attention back to the book. "Go. You now have a shape to strike fear into the heart of others, one more suited to your nature, just as you requested."

The grimoire lay open at an invocation spell, one meant to call and bind one of the lesser demons. So how had this—magic user—managed to summon him, Lord of the Eight Realms, Aziel wondered? What part of the ritual had the hedge-wizard changed?

He pushed the book aside. He'd no need of it now, he already knew the reverse spell. What he did need were the dratted mage's notes. Without knowing the runes, he couldn't return through the veil. Surely he'd scribbled them on some piece of parchment to take down to the cavern. Unless, in killing the mage, he'd destroyed the only record of them? Aziel sighed, his breath turning the edges of the open pages brown. Noticing the faint curl of smoke, he shut the book hastily with a thump.

Methodically, he began to search through the pile of papers on the desk, examining each one in the hope it was what he needed. It wasn't as simple as just substituting a more advanced spell, he needed a list of the actual runes and their positions relevant to each other within the two lines of the circle.

Frustrated, he yanked open the top drawer, then stopped and gazed down at the small crystal orb within. Now this *was* a find, and almost worth the aggravation that the summoning had caused him. But just what was a seeing crystal doing in the midst of such obvious poverty?

A summoning meant that there was a task to be done, one that required more power and magical ability than the mage had possessed. But what would someone as poor as this mage obviously was want done so badly that he'd risk summoning a demon?

Aziel picked up the crystal and held it in the palm of his hand. Not a large one, to be sure, only some four inches in diameter, but it was large enough for anyone with very shallow pockets. Then he noticed what lay below it—a letter.

Lifting the letter from the drawer, he flicked it open one-handedly. The faded ink made the words difficult to read. Obviously, it wasn't new, but to be placed under the crystal, it had to be of some significance. Sweeping the scattered papers onto the floor, he put the globe down carefully in the center of the desk. Then, spreading the letter out, he began to study it.

It took him several minutes to decipher the crabbed writing. It was from The Acquirers' and Facilitators' Guild in Eldaglast, asking the wizard, named, he discovered, Banray, to help them locate their next Guild Master. The fee offered was an amount that was guaranteed to tempt one so poor to risk everything—but nowhere near what a competent Mage would cost.

He frowned, then the corners of his mouth began to lift slightly. So, they were looking to replace the leader he'd slain several months ago, were they? More fools them for being so cheap that they hired an inept hedge-wizard.

A tiny squeak made him look up sharply. Twilby had returned and was sitting on his haunches not far from the desk.

The drudge's voice was thin and high-pitched in his rat body. "Master, the place is empty."

Aziel nodded and returned to his perusal of the letter

"Writing on the other side," said Twilby nervously.

"What?" Aziel turned the letter over. There, hastily scribbled on the back, was a rough diagram of both chalk circles—complete with runes. He had the means to get home—and a means to relieve his boredom.

With a gesture toward his rat-shaped minion, he turned his attention back to the crystal. "Come here. I have need of you."

A minute later, still whimpering with the pain of his second transformation, Twilby was crouched at his side.

"Show me the most unlikely successor for the Guild," he commanded of the crystal, cupping it in both hands and staring into its depths. "I will ensure that he shall be their leader!"

He watched the swirling shapes solidify into a scene, then Aziel's mouth widened into what, for him, approximated a smile, secure in the knowledge that no one could have dreamed that across the gulf of space, a mind as immeasurably old and devious as his regarded them with curious eyes. Slowly and surely, he drew his plans.

⧉———•———⧉

HELL BARROW

"Buffs!" yelled Hurga from his position to the rear of the small group of warriors. "Now, or ye'll have to let the cleric heal ye!"

"I hear you!" Tekkel said, cranking his arm back to deliver a powered blow with his long-bladed knife at the mage's animated corpse. As he did, three arrows, in rapid succession, whistled between him and Davon, narrowly missing his right ear, adding to the dozen or so already embedded in the wight's flesh. "Doing my best, but this bastard just won't go down!" He was already toiling, having taken several small injuries as they'd fought their way through to the main chamber.

"Watch it, Jinna!" Davon snarled, glaring back at the small female standing beside Hurga. "We don't need friendly fire."

The zombie uttered yet another howl of rage and pain as it lurched toward Tekkel, its dead, skeletal hands groping and slashing at him. Tekkel dove to one side, barely avoiding the poisonous, razor-sharp claws.

"Mirri, stun-shot him, in the name of the gods!" he yelled, doing a neat forward roll and coming up behind the monster. He took a moment to glance around the rest of his party. "Zenithia, back off! You're a damage dealer, you can't take damage! Use a spell!"

"But I like hitting them and making them bleed," Zenithia smiled sweetly. "Spells are so... impersonal."

"Just do it, before..."

She let out a low cry of pain as the zombie's left hand managed to scratch her arm. It was only a glancing blow, but it was enough.

Almost instantly, he heard the sounds of the rest of the group charging up their weapons' special attacks.

Shannar's arrows arched overhead, most of them spent as they were brushed aside by the wight.

"Back, sister!" yelled Mirri, letting off another fusillade of arrows that thudded into their target with a dull thump. The animated corpse of the dead mage Tallus staggered briefly, then froze as if rooted to the spot.

"I'm ending this now," Tekkel muttered, throwing aside his shield and pulling his remaining daggers. Powering up their special abilities, he flung himself at the zombie, knives flashing as he sacrificed accuracy and personal protection to double the damage with his assassin skills.

With a low growl of anger, Zenithia's sword rapidly sketching arcane symbols in the air, then she began to cast, her body straightening and standing on tiptoe as she uttered the guttural words of power.

"Heal yourself," Tekkel ordered, continuing to hack away at the unmoving decayed corpse. Thank the Gods of Sondherst that Mirri's stun attack had worked, but time was running out for Zenithia. His senses strained to the limit, he heard Davon begin to mutter a prayer to his deity and silently thanked the gods the cleric was with them.

He glanced up at Zenithia again, seeing her beginning to pale as the poison took hold. "Zen, heal yourself!" he yelled, once again slashing at the exposed zombie's back. "Davon! Cure her, dammit!"

Bits of decaying flesh were breaking off now, scattering in all directions around him as Zenithia completed her incantation. A ball of fire suddenly materialized in front of her, hovered there for a moment before streaking across the few feet that separated her from the wight. It hit with a dull *thwump*, momentarily lighting the creature from within. Then flames erupted from it, and he had to jump back to avoid being scorched himself.

"How dare he hit *me*, one of the Gray Brotherhood," Zenithia snarled, gathering her energy to cast again.

As the final words of Davon's prayer rang out, a bolt of lightning flashed down from the Barrow's ceiling and struck the already blazing corpse. Galvanized into a parody of life again, it jerked like a puppet on strings as the flames became a raging inferno, then, as three more of Mirri's arrows hit it, the flames abruptly went out and the body collapsed in a smoking pile at Tekkel's feet.

Zenithia staggered, falling to her knees as Davon turned toward her and began praying again.

"I said *cure* her, Davon," Tekkel snarled, leaping over the corpse to run to the wounded elf's side. "There was no need for you to attack! We were on top of it then, dammit! Have you any antidotes left, Zen?" he demanded, catching hold of her as she swayed and would have fallen to the ground.

Davon ignored him, continuing to chant as he drew holy symbols in the air. A golden nimbus began to gather around him.

"Ran out of them," muttered Zenithia, her voice so quiet his long ears instinctively twitched forward, and he had to bend his head to hear her.

"Tekkel, catch!" Hurga called out.

From the corner of his eye, Tekkel saw a flicker of green as a phial twisted through the air toward him. Reaching up, he caught it, instantly putting it in his mouth and grasping the cork in his teeth even as he braced himself to take the full weight of the almost unconscious dying elf woman. Davon's cure would be too late. He had to stop the poison now.

He was aware of Hurga's heavy footsteps running toward them, and the dwarf beginning to chant his healing spell as the cork came suddenly free. Spitting it out, he hauled Zenithia around until her head sagged back against his arm. The acrid taste of the zombie anti-venom on his lips made him shudder as he forced her pale ones apart and poured the noxious brew into her mouth. He held her close and still when she began to cough and pushed the phial away. Hurga's silver, healing glow bathed her in its light for several seconds, then faded. Thanks to him, her color was now beginning to slowly improve. Her gray skin was regaining some of its normal blue tint, but there was still an unhealthy green cast to it.

"Drink it, Zen," he insisted, catching her hands in his free one and forcing the phial to her lips again. "Dammit, Davon! How many times do I have to tell you I need you to monitor the party's health?"

"Not my fault my Turn Undead failed," the other muttered angrily. "She was too close, she endangered herself!"

"We knew you couldn't turn this mob before we came," Mirri snapped, running over to join them, an arrow sill nocked on his bow and now aimed at the cleric. "You risked my sister's life! That was a Boss, an Undead Mage. It was agreed you'd be the primary healer and only fight when needed!"

Zenithia struggled to push Tekkel aside as another coughing fit overtook her. Twisting to avoid the edge of the sword she still grasped tightly, he relaxed his hold slightly but remained supporting her as the green of the poison slowly drained from her skin.

"Mirri, put that bow down now. Zen's going to be okay." He locked eyes with the other elf until Mirri had lowered his bow and settled the arrow back in the quiver.

Davon had finished his prayer, and as he sketched the final segment of the holy symbol in the air, the glow around him began to shift, moving toward where Tekkel and Zenithia sat. The white light surrounded them both, bathing them in a sensation of warmth and well-being. Now he could see her complexion begin to return to its normal healthy shade of blue-gray. The glow faded, leaving him feeling energized again and his few wounds also healed.

"I'm well now," she said, taking a deep breath and pulling free of his hold completely.

Suppressing his desire to hold onto her, he sat back on his heels and picked up his knives. This was the closest he'd been to her yet, and slim though she might be, he'd almost felt the gentle curves hidden beneath the showy, half-revealing costume that passed for a female gray elf battle mage's armor. She was usually not as cold toward him as she was today, though…

He pushed the rogue thoughts of her aside and turned to look at the dwarf, now standing, flanked by their archers beside them, guarding them against further danger.

"Thanks, Hurga. Davon, you neglected your responsibilities. You were almost too late," he said coldly, then turned back to Zenithia.

"He's right, though," he said, cursing himself for having to agree with the temperamental cleric. "You took risks too, putting us all in danger. We need to fight as a team to succeed."

"I told you when I joined that I was used to fighting only with my brother," she said, her tone cool as she got to her feet. "It takes time to… accept that others will do their job as well as we do. And then they let us down. I will never rely on Davon again."

"Don't be so damned arrogant," Davon said, taking a step toward her, his hand gripping the shaft of his mace until his knuckles showed white.

"Don't threaten my sister," spat Mirri, suddenly lashing out at the cleric with his knife.

Davon grunted in pain, his weapon hand opening by itself and dropping the mace to the ground with a loud clatter. He looked disbelievingly at the blood running down his knuckles.

"Stop right now," Tekkel commanded angrily, getting to his feet and stepping between the two males. Anger lent him the strength to push even the heavier human back. "I'll have no in-Clan fighting! You know the rules, abide by them. Both Davon and Zenithia were in the wrong for acting independently instead of as agreed. Take this fight to the arena if you must, but not here in Hell's Barrow when the zombies will return shortly!"

He stared at Davon until the large human slowly nodded, then turned to Mirri, the other assassin.

Slim, and with the same blue-gray skin tones as he had, the white-haired elf before him had a sullen look on his face. It was easy now as he stood beside his sister to see that they were twins. He frowned briefly, mind going off at a tangent, wondering why that in them, the slimness of their common race seemed more androgynous than it did for him. There was a femininity about them both that he, with his black hair shot with highlights of dark purple, lacked.

Mirri's pale gaze slid away from his and he shrugged. "As you wish, but I'm still watching you, human."

"Tekkel's right, lads, this is no time or place to be arguin'. Did ye get the token we came for, Tekkel?"

With a start, he remembered their objective and checked his inventory. "Yes, I got it, Hurga," he said with relief as he saw the parchment.

"Then let's leave this charnel house," Jinna said. "Where to now, boss?"

"Who's using the portal scroll this time?" asked Shannar, checking over his arrows.

Tekkel relaxed a little and smiled despite himself. With Jinna, the young goblin lass, and Shannar, one of the light-skinned forest elves, he knew where he was. Longest standing members of his clan, they were always dependable, just like Hurga and Meare...

"Where's Meare?" he asked, looking around the dimly lit main chamber of the Barrow.

"Doing what thieves usually do," grinned Jinna, slinging her short bow over her shoulder. "Turning over the corpses for loot."

"Meare! Get your thievin' ass over here!" yelled Hurga, picking up Tekkel's discarded shield and handing it back to him. "'Less you want to be left here alone..."

"I'm here," Meare said, stepping out of the shadows. "Told you I'd been practicing my sneak skills," he grinned, tossing his head to throw the unruly lock of blond hair out of his eyes.

"Well sneak a portal scroll out of your backpack," said Jinna digging him in the thigh with her elbow. "It's your turn to use it."

"Ouch! You watch it, half-pint!" he said, rubbing his leg and glaring at the grinning diminutive sprite. "Your elbows are sharp! Where to, boss?"

"The Witch's Cave in the Dendess Mountains. I need to give her this scroll and get the key into Iskahar Castle." He lengthened the shield's strap and slung it over his back.

A tingle ran down his spine as he felt a familiar rush of energy course through him. Around him, the world took on a faint bluish tinge. "Hurga, hold the buffs for now, please. We could all do with a short break at the Witch's Cave before going on."

"Good idea," agreed the dwarf. "I'm a mite peckish mysel' and could be doin' with a snack and a drink."

"Fifteen-minute break, then," Tekkel agreed. "We'll be safe in the Witch's Cave."

"And what does this gain you?" asked Zenithia as they waited for Meare to dig out his scroll.

He cast her a surprised glance. "I explained it to you when we met up yesterday. It's a quest to advance myself as clan leader and gain us the castle at Iskahar."

She stood silently, her face still as if she were lost in thought.

Meare activated the scroll, calling up the portal. The air in front of him seemed to twist and bend, refracting the flickering lights cast by the guttering torches that lined the walls of the chamber. A low moaning, like that of a beast in agony, began, building in pitch as a glowing, oval rip formed in the very fabric of their world. The pitch of the wind from the void through which they had to travel, rose, sounding like a banshee in full voice.

"That noise always sends shivers of fear through me," Meare said.

Jinna laughed, reaching up to take hold of the young, light-skinned elf's hand where it lay clenched against the side of his thigh.

"Never fear, my brave boy! I, Jinna, the courageous goblin archer, will protect you!" she chuckled.

Meare snorted and looked down at her but didn't remove his hand from hers. "Yeah, right. You and your empty quiver!"

"Mock me not, elfling! All fear my potent arrow spells!"

"Pity you were out of arrows then!" he laughed.

"It's the multi-shots. They use 'em up at a fierce rate."

"I've plenty spare arrows, Jinna," Shannar said, holding out a large bundle toward her. "Got these from the orcish archers I've been hunting these past few days."

"Thank you, brother," she said, taking them from him with her free hand and stuffing them into her empty quiver. "Appreciate that."

Zenithia stirred, her brows meeting in a frown as she regarded Tekkel. "Ah, yes. I remember now. We get benefits from owning a castle — when you kill its lord."

"He'll kill the lord, never fear, lass," said Hurga. "We do it this way, like a clan of assassins should — through stealth, not numbers."

"Aye, the other clans may have more numbers than us, but we beat them all in stealth," said Meare.

"I don't like this way of doing it," Davon said. "We should do it face to face, in daylight, not use shadows and dark paths of magic to achieve our goal."

"Then time you be changin' your god, laddie," said Hurga gruffly, stepping up to the portal. "You been with us long enough to know how we work."

"And face the penalties? Easy for you to say. Your magic doesn't come directly from your deity," Davon snarled, pushing him aside to step through the portal first.

His departure left an ugly silence, during which the others all glanced at each other, then at Tekkel.

He sighed. "Yeah, I know. I gotta do something about him soon."

"Not soon. Today, Tekkel," said Jinna seriously as she and Meare stepped toward the portal. "He's gotten worse since Zenithia and Mirri joined."

Tekkel chose to reply privately to the goblin woman. *"We need him, he's a useful member of Cabal."*

"He was... 'til the other gray elves joined. No one person is more important than our clan. Your words, Tekkel."

"I'll speak to him after I complete the quest," he promised.

"So what are these benefits to the Cabal Clan?" Zenithia asked as they waited for the other clan members to enter the portal. As was customary, Tekkel would be last through and would see that the portal was sealed behind them.

"Well, we'll own the castle. That means while we hold it, we have access to the special rooms within it. A larger storehouse for a start, to store clan goods in, and a crafting room that allows all of us the ability to put materials together to make personalized and more powerful weapons and armor."

"That sounds a fair reward for such a bold deed as we pursue," she said, smiling gently at him. "Do we all have the skills of the dwarves with metal and gems, and the goblins with their armor?"

He nodded, suddenly aware of the warmth of her body against his. "Um... yes," he said, trying to pull his scattered thoughts back to her question. She was leaning against him, and as he took on board yet another of her sudden mood changes, he began looking around for her brother while wondering if he dared risk putting an arm around her.

She laughed, the sound light and pleasant. "My brother's already gone before us. We're the last. Shall we go through this portal together, Tekkel?" she asked, taking hold of his arm.

"Yes indeed," he replied, risking placing his hand over hers as he led the way.

Taking the headset off and laying it carefully on the desk, Robin sat back in his chair with a sigh. On his computer screen, the waterfall outside the Witch's Cave forming an almost romantic backdrop, Tekkel and Zenithia were still standing close, his hand clasped over hers as she held onto his arm. Around them, the rest of his clan sat or stood while their players took advantage of the break.

He wondered what her real name was. Unlike the others, she and her brother — if he was her brother — steadfastly refused to give any details about their real lives or identities. He knew as much about them now as when they had approached him in the Iskahar market six weeks ago. Since then, she had by turns captivated and infuriated him as he'd gotten to know her.

Her features were different from those of the other gray elfin women that were available. Hers were softer, more delicate, but, like the odd touches in her kit that personalized it and the odd spell that acted just a tad differently, it didn't surprise him. He knew that some of the longest playing members on the server had gotten special bonuses from the *Heroes of the Legacy* game company for their efforts over the long months of beta testing the game.

The phone ringing broke into his thoughts and with another sigh, he reached out to pick it up. He wished she would stop blowing hot and cold on him, then…

"Tekkel, it's Davon. We need to talk."

Resolutely, he twisted his chair away from the screen and gave his full attention to the call. "Yes, we do, Davon. What's gotten into you these past few weeks? You've stopped pulling your weight and become undependable, man. I need the old Davon back, the one who was a cornerstone of the clan."

"Since the two elves joined, you've taken me off offensive duties and turned me into nothing more than a healer. I'm sick to death of it, Tekkel!"

"What do you mean? Yes, you're our main healer, but you are still one of our main fighters, you know that…"

"Bullshit! When was the last time you let me fight? I'm sick of playing nursemaid to the clan."

"You fight every time we go out, Davon."

"If you call that fighting, yes, but I don't!"

"You aren't a pure fighter class, you're a healer and a holy warrior. You're supposed to stand back and bless the party, heal them, and turn the undead as well as fight off anything that comes too close to the weaker party members. We all have our place in the clan, our specialty roles…"

"Yeah, well I'm fed up with mine. It's gotten worse since you recruited those two, as I said. We needed more heavy fighters, I told you that at the time! You shouldn't have …"

Inwardly Robin groaned and glanced at the clock, checking the time. He wanted to be back before Zenithia just in case she decided to change her mind and move away from him. He zoned out, his mind returning to the elf woman as he half-listened to yet another of Davon's rants. They'd been becoming too frequent of late. Jinna had done well to remind him that in his own words, no one was more important than the overall good of the Clan. Davon was beginning to outlive his usefulness.

"Well?" Davon said, raising his voice.

Realizing an answer was expected, he tried to work out what it was. "I realize where you're coming from, Davon," he said, taking a long shot, "but I refuse to recruit any more people. The whole ethos behind our clan is that it should remain small." He tried to keep his tone reasonable. "We want the best, not just anyone."

"Are you even listening to me, Tekkel?"

Robin winced. Over the phone, Davon's voice was even more high-pitched than it was in the game.

"Of course I am!' Another glance at the clock—ten minutes left.

"I finished talking about recruiting five minutes ago! I'm talking about me being the witch's sacrifice."

He sat up with a start. That, he hadn't heard him say. "Not possible, Davon. We need you to heal the sacrifice. They face real character death unless they can be kept alive until I finish my quest. They'll die of the plague she gives them without someone with your skills to keep them alive. " He searched his mind for something that would persuade the cleric to drop his request. "You're vital to the quest in that role."

"You can get outside help for that. We know enough people."

"I don't want outside help, neither do the rest of the Clan, and we don't have time to find someone. We're completing the quest now."

"I told you, I'm sick of doing all the healing and babysitting! I want to feel like I am really contributing something for a change."

"We're running out of time, Davon. I need you as our main healer—only your divine healing spells can save the sacrifice, I made that plain last night at the clan meeting. If you didn't want to be involved in this, you should have said so at the time. Now we both have to get back to the game. I'll see you there."

"Zenithia can heal too—if she uses a Potion of Blessing, her heals will be the same as mine."

"I need her with me. We'll need to fight off any guards we come across once we step through the witch's portal into the castle. She's a damage-dealing class, unlike you."

"Just because you've got the hots for her..."

"Don't go there, Davon," said Robin coldly. "Just do your job and we'll talk about this again tomorrow."

"I find them intimidating. They're up to no good, you know. They aren't real Cabal material, Tekkel. I've been watching them for weeks now."

"Dammit, Davon, this is just a game! It isn't the real world! Get a grip, man!" He slammed the phone down angrily, not caring if he upset Davon to the point where the other logged out of the game and left them to fend for themselves. If he did, at least they'd all get some peace!

He glanced at the clock. Three minutes left, just enough time to grab a bag of pretzels to munch on while they completed the rest of the Quest.

When he put on the headset, then eased his hands into the gaming gloves, he was once more immersed in the world of Sondherst Designed for *Legacy of Heroes*, it surrounded him with the sounds and smells of the world, and relayed feedback from his character, and the others he interacted with, allowing him the sensation of touch. Though the avatars they each used to represent their characters might be stock ones, for those with this interface, they and their world really came alive: even their facial expressions and gestures mirrored those of the players, creating a rich virtual world almost indistinguishable from the real one.

He returned to find Zenithia still leaning against him, in the crook of his arm. Around him, the others were still seated, and there was none of the usual banter going on in their Clan chatting area. He was obviously the first one to return.

"Hi, I'm back," he said to her, using the private chat channel.

"Welcome back," she said, her tone somehow making the ritual words sound more personal.

"Is Mirri really your brother?" he blurted out. *"Or is he… someone special in your life?"*

She'd always avoided this issue, but he had to know because he was already getting too involved with her. If Mirri was her partner, he had to step back from her now, before it was too late.

The look she gave him was one of gentle amusement. *"So intense,"* she murmured. *"I like that in elfin kind, and in my men. Fear not, my dark one, Mirri is indeed my twin brother."*

He felt an easing of tension and a sudden quickening of his heartbeat. *"Do you play in the same room? Can he hear us talking?"*

"He's stepped out of the room for now," she said, turning to look at him. *"Do you have something to say you'd rather he didn't hear, perhaps?"*

"No… Yes."

He was floundering now, and he knew it. It had been so long since he'd dated anyone, not since his disastrous relationship with Anna. It was because of her he'd gotten involved in this game, seeing in it a world that held less pain than the one he woke up to each morning. Until recently, that was.

"Then you should hurry, dark one. Your clanmates are beginning to return, and soon so will my twin."

He gathered his scattered thoughts, and his courage, and plunged in. *"I'd like you to be my partner,"* he said. *"Not just here, but in RL too."*

There was a pause before she replied. *"In Real Life? I wonder what that is. There are so many realities,"* she murmured, then seemed to give herself a little shake. *"You want us to meet? What if the reality of me is not what you expect?"*

"I don't care," he said. *"I know what you're like as a person, that's all that matters to me."*

She put her hands on his arms and looked up into his eyes, her expression thoughtful. *"Are you proposing a betrothal between us? Will you accept my reality, no matter what?"*

He hesitated, wondering if he was ready for such a commitment with a woman he'd not yet met in the flesh. Also, some sixth sense was shouting a warning to him. Sensing her beginning to turn away, he ruthlessly suppressed it and, in a rush said, *"Yes! I will!"*

"Back," said Jinna in their Clan chat. *"Who else is here? That you, Tekkel?"*

"Welcome back, Jinna. Yeah, I'm here."

"Thanks. I see Zenithia is back. You two look rather cozy right now. Welcome back to you both. Not disturbing you, am I?' There was an amused tone to her voice.

"Not really. Just discussing something."

"Ah, clan business," she nodded, putting a knowing finger to the side of her button nose. "I understand. She's very quiet. Lag?"

"Back," said Shannar.

"Me, too," said Meare.

"Welcome back," he murmured, watching Zenithia, wondering why she hadn't replied to him. "I don't think she's lagging. I haven't noticed any delays from her until now."

"Ah, nothin' like a full belly and a drink ta make a dwarf feel good," said Hurga as he got to his feet.

Still watching her, he added his welcome to those of the others.

"You had no right!" he heard her say in a low, almost feral hiss. "Burn it! " Zenithia added, moving closer to him. *Come with me a moment,*" she whispered, then stepped back to draw him toward the waterfall that hid the opening of the cave.

He accompanied her, letting himself be diverted from wondering what was happening between her and her brother.

The roaring of the water drowned out the chatter from the others as they stood on the edges of the fall, a faint mist of water dampening their faces and hair.

"What's wrong?" he asked, concerned.

"Nothing. Was only my brother returning. When this is over, tell me again that you'll share my world, my night creature," she whispered. *"If you do, then I'll be your partner."*

He raised her hand to his lips. *"With pleasure,"* he murmured as he gently pressed his lips to her cool skin. *"You're the moonlight in my life, Zenithia."*

A smile lit her features. *"And you have the ability still to astonish me, my dark one."*

"We must return to the others," he said, leading her reluctantly back to the group. There would be time for them when this quest was over.

"Anyone seen Davon?" Shannar asked suddenly. "Has he logged out?"

"I'm with the witch," said Davon. "Hurga, you better come heal me. I'm the sacrifice."

Tekkel cursed under his breath. "I should have known better than to trust you! You've left me without a healer for the rest of the quest, dammit!"

"You can use your elf maiden," Davon said. "She has a battle healing spell. I know you'd rather have her along than me."

"What the hell do you mean by that?" he demanded.

"That I can see the writing on the wall, Tekkel. I won't let you use me anymore, won't let you relegate me to being just a healer. Hurga, my health is failing. If I die, then so does your precious Tekkel."

"Aye, well you can damned well wait on us now," said Hurga, readying himself to cast. "Ye'll be needin' my buffs now more than ever, Tekkel. Who's goin' with ye?"

"Dammit, Davon, this is only a game you know! It's not real! There's no need to get so worked up about it," said Tekkel angrily. "We each do what's needed for the good of the clan!"

"It's real to me, Tekkel! I've invested several months of my time in this game!"

"Get a life," snorted Jinna.

Tekkel lowered his voice and turned to the goblin woman. "My apologies, Jinna. I appreciate you volunteering to be the sacrifice, but I'd as soon not risk losing you if anything goes wrong. Maybe this will work out for the best. Zerk me, Hurga," he said as the different glows of Hurga's ability enhancements surrounded him briefly, one by one.

"Ye sure, lad?" Hurga asked. "Berserk Rage is a risky buff for one as you. You can't take the damage."

"I know, but we have less time than we thought to do this without you. Zenithia, can you handle healing as well as using your spells?"

"I can, but I'll run low on magic power."

"Just do what you can, please. We'll have to rely fully on stealth to succeed now. Only Mirri and I are close combat fighters."

Mirri stirred and got to his feet. "So what's the problem? You don't need more than us two to succeed."

"You got twenty minutes, lad. Then the buffs'll fade and ye'll have to rely on your special abilities alone. When I think o' what that cleric is puttin' at risk just ta satisfy his own ambitions. Ye face character death if ye fail!"

Tekkel reached out to squeeze the dwarf's shoulder. "Peace, my friend," he said quietly. "I won't fail. How can I? I have my loyal kin with me."

Hurga looked up at him, understanding, and smiling slowly. "Aye, that ye have."

"Do your best to keep him alive. I'll not let it be said we didn't try." Hurga nodded.

"I'll go talk to the witch while you buff the others. Join me when you're done," he said, looking around the ring of grim faces.

"That double-dealing human scumbag..." began Meare. "Never have guessed we were harboring a viper like him!"

"Save it for later," said Tekkel over his shoulder, striding off into the cave. "There will be an accounting for this, you hear me, Davon?"

The witch had teleported them into the heart of Iskahar Castle. It was now up to them to reach the lord's library, where he was closeted with his three advisors, and kill them all. Then Tekkel's Clan Cabal would not only own the castle, but he'd have advanced another level as a leader and assassin and get the corresponding extra skills.

Now they stood outside the library door.

"Jinna, what arrows do you have with you?"

"I've one smoke, and a couple of fire and water left," the young archer replied. "Don't want to use the fire ones in a library, though, won't do the books much good."

"Forget them. That's the last thing on my mind."

"Your health is low, boss," said Shannar. "Too low to carry on."

"You—we—need Hurga with us!" exclaimed Jinna.

He nodded, his thoughts elsewhere as he ran through the battle plan they'd formed, then his possible options now that Davon had screwed everything up.

"You still have several options," said Mirri, uncannily following his thoughts. "Success of your quest doesn't depend on keeping the sacrifice alive, does it? Sometimes a sacrifice is just that."

Tekkel looked at the gray elf leaning nonchalantly against the wall, paring his nails with the tip of his long-bladed knife. "It's a game, Mirri, and he's still kin, despite what he did." He'd thought exactly the same himself but was damned if he was going to admit it.

"None of us are very healthy," said Zenithia sitting down where she stood. "I need to regen my magic powers or I won't be able to heal us and fight. I can gate Hurga here. Tell him to leave the human with a pile of healing potions and join us."

"We still have ten minutes left. We'll rest for two now," he said, sitting down beside her. "We'll take health potions. You should all have enough."

"You're letting one human jeopardize us all!" hissed Mirri, slamming his knife into its scabbard then sliding down the wall into a sitting position with a cat-like grace Tekkel envied.

"Peace, Mirri," said Shannar. "You're taking this too seriously. Only Tekkel and Davon face character death, not us. Sure, we'll lose some of our expertise if we die, but not that much."

Lightning fast, Mirri leaned forward and grasped his sister by the hand, letting loose a stream of what was obviously angry invective even though the language itself was lyrical.

As Tekkel instinctively strained to understand them, Zenithia answered in kind, pulling herself free with an effort that caused her to overbalance into him. As he grabbed hold of her and braced himself, he caught a couple of phrases he did understand.

"Hey, guys, chill out," said Jinna, stepping deftly between them and Mirri. "I'm as angry as the next person, but... Tekkel's right, it is only a game."

Mirri sat back, and Zenithia used Tekkel's shoulder to steady herself as she got abruptly to her feet and stood over him. "I am ready now. Time is wasting."

"Hold on," he said, scrambling to his feet. "What were you two talking about? Who is this one you're looking for?"

"Nothing for you to concern yourself with, elfling," Zenithia said condescendingly in one of her characteristic mood swings.

Confused, Tekkel still caught the tiny by-play between brother and sister as Mirri leaned forward again, mouth open, and Zenithia raised her hand slightly in a negative gesture.

"The plan, Tekkel."

"We go with the area of effect spells, you especially, Zenithia. These will hopefully affect Lord Iskahar and his three guards. Your poison cloud will chip away at their health as we do more damage. My shadow should slow them all down too, making it more difficult for them to see us."

"Then let's get moving," said Zenithia.

"Meare, use your lock-picking skills on the door," Tekkel ordered.

A dull crash, followed by the sound of something spherical rolling across a wooden floor brought Aziel out of his after-dinner nap.

"What?" he muttered, raising his head and blinking. His sensitive ears picked up the low squeal of terror and the scuttling of bare feet on floorboards from the next room as someone ran after the object.

Now fully awake, Aziel focused all his attention on the probable culprit. "Twilby!" he roared. "What havoc have you caused now?" Then he knew. "My seeing crystal!"

Leaping to his feet, wings spread at half height to give him balance, Aziel crossed his sleeping chamber in three bounds

"Not me, Master! Crystal began glowing then leapt to floor!" the drudge whined as the dragon mage's gallop was brought to an abrupt end when his shoulders crashed into the door frame.

To the sound of ominous creaks and groans, a shower of plaster and a few solid chunks of ceiling and wall debris rained down on Aziel.

He snarled, his long neck snaking through the doorway, tongue extended, nostrils quivering and leaking small tendrils of smoke as he sought his servant. Turning sideways, he reached into the room with one huge, clawed hand and grasped hold of the squealing drudge.

"What did you do to my crystal?" he roared, pulling Twilby into his sleeping chamber and holding him aloft.

"Nothing, Master!" he shrieked, grasping hold of the huge claws in terror. "I did nothing! It jumped off the table!"

"You lie!" Aziel snarled, shaking the drudge violently.

"No! I swear!"

Still snarling and hissing in anger, Aziel lowered his hand to the ground then backed up a few paces and, tail scything angrily across the scarred wooden floor, muttered the incantation that changed him into human form.

Moments later, he had Twilby firmly by the ear and was dragging him into his study. "Fetch my crystal!" he ordered, tossing Twilby away from him.

Twilby went sprawling across the floor to collide with the side of a tall press. Scrambling to his hands and knees, he reached under it to draw out the object in question.

"Here, Master," he said, crabbing his way back to Aziel's side, the crystal held up in one sooty, ash-covered hand.

Aziel snatched it from him, rubbing it against the sleeve of his robe as he strode over to his desk to examine it.

"It's not glowing now," he said, gesturing toward the large oil lamp on his desk. As it flared to life, he sat down at his desk, remembering to adjust his weight to human normal as he heard the chair start to crack under him.

"Was when I saw it."

Aziel grunted, his hands cupping the crystal as he ran them gently over the surface feeling for any blemishes. He stopped, passing his fingertips lightly over one point, then leaned closer to the light to look at the surface there.

"It's chipped," he snarled, glaring over his shoulder at the drudge hunkered down in the corner furthest from him. It was only the tiniest of slivers that were missing; with any luck, it would still function properly.

Twilby began to gibber incoherently.

"Get out! You're disturbing me," he said, losing interest in him as a faint glow began to form in the center of the crystal globe. "Ah, the guildsfolk. I see they have found their new leader."

Tekkel's emergency plan had fallen apart the moment they entered the library and found Iskahar's minions waiting for them behind the bookcases that bisected the room.

"Incoming dammit! Skellies incoming! They've changed the whole encounter!" snarled Shannar, backing into the nearest corner and dropping his bow for the long ranger's knife as a skeleton warrior suddenly materialized in front of him.

"Jinna, support him," Tekkel snapped, leaping forward with Mirri to engage the strongest of the three guards. "Use stealth skills, Meare!" He spared a glance at Zenithia, making sure she was standing far enough back from the main attack.

Next he knew, everyone but him had moved and he was staggering and trying to get his balance because Mirri had hit him.

"You got stunned," the elf said as Tekkel recovered then spun round to face the guard again, lashing out at him with a poisoned blade attack.

"Thanks," he muttered, closing in on their mutual target. "Zen, sleep the other two! We can't fight more than one at a time!"

"I'm trying, but he's got too high a resistance. If I attack them, I'll draw their aggro on me."

"Shannar, get your ass out of that corner and root them!" he yelled, wincing in pain as he was hit yet again from behind. The feedback from his game enhancements was getting a mite too realistic; that blow had actually hurt.

"On my way," Shannar called as the skeleton uttered a thin cry and disintegrated.

Tekkel launched a flurry of blows, complementing those Mirri was doing, then, as the guard keeled over, rounded on the one that had been doing him the most damage. A pair of knives flew past him to embed themselves in the chest of the third guard.

"Meare, same target! Support us."

"Sorry, boss, thought I was. Very crowded in there."

"Tell me," he muttered as the third guard began to pound on his back. "Shannar, any time now would be good!"

A bolt of energy zapped past him, making their opponent stagger back. Almost before the spell had dissipated, Zen's next one went off, surrounding the guard in a casing of ice for a few seconds. From behind him, he caught the flash of Shannar's root spell going off.

He nodded, pleased. "Good, Shannar. Nice casting speed there, Zen."

Tearing his attention out of the game, he looked at the monitor screen to check how the rest of the clan were doing. Shannar was back with Jinna and using his bow, the two of them forming a bodyguard for Zen—and she was casting her spells almost without pause.

Checking her interface on the party list, he saw her magic power was dropping rapidly, but that was to be expected. On his and Mirri's right flank, Meare had placed himself against the corner of a bookcase and was throwing volleys of his knives.

A flash of pain suddenly lanced through him and he'd barely time to glance at the clock before it dragged him back into the game.

This time, he really did gasp and clutch his side as his avatar was brought to its knees. What the hell was happening? This was *not* part of the game...

"You left the fight," hissed Mirri as he slashed at the remaining guard. "Foolish! He injured you."

"Checking the time," he said, pushing himself up unsteadily to his feet, trying to keep his mind focused on the encounter. "Five minutes left!"

"He leads them too well," snarled Aziel, the hand holding the crystal clenching until long talons began to replace his fingers. "I wanted a fool, not a warrior!"

With a gesture and brief incantation, the scene in the globe began to form on the top of his desk.

"Time for more direct action..."

"ADD, three Three incoming from behind us!" Meare yelled out. "Undead Knights!"

As one, Tekkel and Mirri sidestepped, forcing their opponent around so they could see the new assailants.

"Zen, all of you, move! Fire protection buffs!" he yelled.

"Shit! This is all wrong! What the hell's happening?" demanded Meare, reaching for his sword.

"Deal with it," snapped Tekkel, powering up another Poison attack as Mirri let off one of his Wounding ones. "Time for that later."

Zenithia, flanked by Jinna and Shannar, headed past them to take up a position further into the room, casting as she ran.

"Undead Knights? And too many, Zen," Tekkel heard Mirri say quietly as Zenithia finished buffing him and began on her brother.

"I know," Zen snapped back tartly. "Just do your job... brother."

To Tekkel, it sounded like Miri's low voice cracked slightly, taking on a higher pitch. Then, uttering a sound like a low snarl, Mirri flicked a small bolt of energy out to zap her: the elf woman stopped dead, frozen to the spot.

"Stop fighting each other!" Tekkel ordered. "Time's running out!"

As Zenithia began to move again, a pulsating circle of fire surrounded the lead knight.

Muttering the incantation to drain health from him, Tekkel instinctively winced then braced himself as the fire flared upward before suddenly exploding outward in a circle toward them.

It hurt, by all the gods of Sondhast Sondherst, it *really* hurt, despite Zen's buffs! Even as he gasped, a sudden icy wave swept through him, cooling then banishing the pain so he could think again. Around him, he heard the other's exclamations of pain and disbelief.

"Fight! I will keep you all safe!" Zenithia called.

Still shaking, Tekkel shifted his grip on his knives. He needed to warn Zen of something, but his thoughts were still scattered. The first knight was nearly upon them and the other two were beginning to cast their fire spells. As he readied himself, he heard Zen and Mirri exchanging a few terse words in their own language.

Calling on his weapons' special abilities, he met the knight with raised blades as two of Meare's water arrows, one swiftly followed by the other, arced over him to hit the casters.

We need them rooted and slept now, he thought.

As he darted inside the knight's defense, blocking with one knife and slashing with the other, he saw their fire spell gutter and die. Then Zen's sleep and Shannar's root hit them.

Seconds later, Mirri was beside him, drawing the knight's attack.

He backed off, checking the party health—all were low, too low, and Zen was almost out of magic. "Potions everyone!" he yelled, leaping back in to attack again. This had to be finished fast.

"I'm out," yelled Shannar.

"Me, too," said Jinna, the tremor in her voice audible. "This is getting scary, Tekkel. I don't like it."

An ear-piercing shriek sounded from behind him. He didn't need to look to know it was Zenithia. "Iskahar!' He'd meant to warn her to watch out for the castle lord!

"It's Aziel!" she screamed.

Aziel? Who the hell was Aziel? He swung round, heart pounding, to see Zenithia held, a knife to her throat, by Lord Iskahar.

Beside him, Mirri let out a string of what he assumed were oaths, then stopped and in a voice altered beyond recognition, uttered one word.

"What the hell..." began Meare, taking cover behind the nearest bookcase.

"Portal, Meare," Tekkel snapped, sizing up the situation, ignoring the thought that this could not be happening. "Hurga, I need you here now," he said quietly, risking a glance back at the knight. He stood motionless, as if frozen to the spot.

"On my way," Hurga said.

"You can't," he heard Davon say. "I'll die."

"Then come," said Hurga.

"Let my sister go, Aziel," Mirri ordered, stepping forward. "You have no business here."

"I want him," said Aziel, raising a long thin hand and pointing at Tekkel. "Give me the human and your sister is free."

"No!" hissed Zenithia, struggling in his grasp. "He cannot be trusted…" Her words were cut off abruptly as the lord tightened the arm across her throat.

Mirri's out-thrust arm pushed him back as he stepped forward. "No," said the elf unequivocally. "He's ours."

"Dammit, Mirri," he began.

"Wait," Mirri hissed, holding him back again. "You're not our leader yet! I brought friends!"

There wasn't time to be confused as a motley crew of beings, including Hurga and Davon, suddenly materialized around them.

Aziel began to laugh, the sound deep and echoing as if it came from the very bowels of the earth.

Tekkel watched in horror as the features of the avatar altered, the hair turning black as midnight, the skin darkening to a tanned hue, the eyes… Oh gods, those eyes! He groaned, shutting his own, but the huge red orbs with their vertical yellow slits continued to grow larger and larger in his mind's eye. Then his courage reasserted itself and he opened his own again, seeing this time, not just a man, but underlying it the form of something else, something that had no right existing in the world of *Legacy of Heroes*.

"This isn't real, it can't be," he heard himself mutter as he stared at the red dragon mage. Around him, the eight newcomers—four elves, three dwarves, and a being he took to be a half-orc—moved forward to surround him and Mirri. Grim-faced and with battered and stained armor, they were very different from the avatars he and the others used.

"You vermin really think you can withstand me?" laughed Aziel, moving his grip till his large hand encircled Zenithia's neck and his knife was in his other hand. "Gate in as many as you wish, elf, they'll meet the same fate as last time!"

"Let the elf maiden go!" Davon demanded in ringing tones as, sword and shield held ready, he stepped forward. "Pick your fight with equals, not women, you coward!"

"No, Davon," Tekkel said as all eyes focused on the cleric. "This isn't the time for melodrama!"

Davon ignored him, stepping closer to Aziel and Zenithia as Mirri let his arm drop to pull his second blade.

Aziel cocked his head to one side and regarded him with obvious amusement. "You want to die now, manling?"

Aziel's attention now off him, Tekkel moved slowly behind Mirri and his friends. He triggered his shadow spell, then using the last of his haste and speed potions, pulled out his bow. Then he stepped forward again, his eyes never leaving Davon and Aziel, watching and waiting for the opportunity he knew must come. This time, his mind was made up that he would sacrifice the cleric for Zen.

"Fight me, man to man, or do you prefer to hide behind a woman." Davon taunted.

"You bore me, manling," said Aziel, flicking his knife toward the cleric and raising his eyes to the rest of them.

As the knife tumbled end over tip, almost in slow motion, toward Davon, Tekkel began his run toward Aziel. Triggering powered multi shots, he let off two volleys of arrows before dropping the bow and reaching for his knives again.

"Be ready!" he whispered, toggling the private channel between him and Zenithia as he leapt high and spun round in a poison blade attack, hitting first the dragon lord, then Zenithia with the pommel of his other blade as he somersaulted over the mage's head. Coming down behind him, he twisted around, landing in a crouch. Pushing himself to his feet, he triggered his backstab ability, checking that Zenithia had collapsed in Aziel's grip before once more launching himself at the mage's back.

Aziel dropped the dead weight that his captive had become. Ignoring the four arrows sticking out of his limbs, he began a half turn to meet him, calling out an incantation to re-animate the death knights again.

The chime signifying a party death sounded loud in Tekkel's ears as he jumped over Zen, and began lashing out at Aziel, forcing the other to take a couple of steps back.

With a roar of anger, the mage began to cast, but not before Tekkel was surrounded by Hurga's healing light — and the glow from other buffs as the newcomer mages worked to protect him.

"Davon?" he heard Jinna call. "Davon! You okay?"

Lightning streaked from Aziel's hands toward him, only to rebound and hit the mage.

"Forget him, Jinna!" Shannar was saying. "Get the knights!"

He pressed forward again, this time doing more damage to Aziel, who began to back off, chanting.

Arrows flew past him, hitting the mage, breaking his concentration as Mirri and his friends came rushing past him.

Mirri stopped briefly beside him. "Dammit, that hurt, Tekkel! Take my sister and back off. Leave this to us. You don't yet know Aziel as we do."

"What?" Tekkel demanded, staring at him.

The elf's face split in a brief grin. "Get my sister. It was me you hit, in her avatar, not her. She's waiting." Then he was gone, racing after his companions.

"Well, my dark one," said a voice he knew well at his elbow. "Are you ready?"

"Ready?" he echoed. "Ready for what? This is a game, it can't be real." A thousand and one questions were racing around inside his head right now.

"To come with me," she said, stepping closer. Snapping her fingers, her staff disappeared, and a portal began to open, one unlike any he'd ever seen before. Reality bent, making the room seem to melt slightly round the edges of the glowing slit that formed in front of them. The wind sighed and moaned through it as flares of colored lightning sparked from one side to the other.

"We need to get you to our realm, away from Aziel," she said, reaching out to encircle his waist with her arms. "I thank you for your gallant attempt to save me, even though it was Mirri playing my poor battle mage at the time, not me."

"Mirri?" Suddenly her mood swings made sense. "You two, you kept switching avatars on me," he said accusingly, even as he put one arm around her. Another thought struck him and he felt the blood rise to his face.

She laughed gently, pressing herself close against him until he could smell the scent of her hair and feel the ample curves he knew were there despite her slim avatar.

"Tell me again you want to share my world, Tekkel," she whispered.

"My clan," he said, pushing her back. "This battle… you. None of it's real."

"You still here?" he heard Mirri shout. "Burn it, Zen, take our new leader home then we can *all* leave!"

"You heard my brother. We all go. Will you come now?" she asked again, gently pulling him toward the portal.

He laughed uncertainly. There was too much that couldn't be explained about this quest, but there had to be a rational one. "Sure, I'll go along with your role-playing, Zen. Just don't expect me to believe in it too much.'

"Tekkel, Davon's gone," said Jinna, stopping beside them. "I can't raise him at all. And his avatar... It's all mangled, and the game doesn't do that to us, or the mobs we kill!"

"Davon?" he called out, looking around for the cleric's corpse. He saw it lying a few feet from them, just as Jinna had described.

"He's dead," Mirri said, running up to where they stood on the edges of the portal. "And so will we be if we don't leave now!" He gave them both a hefty shove.

Tekkel felt himself falling and grabbed hold of Zenithia as everything suddenly went dark and an icy coldness spread through him.

"What the hell's happening?" he tried to say, but his words were torn from him and shredded by the bitter wind that swirled them violently about.

He felt her hand touch his neck, pull his head down to hers, then her breath warm against his ear.

"Is this real enough for you?" she asked before her lips sought his in a kiss as deep and intimate as he'd been wishing for.

Forgotten was the bitter cold of the portal, as was any thought of what was real. The kiss seemed to last forever until suddenly, with a jolt, he felt solid ground under his feet again.

He heard someone cough, then say in a voice that sounded suspiciously like it was trying not to laugh, "Welcome to Eldeglast, Clan Leader Tekkel, and welcome back, Zenithia."

Blinking like an owl, Tekkel lifted his head and squinted over the top of Zen's, seeing an elf bowing at them, realizing with acute embarrassment that he and Zen were still locked in an embrace—and that he didn't care. He looked around the large, sunlit room at the small gathering of assorted elves, dwarves, and other races he couldn't readily identify as the rest of his gaming clan, then Mirri and his companions began to wink into existence.

"This is your new home," said Zenithia, stepping back a little and taking him by the hand. "Welcome to Eldeglast's Guild of Acquirers and Facilitators."

"Better known as the Assassins' and Thieves' Guild," said Mirri, walking smartly over to the speaker. "Merrik, Aziel was there. We caused him some grief, and likely he'll be smarting for a while, but he'll be back. Send up the healers then set guards for now. Oh, and some food would be good—we're all starving."

Still in a daze of disbelief, Tekkel heard a small shriek then a diminutive pixie ran up to him, grabbing at his armored leg and shaking it—just as Jinna used to do.

"Tekkel! Oh, my godfathers! You're a gray elf! A real gray elf!" said Jinna. "And I'm... "

"A pixie," said Mirri, stripping off his mail gloves and handing them to one of the non-fighters. "The goblins of your game don't exist here."

Startled, he looked down at himself, saw the pale gray-blue skin of his hand where it rested in Zenithia's one of the same color. He looked up, seeing not the slim almost ethereal female avatar he was used to, but an elven woman of flesh and blood, and generous curves under the skimpy clothes she wore.

"Well, am I real enough for you now?" she asked, arching a pale eyebrow at him as she pulled him to her side with a proprietary gesture. "I promise I won't let my twin change places with me again."

"He'd better not," said Tekkel, finding his voice at last as he slipped his arm around her waist.

To Catch a Thief

THE SMALL DEMON HUNKERED DOWN ON ITS HAUNCHES, PEERING THROUGH the chinks in the flat wooden roof. Strips of light from the room below bathed his wrinkled brown face, highlighting the two tiny horns that poked through his thick curly hair. From her vantage point, Mouse could clearly see the white underside of his nub of a tail as it began to stir. He leaned closer, hands resting on the unstable surface as he listened intently, his pointed ears twitching to catch every word.

Mouse waited patiently. She had to be sure Kadron actually had Cullen, and that he was still alive.

Deep within her mind, something alien stirred. *This is foolhardy,* came the silken thought from the jewel that lived within her. *The boy is nothing to you – a beggar, a cripple, what use is he? Why risk your life for him? Leave him to this Kadron.*

Anger surged through her. "Leave me alone!" she hissed. "Get out of my head! I don't want you inside me!"

How could she have been so stupid as to break her own rules and accept a contract from a mage? Served her right for cheating on Kadron and taking on a private job in the first place. She focused her attention on Zaylar, using her anger to force the jewel's alien presence back down into her subconscious.

Zaylar glanced uncertainly in her direction. Of late, he'd developed a knack of knowing when the jewel was speaking to her. He stood up, and as sure-footed as any mountain creature, trotted back across to her, his tiny hooves barely making a sound on the rickety wooden surface.

"Boy there," he confirmed quietly. "On floor, in ropes."

"Is he alive?"

Zaylar nodded vigorously as he crouched down beside her. "Must be. Squirms lots."

"How many men?"

"Four. One fat man with loud clothes, and another, stand over boy. Two more hide behind cases opposite door. Is a trap for sure." He peered at her, his ancient, seamed face wrinkling in concern. "Why go save boy? Leave him. Then you no need to sign Kadron's papers, lose Kolin's house, everything, maybe even life."

Even the demon agrees with me, whispered the jewel, taking advantage of her distraction. "Shut up!" she muttered, scrubbing the palm of her right hand against her pants leg as if by doing so, she could remove the jewel itself. If only she hadn't picked the damned thing up, or worn gloves, then it couldn't have seared its way into her flesh and become part of her. How was she supposed to know it was alive?

Zaylar pulled back and began to chitter in distress until Mouse put a hand on his shoulder. The heat from his bare flesh warmed her. "Not you, imp. The jewel," she said, shivering. But the coldness she felt had nothing to do with the chill night air.

Zaylar touched her knee with his small, clawed fingers. "You all right, Lady? Must fight jewel, not let it control you!" His panic was palpable in every line of his body.

"You do this every time I go out on a job!" she muttered, brow furrowing with the effort of fighting the jewel's increased efforts to dominate her mind. Her head had begun to ache and she felt light-headed and nauseous.

You are wealthy, there is no need to steal. All Kolin owned is now legally yours, even the magistrate confirmed this. Let Kadron kill the boy. Why risk your life to save his? Think of all I could teach you about magic. You could become the greatest mage on Jalna, the only female in nine hundred years to achieve this.

"He's my friend! It's my fault Kadron kidnapped him. I owe him!" she said, putting her hands up to massage her aching temples.

"Must not listen to jewel, Lady," said Zaylar urgently, his hand tightening on her knee until his claws pricked her flesh. "We save Cullen, then find book. I teach you demon magics then jewel no threat to you."

With the demon still touching her, she could feel his fears as if they were her own. He was afraid that if the jewel dominated her, he'd have no chance of gaining back the magic his king had stripped from him before casting him out of the Demon Realms and into the world of Jalna and its battling mages. Nor would he be able to get her to make him the talisman that would prevent him ever being bound by another — demon or mage — again. He'd have to continue his life of servitude to her, then the next four wizards after her. Between him and the jewel, she was being torn in opposite directions in a battle for her very soul.

Impatiently, she pushed his hand away and stood up, her anger finally providing enough force to drive the jewel's presence back.

"Let's get moving," she snapped, her hands automatically checking the sword that hung over her left hip. "We got Cullen to rescue."

The day had gone badly from the start. A high-pitched chittering, interspersed with the sounds of objects hitting a wall, had brought Mouse to wakefulness. She groaned. *What the hell was Zaylar up to now?* The demon had been a pain in the butt from the night she'd inherited him.

Throwing back the covers, she sat up and swung her legs out of the bed. As her toes hit the richly carpeted floor, she curled them in pleasure. Not for her the bare floorboards of her old digs above the taproom of the Packrats' Inn, nor the noise of the rowdy drunks celebrating below. That had all changed the night she'd killed Wizard Kolin and she'd inherited this house—and his small demon.

A loud crash preceded a shriek of rage, bringing her back to reality. Sighing, she reached for her pants and tunic, hauling them on before bending to scrabble on the floor just under the bed for her socks and boots. This needed her personal attention. She couldn't leave it to Cullen. One foot done, she hopped toward the door while trying to do the other. The gods knew what Zaylar was up to now, but it didn't sound good. On a sudden impulse, she stopped, returning to pick up the slim volume from her night table.

As she flung open the door to the late mage's study, the sight that greeted her was one of total chaos. Books, obviously flung in temper, littered the floor, lying in every state of disarray, some with their spines broken and the pages floating loose.

"Zaylar!" she yelled, looking around the room for him. "What the hell are you doing?"

He emerged from behind Kolin's desk. "I look for book," he said, scowling.

Mouse surveyed the mess. "That's an understatement!"

"Must find. You need."

She looked back at him, eyes narrowing. "I need, or you? You're supposed to be helping me learn magic, not wrecking my house!"

The demon's brow furrowed beneath the mass of dark curls. "Need Kolin's diary," he insisted. "Magics in there help us. I need them to teach you. Tidy later."

"You damned well better! What's it look like? Maybe I've seen it," she said, picking her way through the piles of books till she was standing over him.

Zaylar made a rude noise.

"What do you mean by that?" she demanded, aware of his contempt for her.

"I read, you can't," he snorted, his brown face becoming even more wrinkled as he frowned. "Jalnians don't teach females to read, everyone knows that!"

Her hand darted out to catch him by one of his pointed ears, as with the other, she pulled the slim book from her pocket, holding it high above him. "Is this the book you want?"

"Yes!" he shrieked, clawing at her hand as he peered up at it. "Let go! You hurting Zaylar!"

"You didn't tell me the truth about yourself, did you? That you were bound, not just to Kolin, but to the next five mages after him. That he only allowed you small magic spells because he considered you untrustworthy."

"He lied! Am trustworthy! Kolin hated Zaylar even though Zaylar did everything he asked!" He stopped, his small body becoming suddenly stiff and rigid. "How you know what Kolin thought?"

"I never told you about my mother, did I?" she said conversationally. "She was from a wealthy family, until she had me. Then they threw her out." She pinched his ear hard, making him shriek even louder than before.

He danced from hoof to hoof in pain, hands once more scrabbling at her in an effort to free himself.

"Mother taught me to read." She let him go and returned the book to her pocket.

Zaylar scowled up at her, rubbing his ear vigorously. "No need to hurt Zaylar. I trying to help you. Promised, I did. You make me amulet, I teach you magic, stop jewel from taking you over."

"The jewel's not bothered me in a while," she lied. "And just how are you going to teach me magic when you barely know any yourself?" She raised a questioning eyebrow at him.

He looked at the ground, shifting from hoof to hoof. "Used to know lots of magic, but king took it away when he banished me here," he mumbled. "Know how to get it back. When I get it, same time I teach you."

"A failed rebel. Some useful demon you are," she snorted. "You can start earning your keep by tidying up the mess you made. You know enough magic to do that, don't you?" she asked sarcastically as she turned to make her way back to the door. "I'm going to the kitchen to get some food. Join me there when you're finished."

He muttered something unintelligible.

Mouse stopped dead and rounded on him. "I didn't hear that."

"Yes, Mistress," he said, baring his needle-sharp teeth at her in a parody of a smile.

She grunted. "Hurry up. You got a bargain to seal with me when you're done."

After having read the contract aloud to Zaylar, Mouse put it down and signed it, then pushed it over to him.

"Your turn," she said. Beneath the table, she slowly slipped her boot knife out of its scabbard and laid it flat against her thigh, ready for the final part of their deal. She'd read Kolin's diary carefully and knew exactly what was needed to bind Zaylar to this agreement. The fact he was bound to her by the terms of the Demon King's punishment wasn't enough; she wanted her own, personal insurance, just as Kolin had done. Except her contract was more comprehensive.

Muttering beneath his breath, the imp glared at her, his eyes taking on a reddish glow as he snatched the quill from her and scrawled his name on the bottom of the page. He tossed it down on the table when he was done. "You not trust Zaylar," he said. "Offended, I am."

Mouse brought her hand up onto the table, knife tucked against her palm, ready to use. "Damned right I don't. Pass it back to me," she said, watching his every movement. Timing was vital in this.

As Zaylar slid it across the table toward her, she pounced on his hand, nicking it with her knife so it bled onto the contract, right over their signatures.

He squealed like a stuck pig, grasping his hand to his chest as his eyes glowed red as coals in a fire. "You cheat me!" he howled. "Insult my honor! I promise you, I sign your precious paper, then you stick knife in me!"

Mouse snatched up the contract and sat back in her chair, regarding him with a faint smile. "Now it's sealed with blood, Zaylar. Yours. There's no way you can break this contract, or betray me, even when our deal is over, because I'll still have power over you." Very carefully, she began to fold it before putting it away in a leather wallet and placing it inside her tunic. Later, she'd find a safer place for it.

"It'll heal in a few minutes," she said, unconcerned. "You know that. It isn't as if I did it after you'd bled on the contract. Then you'd have been in trouble."

His hiss of anger was low, like a kettle beginning to boil. She could feel his resentment. It disturbed her and she looked away, knowing that the sensation would cease when she did.

"So, what do we do first?" she asked, returning the knife to her boot.

"Could help Mistress more if I had more magics," he said sullenly, still nursing his hand. "Kolin only allowed me small ones that enhanced his."

"You'll get more magics the more you help me," she said, pushing a plate of sliced meat toward him. "Here, have some food. You must be as hungry as I was."

As he took the plate, she saw the cut on his hand had already vanished. She'd learned a lot about the demon from Kolin's diary, including his ability to heal rapidly.

His mood had changed already, and as he stuffed the meat into his mouth and gulped down the weak ale she poured for him, once more she was reminded how childlike he was.

Deep within her mind, the jewel stirred. *Don't be misled by appearances*, it whispered. *He's older than you can imagine, and with age comes deviousness.*

She ignored it, pushing the presence down till she could feel it no more.

"We need book," said Zaylar, his voice muffled by the food. "Tells where other demons are. Those trapped here on Jalna by mages like Kolin."

"There're others? Your king must be very unpopular."

Zaylar shook his head. "No. They were called from our world and trapped here by Jalnian mages."

"Trapped? How?" This was news to her. There had been nothing about this in Kolin's notes. She leaned forward to hear him better.

"Mages make amulets to trap us in. Keep amulet near them always, then there to use when needed. Demons can never leave here while mage holds amulet."

"The book gives their location?"

He nodded vigorously, picking up his tankard and taking a large swig from it. Putting it down, he wiped the back of his hand across his mouth. "Says which mage has which demon. Kolin wanted this book, was planning to get you to steal it after he got Living Jewel from you. He control jewel, make him powerful enough to steal amulets."

"He needed the jewel to control the demons."

Again Zaylar nodded. "Told you. Only mage-born can carry jewel. It enhances their magics, makes stronger. One demon safe for Kolin, but more is dangerous. He wanted many."

"Any idea where the book is?"

"No," he said regretfully. "Was hoping in book you have."

"There was nothing about it in there," said Mouse thoughtfully. If she were Kolin, where would she put this information, if not in a diary? "How recent was this plan?"

Zaylar shrugged his naked shoulders. "A day, maybe two, before he ask you to steal jewel for him."

"Must be somewhere in his study. There were still plenty of blank pages in his diary so he can't have started a new one."

"I looked. Found nothing."

"You cleared the books away?" she asked.

"Mistress told me do it. I did," he said, his tone faintly reproving.

"Stop with the Mistress bit," she said, irritated by his use of the word. "I don't like it. I'm a thief, not a Mistress."

"Yes, Lady," he said. "Zaylar not call you Mistress again."

She grunted. Lady was only marginally better. Letting him call her something respectful meant he didn't forget who was in charge.

She got up from the table. "Let's go look properly this time. If it's not among the books, perhaps it's in his desk."

Zaylar looked up at her sharply. "Never thought of desk," he admitted. "Kolin always writing there. Maybe there."

It was. She'd even looked at it the night before when she'd taken a sheet of the expensive reed paper from the desk to draft out her contract with Zaylar.

Resting her arms on the desk, she examined it carefully. "*Demonic Amulets*," she said. "That must be its name. Written by someone called Belamor."

"Mage up in mountain town," supplied Zaylar. "Kolin say book copied and sold to those with amulets. Some mages cooperate, not all fight duels."

"That's comforting. Can't read the next bit," she said, squinting at the spidery writing. "He scribbled it down in a hurry from the looks of it."

"Let me see," said Zaylar, leaning on her thighs and squirming his head and upper body between her arms till he could see over the top of the desk.

Amused, she looked down at him. She could feel his body heat through the fabric of her pants. Though his brown-skinned chest was naked, his lower limbs, resembling those of a mountain sheep or goat, were covered with dense fur as dark and curly as that on his head.

"In house of human Kris Russell, it says."

"A human has it?" That surprised her. Cullen had only spoken about him the night before.

Until two years ago, the spaceport that adjoined Balrayn had been held by Lord Bradogan. His brutal reign had forced several of the local lords to lead an uprising against him. Somehow, the humans and another species of aliens, not unlike the felinoid U'Churians who helped police the Port, had gotten involved. With their aid, Bradogan was overthrown and Lord Tarolyn had replaced him. He'd immediately relaxed the rules governing the flow of off-world goods and, under his more benign rule, the shantytown where she lived had mushroomed in size, becoming a bustling, thriving community. Both species were to be seen more frequently now in the port and around the safer streets and inns of Balrayn.

"Not know. Want me to find out?" Zaylar asked hopefully, squirming away from her again.

"No. You're just a little too noticeable," she said, putting the paper down. "I'll get Cullen to see what he can discover." She stopped, realizing she hadn't seen him yet. "Where's Cullen?"

Zaylar shrugged. "Not Zaylar's job to know that."

That's when her nightmare had begun.

Cullen lay trussed up on the dirty warehouse floor, Kadron and his main henchman Raithil standing over him.

"She won't fall for your trick," he said, trying to put more bravado into his voice than his twelve years of age warranted. "I mean nothin' to her. She'll never come."

Kadron nudged him in the ribs with the toe of his boot. "Oh, she'll come," he said. "You been living up at that wizard's house with her this past week or more. Think I don't know about that, Cullen? You might have been out on the street begging for me like my other brats, but you ain't been sleeping at your usual dosshouse."

"What's it to you?" asked Cullen, straining at the ropes that held his wrists firmly behind him. "You get your money every day. What you leave me ain't enough to live on, you knows that. What if I do stay up at her place? Least I can afford to eat now."

The boot kicked him harder this time. "I don't pay you to eat, I pay you to beg and snout for me!"

Cullen tried to muffle his cry of agony. Already bruised and cut by the beating Kadron's men had given him earlier, he felt the rib give under the blow.

Kadron turned away from him to Raithil. "Go see if there's any sign of her yet," he ordered.

"You want me to look out the door?" Raithil asked. "She'll see me."

"So what? She won't expect me to be alone."

"You told her to…"

"I know what I told her! Just go and look," snapped Kadron, exasperated.

Cullen heard Raithil's metal-studded boots heading away from him, then the sound of the door opening a fraction.

"She's coming," he confirmed.

"She alone?" demanded Kadron.

"Yeah, no one with her."

"Then get back here and watch the boy for me," he said, moving toward the case he intended to use as a desk. "I don't want anything going wrong. And keep him quiet!"

Stifling his groans, Cullen twisted his head around until he could see the door. Somehow, he had to warn Mouse! As Raithil stepped past him, he saw the door begin to open.

A slight figure, barely five feet tall, stood framed in the doorway. Dressed in faded dark pants and tunic, her cloak hung back from her shoulders, she blended into the darkness of the night behind her. Mid-brown hair framing an oval face fell to her shoulders, and from beneath the ragged fringe, her dark eyes cautiously surveyed the room.

Ignoring Kadron, she looked past Raithil, locking eyes with him. "'lo, Cullen." Her voice was soft, almost cultured by comparison to Kadron's and his men.

"It's a trap!" he yelled, struggling furiously against the ropes. "Get outta here, Mouse!"

Kadron spun round and kicked him again, this time aiming for his crippled foot. Cullen screamed, his body convulsing in agony.

"I told you to keep that gutter brat quiet!" he snarled at Raithil.

Instinctively, Mouse started forward, then stopped, knowing it was exactly what Kadron had intended. She would have to play it cool and ignore anything he did to Cullen to get her riled up.

She watched impassively as Raithil stooped to grasp the whimpering boy by the front of his tattered clothing and haul him upright.

Cullen staggered, crying out again as he was forced to put his weight on his damaged foot.

Raithil shook him viciously. "Shut up! One more word from you and I'll finish you right now!"

Cullen choked back his cries as Raithil spun him round, grasping hold of him more firmly.

"I see my prodigal Mouse has returned," Kadron said, returning his attention to her. "Come in, my dear. We're all friends here." His voice was oily, patronizing.

"You're no friend of mine, Kadron," she said, taking half a dozen careful paces into the warehouse. Beneath her feet, she heard the floorboards creak softly.

His flaccid gray face assumed a look of regret. "I'm sorry to hear you say that, child, after all the work I've put your way."

"I've come for Cullen. You've no right holding him like this."

"He'll be released as soon as you and I reach an agreement on the property of the late Wizard Kolin."

"Why should I give you what's legally mine?"

"You'll give me it if you want your little friend to survive, that's why," he snapped. "You're mine, Mouse. When that shiftless mother of yours died, I took you in out of the goodness of my heart, trained you up, and found you work so you didn't end up in the brothels like other girls your age! Treated you like you was one of my own, I did. No sleeping at the dosshouse for you, you had a room at the inn! And how do you thank me? By taking independent contracts you had no business to take! You. Owe. Me." His voice was cold now, the last words spat out like individual stones from the narilla fruits he loved eating. "And I aim to collect right now."

"I owe you nothing. The mage sent for me himself. What was I to do? Refuse him?"

She took several more steps, this time toward the high stack of crates on her left. She knew it was a trap, knew exactly what was in his mind just by looking at him. Kadron intended to get her to sign the paper, then he'd kill her and Cullen to avoid later complications. Her hand clenched over the pommel of her sword, taking comfort from the feel of cold steel.

"You work for me, Mouse, you don't go thieving on your own. You steal from whom I say, no one else! Someone asks you to do a job, you come to me about it! You're going to sign Kolin's property over to me," he snarled, pointing to the chest where paper, pen, and ink lay. "It's mine by rights, and you know it."

"Don't do it, Mouse!" Cullen tried to yell as he twisted in Raithil's grasp. "Leave now while you can!"

She heard the sound of a blow and a yelp of pain from Cullen. Inwardly, she cursed him. Why couldn't he shut up and leave this to her? He was only making matters worse for himself.

"What do I get to keep?" she asked, taking three more steps. She could sense the other two men now, both of them hiding behind the tall stacks of crates that lined the warehouse. One was waiting in the shadows beyond the crate Kadron was indicating, the other was moving slowly round to the door to cut off her escape.

Kadron began to laugh, a deep braying sound of almost genuine amusement. "Your lives, Mouse! Your lives!"

From the corner of her eye, she saw a flicker of movement, heard the creaking of floorboards, then the door as it was closed. She risked a glance over her shoulder, but Zaylar had already vanished behind the crates again.

As she slowly moved further into the warehouse, Mouse's fingers checked the quill pen concealed up her sleeve, praying that the color in it matched Kadron's ink.

"You'll let us go if I sign it? We'll be free of you?" She was level with Cullen and Raithil now. He had the boy in front of him, holding him firmly by the back of the neck and one arm.

Kadron continued chuckling. "You'll be free of me, all right. You think I want to keep a dishonest thief and a useless beggar?"

"He's lying!" shrieked Cullen. "Don't do it, Mouse! I'm not worth…" Abruptly, his voice was cut off as Raithil began to throttle him.

"Harm him and the deal's off, Kadron!"

Kadron gestured to Raithil. "I said shut him up, not throttle him."

Raithil released his neck, placing his forearm across Cullen's throat instead.

Heart pounding, she covered the remaining distance between her and Balrayn's leading criminal. Her fears chased one another inside her head. Would his men jump her now, before she signed the document? No, if they did that, Kadron couldn't be sure she'd sign it properly, and her signature was registered at the courthouse as the legal owner of Kolin's estate. The magistrate would check it for sure when he saw she was giving everything away to Kadron.

"Clever of you to pretend you killed Kolin in a duel. They couldn't get you for murder that way. How'd you do it anyhow?" demanded Kadron. "You got about as much magic in you as one of those wild tarnachs they use to guard the spaceport! You probably walked in and found him lying dead at the foot of the stairs!"

Mouse stopped a few feet away from him. "He got angry and came at me, then he tripped. Like you said. He vanished a few minutes later."

"Vanished?"

She shrugged, feigning indifference. "Vanished. In a puff of smoke."

Kadron looked appraisingly at her. "Right. What'd you do to get him angry? Dupe him like you did me? And what happened to that jewel he sent you for?"

Startled, Mouse looked up at him. How'd he known about the jewel?

Eyes narrowing, Kadron reached out and grasped hold of her arm, pulling her close. "Where's the jewel?" His fetid breath was hot on her cheek.

"What jewel?" she asked, forcing herself to remain still.

"The one you stole from Haram the merchant, that's what jewel!"

"Never asked me to steal a jewel. He wanted me to get him something from the temple at Galrayn. I refused."

"You're lying," he snarled, raising his other hand to hit her. As she flinched, he remembered why she was there and lowered it. "Haram came to me squealing like a stuck pig about being robbed. I got him that Living Jewel in the first place, Mouse. You had no business to go thieving it from him. I said I'd get it back. So where is it?"

Mouse thought furiously as, within her mind, the jewel began to stir again. She couldn't return it, that was why she'd had to kill Kolin. The jewel was part of her now, only her death would release her from their symbiosis.

"I took it," she admitted sullenly. "Gave it to Kolin. That's what killed him."

"How? How could a jewel kill him?" demanded Kadron. "It didn't do anything to Haram or any of the others that handled it."

"How should I know? I gave it to him. He lit up like a torch and vanished. That's all I know," she said, trying to pull free. "Damned thing was magic."

For the space of several heartbeats, Kadron held onto her, then he pushed her toward the wooden crate where the paper and ink lay.

"Maybe you're lying, maybe not, but you got nowhere to sell the jewel except through me. Now sign the papers and let's be done with this!" he ordered.

She picked up the document, trying not to let Kadron see how badly her hand shook. This was not going the way she'd planned. Haram hadn't reported the theft of the Living Jewel to the port authorities, and Cullen had heard nothing about it on the streets, so she'd assumed the merchant had kept quiet out of embarrassment. That he'd gone straight to Kadron had never occurred to her. How many more would come after her just for the jewel?

"What the hell d'you think you're doing?" demanded Kadron. "I said sign the damned thing!"

"I need to read it first."

He grinned. "Read it? You don't need to *read* it, girl, even if you could! Doesn't matter what it *says*, you got no option but to sign it!"

"I want to know what I'm signing," she said, looking over the top of the page at him. "I'm not having you claim later that I signed a contract saying I'd work for you for nothing for the next ten years."

"Hear that, Raithil? Mouse reckons she can read!" But his grin was fading, and he snatched the document from her, slapping it back on the crate. Picking up the quill pen, he thrust it at her. "Sign it now, or I'll let Raithil play with your little friend again."

As Cullen let out another moan of pain, Mouse felt the blood drain from her face. It was no subterfuge when she dropped the quill. Bending down, she let her cloak fall forward, concealing her movements just enough so she could switch Kadron's quill for the one Tallan had prepared for her.

"Cut Cullen loose first, then I'll sign," she said, straightening up.

Kadron gestured to Raithil. "Do it. He's not going anywhere with that lame foot of his."

Raithil removed his arm from across Cullen's throat and, holding him upright by one arm, pulled his knife and slit the rope around the boy's wrists.

Freed, Cullen staggered, clutching at his captor for balance. Raithil grasped him firmly by the shoulder, holding his knife under the boy's ear. "You keep still," he snarled. "And keep that damned mouth of yours shut!"

"No more delays," ordered Kadron. "Sign it now."

Mouse stepped closer to the crate and bending over the document, pretended to dip her quill in the pot of ink. Surreptitiously, she pressed the hollow spine, releasing the special ink just as Tallan had shown her. As she wrote her name at the bottom of the page, she prayed his magic would work.

As soon as she lifted the pen, Kadron grabbed the document and examined her signature. Folding it carefully, he placed it in his belt pouch.

Mouse could only stand and stare at him in horror. His pouch? He was putting it in his pouch? She'd assumed he'd leave it on the crate. How could the magic work shut up in there? As she took a step backward, his hand snaked out and closed over her sword arm.

"Oh, no you don't," he said. "I've not finished with you yet."

She felt herself jerked forward until she was pressed against Kadron's greasy robes. This close, the aroma of stale sweat and beer was overwhelming.

"Think I'll keep you around for a while yet, girl," he said, grasping her chin in one fat hand and forcing her to look up at him. He leered down at her, revealing his broken and stained teeth: his rank breath made her gag. "I was going to kill you and the cripple, but I hadn't realized until now that you'd finished growing up. Raithil, take her weapons."

Shock paralyzed her and she offered no resistance as Raithil, still holding onto Cullen, grasped her sword and pulled it from her scabbard. Then Kadron ran his free hand over her body, looking for knives. Suddenly Mouse could sense his naked lust flowing over her as if it was a living thing. She felt unclean, dirty, as Kadron's hand lingered over her slight breasts before moving lower till he found her belt knife.

"You're a bit skinny yet, but I can live with that."

That Kadron would see her as a woman had never occurred to her. Fighting down the panic that surged through her, she felt the jewel wake fully.

Give me control, it sent. *I can kill this one, and the others, with a thought!*

She gritted her teeth, muttering "No!" under her breath as Kadron pulled her knife from its sheath and tossed it onto the crate beside him.

You want this one to rape you? It won't matter to him that you're not a woman yet. Will you let him kill this boy you value so highly? There is no way out unless you give control of your mind to me.

"No," she repeated, turning her face aside. "If you don't let us go, Kadron, you'll never find the best pieces from Kolin's house. I hid 'em in case you pulled a stunt like this on me."

"You double-dealing little..."

"Let us go, Kadron," she said, her voice shaking slightly. "You gave your word that if I signed your paper you'd let Cullen go and leave us alone."

"So I lied! Kill the brat, Raithil! I'm keeping the girl for now," he laughed, running his hand across her cheek before grasping hold of her other arm. "You'll tell me what I want to know, Mouse, never doubt that!"

"Kill him and I'll never show you," she said, pulling away from him while desperately trying to think up more excuses for Cullen to be kept alive. "Stuff's protected. Magically. Needs Cullen and me both to release the spell."

Kadron's fingers bit deep into the flesh of her arms as he shook her violently. "Wait, Raithil. Spells? What spells?"

A faint smell of burning leather teased Mouse's nostrils. The ods bless Tallan, his ink spell was working! She risked a glance down at Kadron's belt and saw a faint thread of smoke escaping from his pouch.

"Kill Cullen and you'll never get it." She had to keep him talking long enough for the pouch to catch fire.

"Where is it?" he demanded. "Where d'you hide the stuff?"

"My room at the inn," she said.

"You're lying again! Your room's been let. Nothing but garbage was found in it!"

"I had a hiding place." The coil of white smoke was thicker now. Someone would notice it if she didn't distract them. She struggled, kicking at Kadron's legs.

Kadron gave a snarl of rage, releasing her arms to grab her by the throat. "You're lying! Where would you get a spell like that from?" He began to shake her like a rag doll.

Hands clawing at his in a desperate effort to prize his fingers apart, Mouse choked out an answer. "Money. Bought it." As the blood pounded in her ears and her vision started to fade, she heard the jewel again.

You'd die rather than submit to me? Foolish child! Give me the power to...

The roaring in her ears grew louder, drowning the jewel's voice. She felt a surge of power, heard a commotion — swearing and shouting — then suddenly, a weight slammed against her shoulder, knocking her to the floor. She lay there, sucking in deep breaths of air to relieve her heaving lungs, aware of a dark four-legged shape just beyond her turning and launching itself on Kadron. A tarnach? How in all the demons of Jalna had a wild tarnach gotten in?

Kadron's high-pitched scream of terror filled the warehouse. She couldn't stay on the floor, Raithil still had Cullen and the tarnach would go for anything that moved. Coughing and gasping, she pushed herself to her feet, reaching for the knife that hung down the back of her neck as she turned to face Raithil.

He'd dropped Cullen and her sword and was backing away from her, a look of frozen terror on his face.

From behind the crates, two men dashed out, swords drawn, but they ignored her and rushed to Kadron's aid.

Mouse dove for Cullen, grabbing her sword up from the ground as she hauled the boy to his feet.

You're not free yet. What of the tarnach? Let me use you to destroy them all, whispered the jewel.

"Come on," she hissed to Cullen, ignoring the jewel. "We got to get out of here!" The smell of burning leather was stronger now.

"My crutch," he moaned, clinging to her as he looked wildly around the room. "I can't walk without it!"

"You'll have to!" she said, looping his arm across her shoulders as she dragged him toward the door. "Kadron's pouch is about to burst into flames and that'll send the tarnach over our way!"

The tarnach, then. Let me destroy the tarnach. The tone grew sharper now, demanding.

Cullen tried to hop, clutching his side and whimpering in pain as he jarred his broken rib with every step.

Why was the jewel so set on destroying the tarnach? Mouse risked a glance over her shoulder at Kadron and his thugs. The wolf-like beast was straddling Kadron's chest, holding the other three men at bay. Around its neck, the long spines stood out like a collar of deadly spikes: its jaws were wide and slavering as it snarled and howled its anger at them. Then she saw its glowing red eyes and realized how small it was.

Let me kill the tarnach!

Again, she felt the surge of power, but this time she was ready for it.

"Damn you! Leave it alone!" she hissed, concentrating on increasing her pace until she was almost bodily dragging the injured boy. "Stop trying to control me! I want nothing from you!"

Abruptly, the battle for control of her mind ceased. Instead, she felt the jewel's anger as agony stabbed at her temples.

I offer you everything, and you abuse me, put our life at risk! Take care, Mouse, your mage-blood may be waking, but will not always win against me!

Whimpering in agony, she stumbled, sending herself crashing to the ground. Pain gripped her belly too, Cullen landing on top of her. From a distance, she heard the sound of Kadron shrieking again.

"I'm burning up! Put it out! Put it out!"

"Get that damned beast off him first, you imbeciles!" Raithil roared. "It's not an adult, it's only a pup!"

"Mouse! Come on!" said Cullen, shaking her furiously. "We gotta get outta here! The place is on fire!"

Snarls turned to howls of rage, drowning out the voices. Smoke began to fill the warehouse. Mouse lifted her head and peered at Cullen through the haze of pain the jewel was inflicting on her.

"Mouse, come on! They've chased the tarnach our way!"

"S'all right," she mumbled, trying to push herself up on her hands and knees. "Won't harm us." She fumbled around until her hand closed on her sword hilt. With an effort, she got to her feet, pulling Cullen upright beside her. Supporting him, doggedly, she began to stumble toward the door again.

You won't beat me, she said to the jewel. *Because I've had to fight all my life. It's all I know. And by the gods, I'd die rather than give in to you!*

"The tarnach, Mouse!" Cullen's voice was terrified as he clutched her forearm.

She could hear its rapid breathing as it drew level with her. "Forget it," she said, trying to ignore the pain that pulsed inside her head. "No danger." Damn the jewel! It was doing all it could to slow her down, as if it wanted Kadron's thugs to catch them! She began to cough as fumes started to sting her throat and make her eyes water.

"Faster, Lady!" urged Zaylar's voice from beside her. "They follow!"

Ahead of them, the warehouse door slammed open, sending a blast of cold night air eddying around them, driving back the smoke. Suddenly, the jewel and the pain in her head were gone.

The tarnach snarled as Cullen gave a gasp of surprise. Blinking furiously, Mouse peered at the shape silhouetted against the night and lifted her sword, ready to defend them as best she could.

"It's the human," said Cullen, his voice full of relief. "The one I said was asking questions about you and Kolin."

She heard footsteps, could sense someone approaching as she dashed her sleeve across her eyes.

"Take it easy, kids," said a quiet male voice. "I'm on your side. Tell your snarling friend I'm here to help."

She could see him now. Tall, his long pale hair held back by a head-band, he stood with his sword held ready, looking over her head at Kadron's men.

He reached out with one large hand, taking Cullen's weight from her. "Get yourself outside, lad," he said, pushing the boy behind him. "We've got a fight on our hands."

Mouse spun round, thrusting her free hand into her cloak pocket. "No we haven't," she said quietly. "You help Cullen. I'll see to this."

He gave her a curious glance, then nodded briefly before backing up to help the boy.

Kadron, his tawdry finery ripped to shreds and stained by smoke, was leaning on the arm of one of his men, hobbling toward them as fast as he could go. He was yelling at Raithil and his companions as, swords drawn, they advanced on her. Behind them, the fire had taken hold, sending smoke and flames billowing up to the ceiling. The roaring drowned out their words, but she could hear them in her mind. She, not the jewel, had used magic on him. Frightened, she looked at their feet, shutting out their thoughts.

"Look behind and tell me when they're clear," she hissed at the tarnach as she readied the three glass phials.

"Cullen and he are gone," said Zaylar, shifting restlessly on his four paws. "We leave *now* Lady. Or tell me to kill them."

She grunted and slowly backed off. It was her they wanted now, not Cullen.

"Better they die, Lady," insisted Zaylar. "I cannot kill unless you order. Not supposed to help unless you ask me."

She spared him a glance. So the demon had acted on his own, had he? "No. I'm a thief, not a killer," she said.

"They try kill you."

"No," she repeated, glancing behind her. She was almost at the doorway now, and there was no sign of the human or Cullen.

"Get her!" yelled Raithil, lunging forward.

Spinning around, Mouse raced out the door into the yard, then stopped dead to turn and fling the phials into the doorway. The glass smashed on the cobblestones, filling the yard with clouds of thick, white, billowing smoke. The wind caught it, whipping it into the warehouse and sending it swirling around Mouse herself.

Shouts and screams filled the night as the inhabitants of Balrayn realized the warehouse was on fire. Pain gripped her briefly again, making her almost double up as she clutched her belly. Confused and as blinded by the smoke as Kadron and his men, Mouse didn't know which way to turn. Panic flooded through her as a hand closed around her arm.

"Good going," said the human as he pulled her out of the smoke. "Let's leave now, while we can."

In the distance, they could hear the siren of the spaceport's fire service.

"I can manage," she said stiffly, pulling her arm free and running over to where Cullen leaned against the wall of the inn.

"Sure you can," he said, his voice a lazy drawl. "Not as if you'll be noticed, is it? Or that Kadron's thugs might follow you. One small girl and a cripple accompanied by what looks like a young tarnach. Especially when tarnachs are so wild only the Port Police can train them as guard dogs." He sheathed his sword and came over to pick Cullen up. "You need to get off the streets now. I can help you make far better time than you could alone." He headed off down the alleyway.

Mouse stared after him, taken aback by his calm assumption of leadership

"Lady," said Zaylar, pawing urgently at her foot. "Need to go now or Kadron's men will catch us."

"All right!" she snapped. Sheathing her sword, she ran after them, cursing under her breath. He was right, but she didn't have to like it.

Kolin's house was on the edges of the old Market Quarter, last in a row of similar houses. Kris stopped outside the door, setting Cullen down gently on the ground before turning to face Mouse.

"Will you be safe in there alone?" he asked, a concerned look on his face.

"Yes," she said shortly. "We don't need you inside with us."

He grinned. "I wasn't going to offer. You have your strange little friend, after all," he said, pointing to the tarnach. "I suggest you get him to take on a different shape next time he goes out with you, though. A small tarnach isn't much of a deterrent. Or have him on a leash, it looks better. The guard tarnachs are leashed." He turned and began to walk off down the street.

"Thanks," Cullen called out after him.

Mouse turned to look down at the tarnach, blinking as Zaylar seemed to fade before her eyes, only to reappear in his usual demonic form.

Cullen yelped. "That's Zaylar!"

"I know," she said, irritated. Her belly still hurt and the human's attitude had annoyed her. "He could see you," she said accusingly to the demon. "And you didn't tell me you could change shape!"

"Not Zaylar's fault, Lady," he said, looking up at her. "Human different. He see Zaylar without my help. Not allowed to help anyone unless Lady says so, you know that."

"And the shape-changing?"

The little demon shrugged his bare shoulders and looked away from her, shuffling his hooves in the dirt. "I told you Kolin gave me small magics. That was one. Not hiding it from Lady, just you never asked Zaylar about it."

"Huh," she said, digging her key out of her pocket and stepping past him and Cullen to open the door. "Tonight's been just full of surprises," she said, thinking back to how the arrival of the human had coincided with the jewel's abrupt departure and continuing silence.

She turned to help Cullen into the house. "Tomorrow I got to get you a new crutch," she said. "Tell me about this human."

"I told you last night," said Cullen, as groaning, he hopped into the hallway. "He's living down in the Quarters. He's got a seal from Lord Tarolyn himself saying he's free to go anywhere he wants on Jalna. He asks lots of questions and writes it all down in this book he carries around with him."

Mouse shut the door behind them, locking and bolting it securely. "Not many off-worlders get that kind of permission from Tarolyn. What's he want to know about me?"

"Same as everyone else. What you did to Kolin. I was trying to find out more when Kadron's men caught me."

"Zaylar, set the wards," she said. "And fetch me Cullen's old crutch from his room."

"Is there," said Zaylar, pointing to the wooden crutch leaning against the doorway. "Got it already. Knew you wanted it."

She looked at him, hearing his thoughts as if he spoke them aloud. He wasn't usually this helpful, but he knew that the jewel had tried to force her to kill him. "Why'd you come to help me?" she asked. "I know you can't act for yourself, you have to wait for me to order you, so how'd you manage it?"

Zaylar squirmed under her gaze. "Had to. If Lady die then Zaylar sent to another mage, not get talisman. If jewel take you over, then Zaylar still not get talisman."

"Doesn't explain how you managed to help me."

"Zaylar sense Lady want help," he said, looking up at her and spreading his arms wide, his face taking on a helpless look. "Zaylar cannot ignore that."

He was able to pick up her thoughts, just as the jewel was, she realized with an icy shock. She felt the heat of his hand touch hers.

"Zaylar thank Lady for not letting jewel kill him," he said. "Must get book. Must find demon talismans and teach you magics quickly then you can protect yourself from jewel. You still in danger from Kadron. He mad you use your magic on him, mad at fire. He come after you again, this time to kill."

So he knew what she'd done, did he? "I thought I had to learn to use magic," she said, leaning against the hallway wall as the pain returned. "You know, spells and the like. And how come it's never happened before? I've no idea what I did."

"It come on its own this time and last. You mage-born, magic in your blood. Must learn to control it. Need more magics to do this if you to stay alive, keep jewel from besting you, keep mages from challenging you." His small face was creased in real concern.

Mouse wasn't fooled. She knew his concern was self-centered, but for now at least, their aims were the same. "What last time?" she asked sharply.

"Remember firedrake when we steal Living Jewel? Remember guards and 'drake died?"

"You said that was the jewel."

"Was you, not jewel."

She could only stare at him numbly. "But they were crisped—as if they'd been burned in a fire!"

He nodded. "You did. You why mages not let girls with power live. Male childs can control magic when becoming men, not girls."

Suddenly his meaning became clear.

"He's right," said Cullen. "Kadron's got a real grudge against us now."

"I know. You're not going out alone again. Forget begging, we got enough to live on here for a long while." She pushed herself up off the wall and started down the hallway for her room.

"We need help, Mouse," said Cullen, following her slowly. "Someone with muscle living here. You got money now, you can hire someone."

"Sure, and just where we going to find someone honest enough not to sell us out to Kadron?" she asked sarcastically.

"Could do worse than him," said Cullen. "The human. Kris."

Kris. So that was his name. She grunted derisively even as the image of him standing in the warehouse doorway, sword in hand, came to her mind.

"He did help us tonight," Cullen pointed out as he stopped at the study door. "And Kadron ain't going to be the last man to want you," he added quietly, giving her an oblique look.

"What's that supposed to mean?" she demanded, coming to a halt. "You think I can't look after us?"

"No," he said hurriedly. "Knows you can. You rescued me, got us out of there without a fight. I just meant it was odd him turning up like that, 'specially when he'd been asking about you."

And that, along with the fact she hadn't been able to sense Kris's thoughts at all, was just another of the night's surprises.

Paintbox

THE FINGERS THAT PROTRUDED FROM THE TIPS OF ANNE'S GLOVES WERE stiff and blue with cold. With a sigh, she laid her paints and sketch pad down on the ground and reached for her flask of coffee. Steam rose from both flask and cup as she poured herself a drink. She gratefully cupped her hands around the warmth.

Glen glanced at her from his perch on an upturned waste-bin filched from the studio a quarter-mile away.

"Giving in already?" he asked teasingly.

Anne took a drink before answering him.

"Too right," she replied. "We've been sitting here freezing our bums off for the last three hours. I, for one, want a break."

"You have a point," Glen admitted, rubbing his hands together briefly. "It's far from warm today."

"I can't see why Frazer put the studio out of limits, especially in this weather," Anne grumbled.

Doniki looked up from her work. "Probably to stop us getting into bad habits on the first day," she said mildly. "This *is* supposed to be a field trip, after all."

"Well, I think it's cruel. I can easily do my plant study inside, and Glen can see his trees from the window. Can't you?" she asked, turning towards him.

Glen opened his mouth to answer but Doniki forestalled him.

"You just aren't dedicated enough," she said, shaking her head. "It isn't as if we were sitting exposed to the elements on the end of the pier. We're sheltered amongst the trees here."

"We would have been on the pier if it had been up to you," pointed out Glen, putting away his things. "It was only because the others went there that we came in this direction."

"That's beside the point," Doniki replied archly. "The weather isn't as bad as you make out. At least we're here in May and not January like the other first-year section."

Glen grunted and turned to Anne. "You don't happen to have another coffee in there, do you? I could do with a drink to warm me up. I wish I'd thought of bringing a flask."

Anne grinned and reached for the thermos. "I looked at the weather forecast on Sunday, which is why I also brought my gloves," she said, wiggling her fingers at him before pouring a second cup and handing it over. "My older bones feel the cold more acutely than yours do."

Doniki sniffed audibly. "Just no dedication to your craft," she repeated.

"The day of the artist starving and freezing in his garret is long gone, Doniki," Glen said, warming his nose in the steam before taking his first sip. "There's no reason why we shouldn't enjoy our creature comforts too."

As Anne put her cup down, she heard a twig snap. Looking up, she caught sight of a movement in the bushes.

"There's someone there," she hissed at Glen.

"Rubbish," he said. "Unless you believe all that nonsense about the Culzean Castle ghosts."

"Don't be ridiculous," she whispered. "Ghosts don't snap twigs! There's someone there I tell you."

She got to her feet and moved silently forward, motioning Glen to go round the other side of the small thicket ahead of them.

Amused, he got to his feet.

There was the rustle of leaves as something moved its feet.

Anne saw a flash of black at the heart of a rhododendron bush and pounced.

There was a sharp squeal and a female voice said, "Don't touch me! I didn't mean any harm. I was only watching you."

A small figure backed defensively out of the bushes followed by Anne.

"It's all right," Anne assured her, "we won't hurt you. We just wondered who it was."

The girl was slightly built, with elfin features set in a pale face topped by a mass of long ginger curls. Probably about sixteen at a rough guess, gauged Anne.

"This is Glen, Doniki, and I'm Anne," she said, pointing to the other two in turn. "Are you a local, or a visitor like us?"

"I live over there. My name is Cassandra," she said quietly, her voice almost a whisper. She pointed through the bushes to the headland beyond. "You're art students, aren't you?"

Anne nodded. "We're here for a week's study."

"My family don't like me mixing with strangers so I don't get to meet many people. Can I see what you're doing?" she asked, some of the tension leaving her face.

"Of course," said Anne, warming to the girl. "Come and have a look." She led the way over to where her sketch pad lay propped against the tree stump.

"I've been doing some plant studies in watercolors," she said, picking the pad up. "That's the fern over there."

Cassandra gazed at the sketch, a look of rapture on her face. She reached her hand out then stopped, fingers hovering just above the paper.

"Can I touch it?" she asked. "It looks so real, and the colors are beautiful."

"Yes, of course you can," mumbled Anne, embarrassed. "It isn't really that good."

"Oh, it's lovely," she said, turning an intense look on her. "I've never seen anything like it before. How do you do it? What makes the colors?"

"The paints," said Anne, confused. Surely Cassandra knew what paints were?

The girl answered Anne's unspoken question. "What are paints?"

Baffled, Anne picked up her paint box and showed it to her. "These are. It's a colored paste that comes in tubes, and I squeeze a little of each color into my box."

The girl pointed to the paintbrush. "You use that to put the colors on the paper?"

Anne nodded.

Cassandra touched the crimson carefully with one finger, then rubbed it onto the back of her other hand. "I love bright colors, but Mother won't let me wear them." She looked down at the long black skirt that she wore and smiled wryly, an oddly adult expression. "She says it would only make people notice me."

"Why can't they notice you?" asked Glen, intrigued by the image of seclusion she was painting.

Cassandra shrugged. "They just mustn't," she said. "I shouldn't be talking to you now. If my brother catches me, I'll be in trouble."

"Just for talking to us?" exclaimed Anne.

"Yes," she said simply. "Can I look at what you're doing?" she asked Glen.

He showed her his sketches of the trees, and after admiring them, Cassandra was about to move over to Doniki when the other girl closed her pad and stood up.

"I don't like people looking at my unfinished work," she said coldly, bending down to pack away her things. "May I remind you that we were told to stay away from the families living on the estate. It's nearly teatime. I'll see you two back at the hostel when you're finished with your captive audience." With that, she strolled off.

"Did I upset her?" asked Cassandra, a worried frown on her face.

"No," said Glen. "She's always like that — arrogant about her work, and short on manners."

"Forget her," said Anne, dismissing Doniki with an airy wave of her hand. "You don't seem to know much about art. Didn't you do any painting or drawing at school?"

"I never went to school," Cassandra said. "My brother did, though, and he says I didn't miss much."

"How come you didn't go to school?" asked Glen, sitting down on his bin again.

"I told you, I'm not allowed to meet people," she said, frowning. "Mother says it isn't safe."

"Isn't safe for whom?" asked Anne. "The world isn't that bad a place."

"I wouldn't know," she said sadly. "You're the first strangers I've spoken to in years. If I get the chance, can I come over and talk to you again?"

"Of course, you can," said Anne, reaching out to touch her. "I just don't see..."

"Hush!" said Cassandra suddenly, ducking the gesture and putting her head on one side. "I hear someone coming. It has to be my brother." She looked around frantically. "I'm not supposed to be out at all! I must go." She left so quickly she seemed to melt into the bushes.

Anne and Glen looked at one another in bewilderment.

"What do you make of that?" he asked.

Anne shook her head. "I just don't know," she said. "She seems so naive, yet..."

Glen nodded. "I know what you mean."

They heard footsteps nearby and looked up. A dark-haired youth in his early twenties dressed in a green waxed jacket and jeans stepped into the clearing and glanced around. He carried the blood-stained bodies of two rabbits slung over his shoulder. In his other hand, he held a shotgun, broken open to show it was unloaded.

Anne blinked. His features were perfect—he looked like one of the old classical statues come to life.

As he caught sight of them, he stopped, his face creasing into a scowl. "You're trespassing," he said shortly. "This is private land here. You students have been told stay inland, not come wandering in the woods."

"We're allowed here," said Glen, getting up. "I made a point of checking the map of the estate. So long as we stay off the headland, we can go where we want."

He continued to stare at them. "Have you seen anyone else today?" he asked abruptly. "A girl, ginger-haired?"

"No," Anne said quickly before Glen could answer. "We've seen no one."

He nodded, the frown easing slightly. "You see her, you stay away from her. She's my sister. I don't want her mixing with the likes of you."

Once the sound of his footsteps had faded, Glen let out his breath. "If that's the brother, I don't blame her for being nervous of him. Did you see what he was carrying?"

"The rabbits? Yes," she said.

"The shotgun, actually. I didn't like the look of him, Anne. I think we'd better head back to the hostel too."

Anne glanced at her watch. "It is teatime," she agreed readily, bending down to pick up her things.

The next morning dawned bright and warm. Doniki and Anne had drawn the short straw to make breakfast that morning, and the prospect of good weather had made everyone anxious to have an early start. The kitchen, roomy enough for three, was totally inadequate for the twenty students each trying to "help" by getting their own meal. By dint of shouting, pushing, and outright threats of violence, Anne finally managed to chase them out into the common room to wait their turn. Doniki, nose in an art book, stood guarding the small oven's grill.

Several minutes later, Glen stuck his nose cautiously round the door.

"Can I help?" he inquired. "I'll take the milk and cereals through for you if you want."

"You just want to get fed first like the rest," muttered Anne, banging the offending packets onto a tray alongside the bowls and milk.

"Yes," he agreed complacently, venturing into the kitchen. "But unlike the others, I'm genuinely offering to help."

"Take them!" Anne said, amused and exasperated at the same time.

Glen lifted the tray and headed back out. He paused at the door.

"I should have a look at the toast if I was you, Doniki. I don't think it's supposed to be served flambé."

Glancing up from her book, Doniki pulled the grill tray out and surveyed the ruined toast critically.

"He's right," she announced after a moment. "It shouldn't be that shade of burnt umber, more a sort of yellow ochre."

"It's a piece of bloody toast," exclaimed Anne, snatching up the pieces of smoking bread and hurling them in the direction of the bin. "Not a work of art! Just don't burn the next lot or we'll never get finished!"

Breakfast finally over, everyone made their way into the great outdoors to start sketching. Anne declined the invitation to join Glen and Doniki on the beach. She'd had enough of the younger girl to last her the week, let alone the rest of the day.

"I want to have a look around before I settle down to paint today," she said by way of an excuse.

"Don't take too long," warned Glen. "Frazer missed us yesterday and you can guarantee he'll make a point of seeing our work today."

"I won't," she assured him, setting off along the path to the woods.

She strolled leisurely, in no particular hurry despite Glen's warning, reveling in the solitude after the hubbub of breakfast. Presently she came to the little clearing near the studio where they had worked the day before. She stopped, surprised to find herself there when she hadn't intended to return to the same spot. Coincidence? She'd been thinking about Cassandra, perhaps subconsciously she'd taken the same route. Well, now she was here, she might as well indulge her curiosity and see if she could find out where the girl lived.

Looking carefully around, Anne finally spotted the path — more of a rabbit track — that Cassandra had taken when she left. Pushing through the bushes, she followed it until the trees thinned out, giving way to a grassy slope. Over to the left, some distance away, was a small croft on which there was a cabin.

Now what? she wondered. She couldn't exactly go and knock on the door and ask if a girl called Cassandra lived there, especially if her family did dislike strangers. She shrugged. Still, she could always walk nearby and see if Cassandra was about.

Anne was only a few hundred yards from the cottage when a slight figure came out of the door. Recognizing the girl, she opened her mouth to call out just as Cassandra spotted her.

The girl's hand flew to her mouth in a silencing gesture and Anne stifled her greeting.

Cassandra looked warily around before running over.

"You shouldn't have come here," she said breathlessly, coming to a stop beside her. "We'll both get into trouble if I'm caught talking to you."

"How can I get into trouble?" asked Anne indignantly. "I'm doing nothing wrong. This land belongs to the Castle, doesn't it?"

Cassandra sighed. "Just believe me, please. If my brother finds you here then he'll make sure I have no chance of getting out on my own before you leave, and I do want to talk to you again."

"You make it sound as if he keeps you virtually a prisoner here. Why can't you mix with other people? What about your parents? I don't understand. The whole thing sounds cruel and pointless."

"They're only trying to protect me," said Cassandra defensively. "Last time there was an accident, and someone got... hurt," she faltered.

"Hurt?" queried Anne. "What happened?"

"Never mind," she said hurriedly. "I can hear Mother calling me. You must go."

In the distance, Anne could hear someone shouting.

"Please. Just leave," she begged when Anne hesitated.

"Very well," Anne agreed reluctantly when she heard the voice drawing closer. She turned and walked away, wondering about the family's paranoia, and how on earth someone could have got hurt. Perhaps Cassandra was exaggerating. Girls her age often did to make themselves appear more intriguing. *Well if she was,* Anne thought wryly, *it was certainly working!*

When she reached the edge of the trees, she glanced back toward the croft and saw Cassandra standing with the dark young man of the day before. They were moving back toward the cottage.

"Ah, Anne!" she heard a voice hail her from across the other side of the headland. "I've been looking for you. Haven't you found somewhere to work yet?"

"Oh no," she muttered to herself. "Hello Mr. Frazer," she called, walking toward him. "I was just having a look round before deciding where to settle."

"In that case, I suggest the pier," he said decisively, pointing out toward the sea. "There's a path leading down to the harbor over there. On the shingle you'll find a lovely collection of lobster kreels beside a beached dingy. Lots of mussel colonies to draw too. Not the sort of thing you see much of in the city."

"No, Mr. Frazer," said Anne obediently.

"Off you go, then. I'll be round again in an hour or so to see how you're doing." He nodded to her then set off briskly toward the woods.

Anne watched his retreating figure with a grimace. Damn! She would have to bump into him. She didn't like harbors or piers, and seafood made her throw up. The thought of spending a day sketching the blessed things did not appeal to her in the least. She heaved a deep sigh and set off in the direction he'd indicated.

By Wednesday morning, it looked as if the good weather would last out the week. Anne decided to get off immediately after breakfast so as to make sure she didn't meet Frazer until she was firmly ensconced in the day's work. She couldn't face another session at the smelly little harbor.

Glen and Doniki were returning to the beach to continue their paint studies and this time Anne decided to join them. They made their way along the drive toward the Castle, cutting off down the small track that led to the beach. It was a pleasant walk, leading through a lightly wooded area. As they approached the sands, they saw a familiar figure bending over a group of rocks near the path. She looked up as they approached.

"Hello," said Cassandra, smiling shyly. "I hoped you might come this way."

"I see you managed to escape again," said Anne.

"Yes," said Cassandra, totally serious. "My brother has gone into town today, so I have some time to myself. Mother doesn't watch me as closely as he does."

"Hmm," Doniki grunted disbelievingly.

"I've been trying to paint," Cassandra went on, standing back a little from the rock. "Would you have a look at it and tell me what you think? I've never tried before," she confided to Anne.

On the rocks she had attempted to draw a group of figures, but they were naive representations of the human form, almost childlike in their simplicity of structure.

"It's supposed to be you," she said, indicating all three of them. "I tried to get the colors right, but it wasn't as easy as I thought it would be." She waited, obviously anxious for their approval.

Doniki was the first to speak. "Are we going to stand here all day admiring this child's primitive daubs or are we going to get on with some work?" she demanded. "You can waste your time with her if you like, but I've more important things to do," she said, sweeping off down the path without a backward glance.

Anne looked at Glen, trying not to see Cassandra's stricken face as the girl gazed at Doniki's retreating figure. He raised his eyebrows questioningly at her.

She turned back to Cassandra. "They aren't bad for a first attempt," she temporized, "but you've a lot to learn. You can't become an artist overnight, you know."

"The colors are very good," added Glen lamely, shifting his bag from one hand to the other. "I don't think my first picture was as good as that."

"It's rubbish, that's what you're saying, isn't it?" Cassandra said, looking as if her world had just collapsed. "I'm no good at painting, am I?"

"I didn't say that," said Anne hurriedly. "We're not great artists either, that's why we go to art school, to learn more."

Glen began to fidget. "Look, Anne, I've got to go after Doniki. You know what she's like if she gets into a mood. I'll see you down there, okay?"

Anne nodded. "Go on," she replied shortly. Kneeling, she put down her bag and portfolio and got out a soft dark pencil.

"Let me show you," she said, beginning to sketch round the outline of one of Cassandra's figures. She looked up at the girl, seeing her dash tears from her eyes with the back of her hand. "Come and watch," she said softly. "Some of your mistakes are fairly easy to correct."

"No," Cassandra gulped, rubbing furiously at eyes that wouldn't stop overflowing. "It's just another thing I'm useless at. For once, I'd like to find something I can do well."

Anne sat back on her heels. "You can't expect to paint a masterpiece first time, you know," she said kindly. "It takes years of hard work, and even then very few people become great painters. Don't take what Doniki said to heart. She's no authority you know, just another student like me."

"Forget that I mentioned it," said Cassandra, pulling herself together with a visible effort and giving a final dab at her tear-stained face. "I have to go now, and you've got your painting to do." She began to back away up the path. "Maybe I'll see you again before you leave."

"Don't go," called Anne, but the girl had left in a flurry of black skirts.

Anne sighed, looking again at the rock painting. She frowned and leaned closer, reaching out to touch it. The paintings were very immature, having more in common with a bad copy of Lowrie's matchstick men than any realistic representation of people. Her use of color, however, was another matter. She seemed to have a natural appreciation of tonal relationships. There was a vibrancy about the colors which was unique.

How had she done it? Anne couldn't remember Cassandra having a paintbox or any colored pens with her. What had she used? She began to scrape at the figure depicting herself but the paint seemed to have sunk into the surface of the stone. Wetting her finger, she rubbed at it, but again none came off. She looked more closely, then on an impulse pulled out the small knife she carried and began scraping, then digging, at the surface of the rock. The paint seemed to be embedded into the actual fabric of the stone.

"That's impossible," she murmured, sitting back to think for a moment. She leaned forward again and began to dig more deeply this time. Stopping momentarily, she prodded an unpainted piece beside the figure. The stone was definitely softer under the paint, and the color seemed to go deep down into the rock. She tested several other areas and found that everywhere Cassandra had painted, the pigment had changed the actual substance of the stone and become an integral part of it.

"How the hell did she do that?" she wondered aloud. This time, Cassandra didn't need to try to be intriguing, she genuinely was. How could she possibly have altered the rock and put colors into it? Anne shook her head in bewilderment as she put her pencil and knife away again. Maybe she had a strange talent, like the chap who could bend spoons. Well, at least rock paintings, even if they were this simplistic, were more interesting to look at than a pile of bent silverware.

She got to her feet and picked up her bag and portfolio. Tomorrow she would try to pin the girl down long enough to ask her about the paintings. A talent like that would be wasted if it wasn't used and developed.

Cassandra did not reappear that day, nor did Anne see her the next day until late afternoon when she was making her way back to the hostel. The meeting was a chance one. Anne had struck out on her own to sketch by the inappropriately named Swan Lake and was cutting back through the woods when she came across the girl in the clearing near the studio.

"Cassandra," she called, "just the person I wanted to see. Don't run off, I've got something for you," she said, digging into her bag with one hand as she hurried over to her.

Cassandra hesitated, a sullen, unhappy look on her face.

"I had another look at your paintings, and your use of color is lovely. You do have a talent. Don't worry about the drawing, that will come with time and practice. I wish you'd tell me how you got the paintings into the rock the way you did. That's a rare gift." She came to a halt beside the girl and held out a small box.

"Here, take it," she urged. "It's a paintbox." She gestured with the box. "Please take it. I thought you could use the paints when you aren't able to get out." Anne let her voice trail off. It was obvious that Cassandra was upset and had been before Anne arrived.

"Look, I can see something's wrong. Is there anything I can do to help?" she asked.

Cassandra's face changed to become a mask of fury. She lashed out at the paintbox, knocking it from Anne's hand and sending it flying.

"I don't have a gift, I have a curse!" she said harshly, her voice pent with barely controlled fury.

Anne stepped back, shocked and frightened at the change in this quiet girl.

"I don't want your or anyone's help. No one can help me anyway, so just leave me alone — pretend you never met me," she said. "It would have been safer for you if you hadn't."

Anne watched stunned as Cassandra stalked off into the trees. She had never expected an outburst like this. What had happened to upset her so? She walked over to where the paints had fallen and bent to pick them up. As she touched them, the box seemed to collapse in on itself, settling into a little pile of dust. Horrified, she drew her hand back. A shiver went down her spine and she looked up sharply expecting to see someone. There was no one there. Straightening up, she backed away from the clearing. Something told her to run, and without questioning the impulse, she turned and fled. Short of breath and shaking, she eventually arrived at the hostel.

Glen looked up from where he was sitting as she entered the common room.

"You look as if you've seen a ghost," he said, noticing her pallor.

Anne's legs refused to hold her up any longer and sedately, she slid to the floor.

Leaping to his feet, Glen rushed over to her. "Are you all right?" he asked, feeling her forehead.

Anne nodded weakly. "I am now."

"What happened?"

"You wouldn't believe me if I told you," she said. "Let's say I had a fright."

Glen hauled her to her feet. "Then what you need is a cup of hot, sweet tea," he said, conducting her to the kitchen.

"Not tea, coffee," she protested. "And not here!"

"There's still half an hour before our amateur chefs take over. You've plenty of time to tell me what's happened," he said, pushing her onto the stool and plugging in the kettle. "Now talk."

"It'll just sound as if I'm being foolish and irrational," she objected.

"Never mind, just tell me," he ordered, leaning back against the work surface and folding his arms.

Anne explained what she'd discovered about the rock paintings, and of her meeting with Cassandra in the clearing quarter of an hour before.

"That damned paintbox just disintegrated before my eyes, Glen! That sort of thing just can't happen, can it?"

"I don't know, Anne. I'll tell you what we can do, though. We can go back and have another look at those rock paintings. Now finish your coffee like a good girl," he said grinning at her.

"Don't patronize me," Anne grumbled, draining her cup before getting up.

"Are you sure these were the rocks?" Glen asked after half an hour of fruitless searching.

"Can you see any others beside the path?" demanded Anne, scrutinizing the boulders yet again. "You know as well as I do that yesterday there were paintings on them, and now they're blank! And the marks I made with my knife have vanished too."

"I know I saw the paintings, and I'd swear these are the rocks, but the fact remains that if you did scrape away at the stones, it couldn't have been these," Glen replied patiently.

"Then where are the paintings?" Anne demanded in exasperation.

"There's any number of rational explanations for the lack of the paintings," he said.

"Give me one!"

"The rain washed them away."

"It hasn't rained in the last two days."

"The dampness and the salt air then," he said promptly. "It really doesn't matter why they're not here. The fact is they aren't. Are you absolutely positive that you did stick your knife into them?"

"Absolutely!" Anne snapped. "You don't imagine things like that unless you're having a breakdown," she glared, daring him to say anything.

Glen sighed. "Shall we go and have a look at the clearing?"

"What for?" she asked, suddenly weary. She started back up the path. "All you'll see is a pile of dust that could have been anything. Let's get back for tea."

Glen came up beside her and wrapped his arm around her shoulders. "I'm not suggesting you imagined it all," he said. "Let's go and have a look by the studio. It's my bet that you'll find your paintbox lying on the ground in one piece. Did it occur to you that these two incidents happened when Cassandra was upset, and that perhaps you saw what she wanted you to see?"

Anne frowned. "What do you mean?"

"The power of suggestion. She's a young teenager, and they're capable of all sorts of strange things. Maybe you saw what she wanted you to see rather than what really happened."

Anne considered it for a moment. "Impossible," she said. "The nature of both the rock and the paintbox was changed. They had become..." she searched for the right word but couldn't find it. "...different," she ended lamely. "No, I don't want to go and look for the box. We're leaving tomorrow, and as far as I'm concerned, Cassandra can keep her secret, whatever it is."

"I think you're wise," he said. "Let's get back and eat. We need to line our stomachs if we're going to do some serious drinking on our last night."

"I don't know if I feel up to walking to the pub."

"It's not far."

"Not far! It's a four-mile walk there, never mind back."

"Just a brisk stroll," he said airily. "As for the walk back, you'll never notice it with a wee dram inside you to keep out the cold."

The pub in Kirkoswald was warm and comfortable. High-backed wooden settles kept out all but imagined draughts, and the log fire burning quietly in the grate complemented the subdued lighting, lending an old-world charm to the place. The publican and the locals were a friendly lot, used to the weekly turnover of students. All too soon last orders were called, but the little group they had joined around the fire didn't move and shortly the publican brought his owdrink over and sat down with them.

"Now yon ghosties," said one old boy, puffing mightily on his pipe till a cloud of dense smoke all but obscured him. "Yon ghosties up at the Castle. Ye must 'a seen them, have ye no?"

"Ghosts?" queried Glen, feigning innocence. "What ghosts are those, Mr. McNabb?"

"Ye mean ye've no seen them? Och, come on, laddie," he said, poking him in the arm with an authoritative pipe stem. "Ye canna get me to believe that ye havna seen one of the Culzean ghosts!"

"One of them!" exclaimed Doniki, rising to the bait. "How many are there?"

Satisfied, Mr. McNabb sat back, puffing once more on his pipe.

"Oh, a great many if truth were known," he nodded sagely.

"Aye," echoed one of his cronies, "there's a fair few up there."

"Tell us about them," said Glen, taking a mouthful of his beer.

"Aye, and so I would," said McNabb, lifting his empty glass sorrowfully, "if my throat werena' so dry."

Glen laughed and raised an eyebrow at the publican.

A few minutes later they returned to their nook with recharged glasses. McNabb took a long draught and smacked his lips appreciatively.

"The ghosts," prompted Glen gently.

"Ah, the ghosties. Now ye'll have heard of the Kennedys, I'll be bound. The American family that was big in politics twenty or so years past? Well, they left Ireland, making their way o'er here first. They bided here for a couple o' hundred years, then went on to America."

Anne groaned. "Don't tell me there's a ghostly piper!" she said.

"Dinna ye laugh, lassie," said McNabb tartly, stabbing the air with his pipe. "It's no joke in the dead o' night to hear they bagpipes skirlin' and know no mortal man is playin' them!"

"I don't believe it," said Doniki firmly.

"Ah, well you'd be wrong then," said the publican seriously. "He's been heard the night before any of the Kennedys have died. We heard him back in '63"

"Aye," nodded McNabb. "The night before he was shot. You could hear the lament o' the pipes for miles."

Glen shifted uncomfortably. He had been hoping for ghost tales, but this was getting just a touch too heavy.

"What about other ghosts?" he asked.

McNabb broke out of his reverie. "Tam, you used tae work at the restaurant in the summer season. Where was yon one you told me about?"

Tam began to grin. "Ach, they willna' want to ken about that one," he said.

"It's their last day the morn," said McNabb. "They're no' likely to meet it now, if they havna already."

"Ben the Ladies," he grinned.

"The Ladies?" said Anne. "In the Ladies' toilet? You're joking!"

He shook his head. "It doesna happen a' the time, just now and then."

"What happens?" asked Doniki, her face beginning to turn a little pale.

Tam shrugged. "Things get flung about. We had some students here havin' photos taken. The lassies, they didna half start a song and dance when their bits of makeup went flyin' round the room."

"I'm not surprised," murmured Anne, taking a sip of her lager.

"Is that all?" asked Glen.

McNabb gave him a long look.

"What more d'you be wantin', laddie?"

"I meant, did the ghost do anything else?" explained Glen.

"Well now, I'd have said by looking at yon two lassies, that was enough, but I'm no judge o' things like that," McNabb replied, indicating Anne and Doniki, who were definitely looking a little uneasy.

"You forgot the ghostly walker," said the publican. "You know, the one who walks beside folks out for early morning strolls."

"Where does he walk?" asked Glen.

"On the path down to the beach. You can hear his footsteps stirring the fallen leaves at the side of the path, even if there are no leaves on the ground."

"What about the one in the hostel?" put in Tam.

"Ah, now that's a sad one," nodded McNabb, sucking on the pipe stem. "Story goes that last century, the daughter of the Laird had an illegitimate child. The parents took the bairn away as soon as it was born and she never saw it again. She died young, o' a broken heart they said, and her ghost still searches for the lost bairn."

Glen looked surreptitiously at his watch.

"Remember last night I told you I thought I saw a dark figure by the dorm door?" said Doniki, turning to Anne. "It must have been her," she ended in hushed tones.

"You were half asleep at the time," said Anne, "and when I looked, I couldn't see anything. There's no reason to believe it was a ghost."

"Maybe it was, maybe it wasn't," said McNabb wisely.

"We'll have to go, I'm afraid," said Glen, finishing his beer. "It's twelve-thirty, girls, and we've a four-mile walk back."

Anne and Doniki downed their drinks and grabbed their coats.

"Thanks for a great evening," said Anne, stopping at the door.

"Pleasure t'meet you, lassie. You watch out for yon ghosties on your way back, ye hear?" said McNabb with a wave of his pipe.

The cold air hit them like a slap in the face. As they walked away from the comforting lights of the pub, they could hear the sound of uproarious laughter.

"They were just winding us up," Glen said as he linked an arm with each girl.

"I don't think so," said Doniki. "I got the feeling he believed his own stories."

"He's probably told them so often, he's forgotten he made them up," Glen retorted, leading them onto the roadway. "Come on now, best foot forward. We've got a full moon and a nice clear sky. We should reach the hostel in no time."

"It's Beltane tonight," observed Doniki, glancing at the silvery disc of the moon.

"So what?"

"It's a pagan festival," she murmured, stumbling over a stone on the road. "Strange things happen at this time of year."

"You don't believe in that rubbish, do you? Those old codgers in there have really got you going, haven't they?" laughed Glen. "Come on, there's nothing magical or mystical about a full moon, except that on a clear night you can see for miles, which means we can't lose our way."

"You mentioned the ghosts to me once before, Glen," said Anne. "Remember? When I said I heard someone in the bushes by the studio?"

"When you found Cassandra?" he asked. "Yes, I remember."

"How come you knew about them then?"

"One of the third-year students told me about them when he heard we were coming down here this week."

"If they knew about them, then the stories they told tonight must be true."

"Not necessarily. They'll tell the same stories to every section, and I haven't yet met anyone who has personally experienced one of the ghosts. Plenty of people who know someone who... but no one who has actually met them. I really wouldn't think about it anymore," he advised, setting an even smarter pace so that they were almost trotting to keep up with him. "You'll get yourselves so spooked that the first owl that flies near us will have you shrieking as if all the devils in hell were after us."

They walked, or trotted, in silence for a while until Glen suddenly veered off the road toward a field.

"There's the stile," he said. "Over you go." He helped Doniki up then went over himself, waiting in the middle to help Anne. "Nearly there," he said, looking over at the trees. "The path leads through the woods and brings us out at the bottom of the drive beside the hostel."

"Is this the way you came back last night?" asked Anne, jumping down.

"Yes. I thought we'd take the pretty way there, but the short cut back."

"I won't go through the woods," said Doniki, obstinately refusing to go any further.

"What?" said Glen incredulously.

"I refuse to go through the woods," Doniki repeated firmly.

"Why?"

"They're haunted, McNabb said so, and I won't go through haunted woods on Beltane Eve."

"I don't believe this," exclaimed Glen. "Do you seriously expect us to go all the way down the main road, not to mention the drive — which incidentally is wooded too — just because of the tales of a couple of old men in a pub?"

"Yes," she said firmly.

"Get a grip on yourself, girl! Where's this much-vaunted impartiality of yours? There is no way I am making a four-mile walk into a six-mile one just because you choose to believe the ramblings of a bunch of old drunks," he snapped. "You want to take the long way, fine, but I'm going through the woods. Are you coming, Anne?" he demanded.

Anne looked from Doniki's stubborn expression to Glen's angry one.

"I think we should all go the same way," she said, moving toward Glen.

"You can't leave me!" exclaimed Doniki.

"We aren't leaving you. It's you who is staying behind," said Anne peaceably. She felt no sympathy for Doniki. Living with her this last week had made her intolerant of the other's continual moods and demands.

The light began to fade and Anne looked up. Clouds had formed and were drifting across the face of the moon.

"Looks like weather might be coming in," she said, following Glen across the grass.

"At least we had the best of it," he replied. In a whisper he added, "Don't worry, she'll catch up with us in a minute. Less, now the light's going."

Sure enough, a few minutes later they heard Doniki yelling.

"Wait for me!"

As they reached the trees, the cloud bank totally obscured the moon, and they were plunged into darkness.

"Damn!" swore Glen, stumbling into a tree. "Here, take my hands you two. We don't want to get separated. I think we go this way."

Anne stumbled along through the undergrowth, trying to keep up with Glen. Her foot caught in a root and down she went, falling heavily on her knees and ripping her hand free.

"Ow!" she yelled. "Hold on, wait a minute!"

Glen bent down and lifted her to her feet. "You all right?" he asked.

"I think so," she replied, rubbing her bruised kneecaps. "Do you have to go so fast?" she complained.

"I'm not sure where we are," he said. "I want to find some recognizable landmarks."

Gradually it began to grow lighter again, and Anne squinted up through the trees. "The moon's back. We should be able to orient ourselves now."

Glen look around for a moment, then pointed off to his right. "Over there, I think."

They started off again, making slightly better progress now they could see. Suddenly Doniki stopped.

Anne bumped into her. "What're you stopping for?" she demanded.

"I can see something in front of us," she whispered, trying to hide behind the nearest bush.

Glen peered over their shoulders. "There's nothing there," he said.

"There is," Doniki insisted, keeping her voice low. "I'm not moving until you find out what it is."

Glen made an exasperated noise. "I'm getting fed up with you ordering me about, Doniki." Unceremoniously he pushed her aside and moved forward a couple of steps. "I can't see anything."

"The moon's gone behind another cloud now, but I saw a patch of black by that tree over there," she insisted, her voice beginning to quaver.

"There's nothing there."

"There is!" she insisted.

Glen grabbed her by the hand and hauled her toward the tree.

"Now you show me..."

Doniki's terrified shriek split the air. A shaft of moonlight picked out the frozen tableau at the foot of the tree just as surely as if it were a spotlight. Something was hanging from a branch above their heads.

As Anne looked up, she felt everything around her begin to take on a slowness, as if time itself had become stretched. The scream seemed to go on and on forever. There was the sound of a sharp slap, but it was she who put her hand up to a smarting cheek and found Glen shaking her violently.

"Snap out of it, Anne," he said urgently. "You can't help her now, she's beyond it." He stopped shaking her and held her close for a moment, releasing her when she feebly pushed him away.

"Cassandra?" she asked.

He nodded. "She's dead."

Like a sleepwalker, Anne moved toward the body, but Glen held her back.

"I wouldn't," he said.

"I have to see!" she insisted, pushing his restraining hand away.

She walked over, gazing up at Cassandra's body. The girl hardly seemed dead unless you looked closely. Her feet were only a few centimeters off the ground—it was as if she was standing waiting for them.

A faint breeze seemed to catch the body, and it began to rotate slowly at the end of the creaking rope. Anne frowned. There was something wrong, something that didn't fit if only she could see what it was.

A hand clutched at her arm. "Don't look, Anne," urged Glen, pulling her away.

She turned to face him, seeing for the first time that he was ashen and sweat was beading his forehead. From nearby came the sound of Doniki retching.

"Let's leave. We need to tell the police and there's no point in staying here, we can't do anything for her now," he said.

"Her family, they'll have to be told," Anne said abruptly. "I know where she lives. I'll get them. You wait here with her."

She could hear Glen calling for her to stop, but she ignored him in her need to do something positive. If she did something—anything—then she wouldn't have to think. She wouldn't have to face the reality that perhaps they had contributed something to Cassandra's despair, perhaps the final straw.

It was a mad race through the trees. She had no real idea where she was let alone in which direction the headland lay. Instinct must have guided her for eventually she ran free of the brambles and thorns and found herself at the edge of the woods with the lights of the croft ahead of her.

Up the slope she ran, panting now, to collapse against the doorframe with barely enough strength left to knock. The door was flung wide, almost catapulting her into the light and warmth of the main room.

She looked up into the face of the brother, dark and angry with her for not being his sister.

"Cassandra," she blurted out. "You must come. She's... hurt." She steadied herself against the door frame and made to move away.

The brother's arm snaked out, catching hold of her.

"Hurt, is she?" he said harshly. "What've you done to her?"

"Nothing," said Anne. "She did it herself."

The grip tightened. "How hurt?"

Anne looked away. "Dead. She hanged herself," she said, her voice devoid of emotion.

"Where?" he demanded. "Show me."

"Have they found Cassandra?" asked an older female voice from inside.

"They found her," affirmed the youth over his shoulder. "She's gone and hanged herself. I'm going to get her now." He turned back to Anne. "Where is she?"

"We came over the fields from Kirkoswald and cut through the woods. We found her in a tree beside the path."

"It's your meddling that brought her to this," he snarled, his face twisting in anger as he shook Anne. "If you'd left her alone..."

"Paris! Enough!" said the peremptory voice from inside. "It's no one's fault. Fetch a torch, you'll be needing one."

He let her go and with a look of pure hate, stormed from the room. Anne heard the distant sound of raised voices then Paris returned with the torch and a blanket.

"Let's be going," he said, shutting the door.

"Shouldn't we phone the police or something?" faltered Anne, backing away from him.

"Mother'll see to that," he answered shortly, setting off across the headland.

It was a silent journey. There was nothing really to say. When they reached the spot where Cassandra was hanging, Doniki was still lying in a heap on the ground sobbing with Glen sitting beside her.

He looked up as they arrived. "You found the house safely, then," was all he said.

She nodded.

The youth spread the blanket down at the foot of the tree and reached for his belt knife. Clasping Cassandra's body around the waist, he began to saw through the loop of the rope where it extended above her head.

Glen got to his feet. "Can I help?" he asked.

"We look after our own," was the short reply. "My thanks for telling us," he grunted, "but you see to your own women and get them home."

The rope parted finally making Paris stagger briefly as he took the full weight of his sister's body. Laying her down on the rug, he wrapped the blanket around her before putting his knife away. Silently he lifted Cassandra's body and vanished into the night, leaving them alone.

"I think we'd better get back," said Glen lamely. "There's nothing we can do now."

Anne nodded.

"Get up, Doniki," he said, giving her a nudge with his foot.

She didn't move.

"For God's sake, girl, get up!" he said, leaning down and pulling her to her feet. "And stop that awful whimpering. If anyone has a right to be upset, it's Anne, not you. You didn't give a damn about the girl and made it obvious to everyone."

Glen turned his back on her to put an arm around Anne.

"Are you all right?" he asked, drawing her along the path with him.

"I'm fine," said Anne quietly. Her grief was a cold knot inside her that wouldn't dissolve.

"Follow when you're ready, Doniki," said Glen. "We're leaving now."

"Just a minute, there's something I want to check," said Anne, ducking out from under him and going over to the tree. She took hold of the end of the rope. She'd noticed something strange about it when Cassandra's brother had been cutting the girl's body down. She teased at the loose fibers on the cut end. They looked different from the rest of the rope. There was a strange elasticity to them. She pulled, feeling them stretch slightly. There was a resilience where the rope had been in contact with Cassandra's neck. Thoughtfully she felt above the loop but it was just a piece of hemp. Once again, something the girl had touched had been altered.

"Anne, come away," urged Glen. "Whatever you've found, it doesn't matter now. All I'm concerned about now is getting you back to the hostel."

Reluctantly Anne released the rope, letting it swing back against the tree. She turned and walked back to him, feeling her legs begin to wobble slightly. He was right, if they didn't get back soon, she was likely to collapse on them.

It was a bleary-eyed face she presented to the world late the next morning. She had lain awake for several hours puzzling over Cassandra and her strange talent, replaying all their meetings with her and worrying that they might have been the cause of her suicide. She hadn't come to any conclusions and eventually, sheer exhaustion had taken over and she had slept.

Most of her section had left to get in a last few hours' work before the bus came after lunch to take them home, so she was spared the necessity of telling anyone what had happened. Those who demanded the grisly details had gotten them from Glen the night before or over breakfast. In fact, the hostel was empty except for the three of them.

After a meager breakfast, Anne announced that she was going for a walk.

Glen looked at her in concern. "Would you like me to come with you?" he asked.

Anne shook her head, smiling. "No thanks, I'm fine. I just want some fresh air to clear my head, and to do a bit of thinking."

"Take care, then," he said, reaching out to touch her cheek gently, and intimately. "I'd hate anything to happen to you."

"I don't believe it!" said Doniki indignantly. "Now's not the time for a testosterone high! How can you be so insensitive when we've all been through such a trauma?"

"Can it, Doniki," said Glen, letting his hand drop. "Anne's been through more than us. She lost a friend. I want her to know I care about her, that's all."

Embarrassed, Anne nodded and headed for the door, but Glen followed her.

"Stay away from the woods where we were last night, Anne," he said quietly, taking her jacket off the peg and holding it out to her. "I don't trust that brother of Cassandra's. Head for the beach. If you're not back in an hour, I'll come looking for you."

"There's no need," she protested.

He held onto her jacket as she tried to take it from him. "I meant what I said in there." His voice had deepened, become more intense as he leaned toward her. He hesitated, taking a step back and letting her jacket go as he realized now was not the time for more. "Please don't take any risks."

"I'll take care," she promised.

The day was grey and overcast and a fine drizzle had begun to fall. As she headed out of the courtyard for the shelter of the trees, she smiled gently to herself, Glen's sudden interest in her lightening her somber mood.

Once under the canopy of leaves, she slowed down, content just to amble where her feet took her. For once, Frazer had shown some humanity and had given the three of them the morning to themselves. She aimed to take advantage of it.

The path forked in two, one branch leading to the studio, the other toward Kirkoswald and the route they'd taken home last night. With a shudder, Anne took the lower path down to the studio.

Her thoughts returned to Cassandra, trying to make some sense of the past week. Cassandra had been brought up isolated from everyone except her family. Not only that, but she had been constantly watched by her brother to make sure she didn't meet people, and the last time she had, she said there'd been an accident. What kind of accident? Obviously not an ordinary one, otherwise why isolate her? Could it be to do with her gift? She could obviously change the structure of things she touched, but if she could do it at will, why try to commit suicide then change the rope, make it stretch? That didn't make sense. Perhaps Cassandra had no control and everything she touched changed.

Anne had reached the clearing where the studio stood and crossing over to one of the windows, she perched on the ledge. Despite the fine drizzle, she didn't want to go inside. The smell of damp earth filled the clearing and she found it refreshing, touching something deep in her soul that brought her a measure of peace.

If Cassandra had no control over her gift, could circumstances around her be triggering it? When Cassandra had altered the rocks, she'd been happy and the "paintings" had reflected this. The second time, she'd been upset and angry and when she'd lashed out at the paintbox, it had gone flying as one would expect, but the structural change had been one of decay—It had crumbled to dust on being touched. Perhaps her mood dictated the type of change.

That sounded good so far, but how did the change in the rope fit in? Maybe her ability had a built-in survival factor and she couldn't stop the rope from changing. Anne sighed. As a survival factor, it hadn't been particularly successful.

The sound of footsteps, followed by the flash of black skirts and swirling ginger hair made her look up.

"Cassandra!" she yelled, leaping to her feet. "My God, you're alive! Come back, it's me, Anne!"

Anne raced across the clearing. "It can't be her, she's dead. Oh, please God, let her have survived," she said pushing the bushes aside as she tried to follow.

Beyond lay a narrow rabbit track. Dark footprints on the damp grass showed she was on the right path. Not stopping to think, she ran along it, following it till she burst out of the trees onto the headland not far from the croft where Cassandra's family lived. Sides heaving, frantically she looked around but apart from the croft, the grassy slopes were absolutely empty of human life. Maybe she'd overtaken her in the dash through the woods.

Logic told her that she couldn't possibly have seen Cassandra. Briefly she considered going up to the croft, but she knew she'd no right to disturb the family in their mourning. Turning to leave she let out a muffled shriek as she came face to face with Cassandra's brother.

"God, you frightened me! I didn't expect to see you here," she said, backing off hurriedly.

"Who'd you expect to see? Cassandra?"

"No," admitted Anne, suddenly aware he was carrying a dead rabbit and a shotgun. "But I thought I saw her back by the studio. It must have been my imagination playing tricks on me."

"Must have," he agreed laconically, his dark eyes never leaving her face.

"She had a great talent. It's a pity that she didn't have the chance to develop it," she said, stumbling for something to say.

"Cassie didn't have a talent," he said, frowning.

"But she did. She was able to alter the rocks and paint into them. You must know she could change things."

"She never painted into any rocks that I knew of. Where d'you see these paintings?"

"On the path down to the beach."

Paris shook his head, a lock of black hair falling over his face, shielding his eyes from her. "I was down that way on Thursday and there weren't any paintings then. Reckon it's your imagination again."

"The paintings were there on Wednesday," began Anne, then stopped, her hand flying to her mouth in shock. "Cassandra," she whispered, pointing a shaking finger past him toward the croft.

"You should have listened to Cassandra and stayed away from us," he said sadly, shifting the rabbit off his shoulder and letting it dangle at his side. "Pity you had to find out. Cassie has our gift all right, but it's wild in her. She can't control it. What she touches turns depending on her mood at the time."

Anne pulled her gaze away from Cassandra and looked back at the brother, sensing the menace in his tone.

"It was you who erased the pictures," she whispered, color draining from her face.

"To save you, missy, if you'd had the sense to let be," he said harshly. "You pushed her, reminded her what it's like to be one of your kind. It was just your bad luck that you were the one to find her body." His eyes narrowed and he lifted the rabbit. "Our gift can create and heal, which is how we saved Cassie, but it can destroy too." He tightened his grip on the rabbit's body and as he squeezed, before Anne's horrified eyes, it began to decay. The skin swelled, oozing a yellowish-grey liquid. The stench of putrefaction hung heavily in the air.

Anne glanced back at Cassandra, a small figure in front of the croft, but near enough for her to tell that the girl was no less terrified than she was.

"We can't let you leave now, you know that, don't you?" he said almost conversationally, tossing the decayed body to one side. "Every time this happens, we have to move on, keep hiding from the normals like you. After thousands of years, we finally thought we'd found a place where we'd be safe."

His stare became hypnotic, and Anne found she was unable to look away. Her willpower gradually began seeping from her and though she stood passively waiting, her mind screamed in raw terror.

He stepped forward and his hand reached out for her.

"You should have listened to Cassandra, she knows the truth, but then, you're not the first to ignore her warnings of danger. It's her curse, you see."

WARRIOR IN THE MIST

With many thanks to Pete James of "The Vikings!" for his technical help.

I AM LISANNE NORMAND, OF THE CLAN MACLEOD, AND I FIRST CAME TO these shores in 1066 with Duke William of Normandy, heir of King Edward the Confessor of England. But it's not of that time I wish to tell.

It's the evening of Saturday, October 13th. Dusk is falling on the slopes of Senlac Hill. The year is 1990, and the event is the largest ever recreation of the Battle of Hastings, otherwise known as the battle of Senlac Hill. The site was aptly named Senlac—Sangue Lac—the River of Blood, because for years after, when it rained, the blood that had been spilled that fateful day would rise red to the surface and its stench once more would fill the air.

Today's battle is over now and darkness is falling. I am the last of those who played the parts of Norman archers, and I am doing a final sweep of Senlac Hill with my young son for any lost arrows.

"Was this really where the Battle of Hastings was fought, Mum?" Kai asked as we trudged back toward the campsite where all through Friday night, from cities and towns across the length and breadth of Britain, some seven hundred re-enactors, most warriors like me, had gathered on the wooded slopes to the east of Senlac Ridge.

I glanced briefly up the hill to my right where the Abbey squatted on the brow of the hill, its ruined walls a forbidding presence.

"Yes, this is the place. The Normans defeated Harold up there where the Abbey now stands on the top of Senlac Hill. They say he died where the altar stood."

"Did your side win today, then?"

"Of course. We're real Normans, aren't we?"

"Our family," he said with quiet pride.

"We didn't do so bad a job. Britain's never been invaded since." I looked down at his earnest five-year-old face and smiled, ruffling his fair shoulder-length hair. Then I stopped to pick up an arrow that lay concealed by my foot in a tuft of grass.

"How d'you know the arrow was there?" he demanded.

I shrugged, tucking it into the quiver that hung on my right hip. "A knack," I said. "Arrows take a long time to make and they're too expensive to lose. The horses broke six of mine today."

"Tell me what happened in the battle," he said, losing interest in the arrow now that it was out of sight.

"We formed up at the bottom of the hill in three divisions," I began. "The Breton mercenaries, William's own Norman troops, and the French mercenaries. As archers, we were out in front with Roy. He was in charge of us all, but my unit was at the far end of the line, on the right, in front of the left-hand flank of Saxons. It happened in the second half of the show, after Harold's right flank had been destroyed."

"Did you follow the real battle plans?"

"More or less."

"How d'you know what happened that long ago?"

"The Normans left a history of it embroidered on the Bayeux Tapestry, and a Norman poet called Wace, who lived then wrote everything all down in a poem called 'Roman de Rue.' Oh, and there's the Chronicles of Battle Abbey, documents written about the battle and the founding of the Abbey," I added. "Now, shall I tell you what happened?"

I skidded to a halt by Roy on the damp grass in the gap between the Norman and Breton cavalry. "We're running out of arrows down our end," I yelled over the noise of the battle raging at the top of Senlac Ridge. "There's dozens of them lying ahead of us near the Saxon left flank but the scurriers can't reach them safely. If we don't get them now, they'll be trampled when the French do their second feigned retreat!"

Roy glanced across to the Saxon left, then behind him to where William's cavalry waited, the horses snorting and pawing the ground, impatient to be off again.

He leaned closer so I could hear him. "Do it," he said. "You've seven minutes before the next cavalry charge. If we don't get them, they'll be turned to matchwood by the horses. When the French retreat, the Saxon fyrdsmen will break ranks to follow. Let them through then have your unit loose three volleys at the remaining Saxon to pin them down, giving our men a chance to turn on the fyrdsmen. Pull back to the trees until after the cavalry charge, then join us when we form up behind the Norman infantry."

"Fyrdsmen?" interrupted Kai. "What are they?"

"Ordinary men called from their farms to increase the size of the small permanent army Harold had. A militia. It's thought Harold only had about two thousand fully trained and armored men, the remaining five thousand were his fyrdsmen, most of whom didn't have armor or even a shield."

"And William?"

"Probably about the same number, but they were a well-armored and disciplined army, and twenty-five hundred of them were his knights on horses. Now hush, I thought you wanted me to tell you what happened to me."

Giving Roy a thumb's up, I quickly checked the watch in my pouch as I ran back to the far end of the line of archers. "Follow me!" I yelled, heading toward the woodland bordering the battlefield. "You, too," I said, touching two scurriers as I passed. Twenty yards from the tree line, I stopped.

"Everyone got at least four arrows?" I demanded, looking 'round my group of ten men and women. Getting nods from everyone, I briefed them and gave the order to move out.

In a loose file, keeping to the rough ground, we ran up the hill until we were just beyond the scattered arrows. I pulled out my watch again.

"Katie, Kevin, you got two minutes. Get as many arrows as you can then get back to the French lines. We'll cover you. Colin, form an open order line in front and just to the left of the arrows. Space yourselves to let the French and the Saxons through," I ordered, leading the way out onto the field, my eyes focused on the combat sixty yards ahead of us.

I placed myself beside Colin, but slightly in front of him, checking my watch every now and then. The French line was wavering, getting ready to retreat.

"Thirty seconds!" I yelled, looking back at the scurriers to find Katie beside me, holding half a dozen arrows.

"We're finished," she said breathlessly. "You've all got six more."

"Well done. Now go!" I grabbed the arrows, pushing them easily into my almost empty quiver. The large rubber blunts on the ends usually made this a task that needed both hands. "Rest of you, hold fast and let the French and Saxons through!"

The gap between the two lines grew larger. I pulled out two arrows and holding one against the bow with my left hand, I nocked the other, latching my left forefinger over it to anchor it to the bow. Having an extra arrow ready had saved me from enemy re-enactors many a time. I fell back in line with Colin and glanced to my right at the other six archers, making sure they were ready and far enough apart. All we had to do now was wait.

As the French line broke and began to run downhill, I knew I'd placed us well. They, and the Saxons, should pass at least five feet clear of us. I hadn't been happy at the thought of standing like trees in the middle of a hurricane of fleeing armed warriors. Accidents happen, and apart from helmets concealed beneath soft hats, we were unarmored.

Suddenly, something heavy slammed into me, sending me reeling. I was dragged violently to one side. The ground shook as the huge dark shape of a horse thundered past.

"Looks like Delon got bored," said Colin's voice calmly in my ear.

Stunned, I could only watch in horror as five more mounted knights followed the first, each of them sending clods of grass and earth flying into our faces as they passed.

Colin let me slide down to the ground. "You all right?" he asked. "You look a little pale."

"I'm fine," I said shakily, one hand tightening on my bow, the other going automatically to check that my quiver still hung at my side. Numbly, I looked across at the others. Their faces were as pale as mine probably was, but everyone was still there and unhurt, thanks to Colin's quick actions.

"You nearly got run down by a horse?" interrupted Kai, his face scrunched up with worry. "Didn't the rider know you were there?"

"He didn't care. He expected me to get out of his way."

"But you couldn't see him!"

"I know, but I'm here, aren't I? Let me finish the story."

"Thanks, Colin," I said as he went back for his bow. "Dammit! The man's a maniac! What the hell does he think he's doing? He could have killed me! He's not supposed to go yet! His cue is to wait for the French to turn and kill the fleeing Saxons then all the cavalry charge to destroy what remains of the Saxon left!"

Colin shrugged as he came back, nocking his arrow again. "That's what happens when you use display riders like Delon as cavalry. We've had trouble from him before, at the Isle of Man Millennium show."

The shock of what had nearly happened to me was just beginning to penetrate. On autopilot, I looked over to the far side of the field where Roy stood with the rest of the archers. With Delon messing up the script, I knew I needed to check for fresh orders.

Roy raised his arm, making the signal for me to carry on. I gestured my acknowledgment and turned my attention back to Delon and his riders. Discovering the Saxons hadn't yet broken ranks to run after the French, they'd charged to the other side of the field where the Norman and Breton infantry were attacking the Saxon center. From behind their lines, Delon and his riders shouted insults and taunts at the Saxons while making their horses rear up and prance on their hind legs.

The French had almost reached us now, and the Saxon left had begun to split with more than half of its force following our fleeing soldiers. "I hope Delon's not completely forgotten his cue," I muttered, checking again on the maniac. An adrenalin rush had kicked in and I was getting increasingly bad feelings about our position. "Pull back, Colin," I said abruptly. "Head back to the trees!" I began to run in front of my archers. "We'll wait there till they're all past us!"

"Incoming!" yelled someone.

Stopping in my tracks, I instinctively ducked, turning my head away to look behind me, praying the others would do the same. I glanced sideways along our line — in time to see Stewart look up, and an arrow smack him hard in the center of his forehead.

"Jesus!" I swore, then "Go!" I yelled to the others, rushing over to him.

With a look of incredulity on his face, Stewart staggered back a few paces, then fell like a stone. Dropping my bow and arrows, I flung myself on the ground beside him, holding him down when he began to struggle to sit up.

"How many times have I told you to keep your head down when you hear Incoming?" I raged at him, checking his face, relieved to find the skin on his forehead unbroken, though a large lump was beginning to form. Around us, the French foot soldiers were streaming past, thankfully giving us a wide berth. Reaching out, I snagged my bow closer to my side. "Stay put. You could have a concussion. At least you kept hold of your bow."

Jumping to my feet, I grabbed the nearest man. He swung 'round, eyes staring, mouth set in a snarl of fury as he raised his sword to hit me, then hesitated.

"Take him to a medic! He took an arrow on the forehead!"

His breathing labored, he glanced briefly over his shoulder. The Saxons were only thirty yards away and closing fast. "Take him yourself," he said, trying to pull free of me. "I got Saxons to kill!" Sweat was running in rivulets down his face, and as he shook his head, droplets sprayed onto me. The light of battle was fading from his eyes.

"Unit commander, I can't," I snapped, pointing to the band of red I wore around my upper arm. I let him go and pushed him toward Stewart. "Got a volley to do right now!"

He nodded and reached down to drag Stewart to his feet.

"Watch out for the cavalry!" I yelled after them, as I grabbed for my weapons and the arrow that had hit Stewart, then I sprinted back to the others.

"Is he okay?" asked Judith, face creased in concern.

"Trust him to do a Harold," grinned Pete. "Told you that Stewart the halfling was on the wrong side. He should have been a Saxon."

"Yeah. Well, maybe it'll knock some sense into him, but I doubt it," I said, gesturing them to follow me up the hill as I stuffed the extra arrow into my quiver. "Let's move out. Keep level with me. We've got to shoot before the cavalry charge."

The hill was steeper now, and by the time we'd outflanked the Saxon fyrdsmen following our soldiers and taken up our positions opposite the remainder of the Saxon left, we were all short of breath and sweating in the heat of the October sun.

Behind us, the French had turned on the Saxons and were slaughtering them. There'd be no danger to us from that direction. I checked the Saxon center, but Delon's horses had returned to the bottom of the hill with William's infantry. I suddenly realized that the battlefield was empty and we'd be virtually alone in the center. The eyes of the audience of ten thousand people would be on us.

This better look good, I thought. "Showtime," I said, glancing over my shoulder at my unit. "In single file, we jog out and line up with an arrow ready. Make it look nice and military. If you miss my call, don't loose, wait for the next volley just as we've practiced. Nothing looks worse than a trailing arrow."

Heart pounding, I led us out to face the Saxons.

They greeted us with yells and screams of anger and derision. They only had four archers, there just to provide return fire so we didn't run out of arrows like the real Duke William's archers had until this final stage of the battle. And yet, despite all our plans to avoid it, so had we. It was strange how our show was paralleling the real battle.

"Open order. On my command, three volleys, then fall back in good order to the trees. Low shots, aimed at their shield wall. Try to get some kills. It's about time some of those Saxons died." I searched for a Saxon to target in the front rank. I found one, and as we locked eyes, he began to strike the back of his shield with his sword pommel, yelling, "Out! Out!"

"Nock," I commanded, "Draw. Loose!"

Like a wave, our arrows flew, bouncing harmlessly off their shields. Twice more I gave the command, and with the last volley, as the warriors lifted their shields slightly in anticipation, some of our arrows hit home. Two front-line soldiers, mine one of them, were reeling backward, their comrades immediately closing to fill the gaps in the shield wall.

"Yes!" I yelled exultantly as we ran back to the trees. "Good shooting!"

This time I could feel the ground vibrating beneath my feet with the beat of the horses' hooves as all the cavalry charged up Senlac Hill, encircling the Saxons and cutting them off from their central unit.

"The whole Saxon left will collapse now," I said, crouching down to catch my breath, watching our French infantry surging up the hill in the wake of the cavalry. "They'll run for their lives, a few of them breaking to come this way. Let them pass unchallenged. A small group actually escaped the Normans, and they're scripted to be it. As soon as they're gone, we watch for Roy and the rest of the archers. Get an arrow ready, we've got to look like we mean business."

The cavalry wheeled about, pulling back to let the Saxons break and run—straight into the waiting French infantry. Six fyrdsmen broke from the rest, heading toward us. They hit the rough some fifteen feet below and crashed into the cover of the trees.

We formed up at the end of Roy's line of archers, behind the combined ranks of William's infantry, facing the remains of the Saxon army which had now regrouped closely around Harold's banners of the Fighting Man and the Red Dragon of Wessex. The huscarls were packed so close together they really would be unable to lift their shields to protect themselves from our arrows.

Stewart rejoined us as the arrow scurriers rushed up and down our line handing out fresh arrows. Katie and Ken, remembering my earlier instructions, made sure that as many of my distinctive turquoise blue-and-white-fletched arrows as possible were returned to our unit.

"I'm fine," he said, touching a hand gingerly to the huge swelling in the center of his forehead. "Couldn't miss the final part."

"You'll have a shiner tomorrow," I said, hiding my anger at the Saxon archer who'd injured him. High lobbed shots were only to be used at scripted sections of the battle, and none were warranted by the Saxons. It had been deliberate. There was one archer up there who'd been targeting our little group throughout the battle, and I knew who he was. He was in the center now, and he was mine.

"Six volleys, then hold your ground," Roy yelled. "High angle lobs to fall down on them from above, then shoot at will. On my order!"

There'd be no incoming fire this time. All four Saxon archers would have downed their bows for the final assault on their position.

We were about halfway up the hill, and with our underpowered bows, which were all the safety rules would allow, we'd be hard-pressed to reach the Saxons on the brow of the hill—if it hadn't been for my speed-fletched blunts. Having only three feathers like a regular arrow rather than the four we normally used; we had an edge over the other archers. I knew that Roy, being a member of the Ancient Guild of Bowmen and Fletchers, planned to use one of his more powerful bows to enable him to reach the top of the hill.

I called my seven archers into a huddle. "We've six called volleys. Get a rhythm going and try to punch your bow forward as you draw back on the bowstring. Don't aim too high or the arrows will go into the Abbey grounds or the woodland and be lost. We did ranging shots from here this morning, so you know the angle of shot you need to make to reach the top. Track your own arrows and adjust your aim accordingly. Use the speed blunts first, those are the shots the audience will be watching, so we want them to count."

They nodded and fell back to their positions.

"You punch the bows forward?" asked Colin as we readied our arrows. "That's a new one on me."

During the break in the middle of the battle, while we'd waited for the water carriers to come around, Colin and I'd shared a surreptitious cigarette, puffing the smoke down into a small pothole beside us, and chatted about archery. I'd been surprised to find out just how much he knew. I remembered then had it not been for the fact his armor hadn't passed the authenticity check that morning, he'd not have been doing archery with us—and wouldn't have been there to pull me out from under the hooves of Delon's horse. I shuddered, glad that I'd followed my instincts and spoken to Roy about him joining my unit.

"Roy lent me a book about the history of archery in warfare," I said, reaching down to pluck a tuft of grass and throw it up into the air to check the wind direction. I knew it had veered slightly. "He taught me how to set up and run my specialist archery display team. Punching the bow away from you was a trick they used with the longbows to get more power behind the shots. I know ours are only lightweight self bows like the Normans used, but it does work. I've only been able to do it a couple of times, but then we don't usually have such a large arena to shoot in."

"I'll have to give it a try," he said.

"Wind's changed," I said over my shoulder to anyone who was listening. "Coming across the field from right to left now."

Then all talk ceased as Roy gave the command to nock arrows.

The arrows flew high, like a dark cloud over the heads of our army, out into the field, many falling spent at the feet of the Saxon shield wall, but not our arrows. Straight and true, they dropped down into the Saxon center.

It was our fifth volley before a cry from the Saxons signaled that the man playing the part of King Harold had been hit. A small gap opened up in the middle of their ranks and as we loosed our last volley, we could plainly see him staggering, holding his hand to an arrow protruding from his head.

The cavalry, led by Jim Alexander who was playing Duke William, passed safely between us, in an ordered charge this time, and headed up the hill, followed by the rest of William's infantry.

I began shooting at will, thinking of the Saxons on the brow of the hill—Chris from my group, so proud to be chosen to be one of Harold's huscarls, John himself, and his wife Gina, Ralph, and the others. They had no way of protecting themselves from the arrows falling from above, they were too tightly pressed together to lift their shields. But they'd been trained as well as my people—better, probably—to keep their heads down when under a barrage of arrows. I thought then of the archer who'd shot Stewart. It hardened my heart. We all had our jobs to do today, and mine was to rain arrows down on the Saxons, hopefully hitting the man who'd targeted Stewart.

I started to build a rhythm with my shots: as soon as I loosed one, I plucked another arrow from my quiver, nocking it, raising the bow, and punching it forward as I drew back the bowstring. Each arrow flew true, soaring high above the shield wall before the weight of the blunt pulled it down in a sharp arc to fall in the center of the remaining Saxons.

It was a different kind of battle fever I experienced, and it was exhilarating. For the first time, I understood what the others meant when they said it was hard to control the fighting spirit of the ancient Saxons that filled them whenever they fought at Battle Abbey. Only what I felt was the battle fever of the Normans.

Before long, like the others around me, I'd run out of arrows.

We watched the cavalry retreat to let the infantry close in. The Normans ran forward, shouting enthusiastically, then the whole line seemed to hesitate, to waver briefly before engaging.

The fighting was fiercest in the center. But then, John had chosen his men from among the best warriors across the length and breadth of England.

There was nothing left for us to do now, save to pick up what arrows we could and wait for the end, then go up the hill to help in the final slaughter as we gave the *coup de grace* to the dying Saxons and pulled our arrows from their bodies.

"Why did the Normans not go rushing in?" Kai asked.
"I found out when I got to the top of the hill."

"Let go of the arrow, Ralph," I grinned, putting my foot on his chest to give me extra leverage as I tried to tug free the arrow that he was holding firmly against his body.

His bearded, blood-spattered face leered challengingly up at me. "Shan't! You want it, you got to pull it free!"

"C'mon, give it to me."

He let go suddenly, sending me staggering away. I recovered my balance and went back to him, pulling out my battle knife and kneeling down to pretend to be looting his corpse.

"What's with all the fake blood?" I asked.

He laughed, a great, deep belly laugh that went all the way to his eyes. "Did you see the Norman line falter?" he asked.

"Yeah. What did you do?" I asked suspiciously.

"Just before the final charge, the whole front line, which was us of course, stepped back and we squirted stage blood into our helmets. Then when the Normans charged, the front line opened up and we stepped through. The first thing they saw was us, covered in blood! They thought it was real. Gave them a hell of a fright!"

"You're a bunch of mean bastards! We could see the line waver even from our position halfway down the hill."

"Well, if we had to die, we were going to do it in style."

"Did they really do that?" laughed Kai, delighted at the gory tale.

"Yes, they covered themselves in lots of fake blood," I said as we headed back to the fence that divided our campsite from the battlefield.

"And you're going to do it all again tomorrow?"

"Not quite all of it," I said. "Tomorrow is the actual date that the real Battle of Senlac Hill took place. October the 14th, though it happened on a Saturday, not a Sunday."

Full darkness had fallen as we'd been talking. A low mist was beginning to rise from the ground, and moonlight filtered down through the scudding clouds, giving the land an unearthly quality. As we reached the fence, the small hand within mine clenched, pulling me 'round.

"Mum! Over there! One of our knights!"

I looked. Emerging from the mist was a horse, its rider dressed in full battle kit.

"The horses have all been stabled for the night and aren't due out until tomorrow morning," I said, frowning as I looked in the knight's direction. Around him the mist eddied and swirled, hiding him from clear sight.

A tug on my arm and, "I want to go back to our tent now, Mum."

"I need to see who it is first. He might be lost, wondering where they're camped." My voice was as quiet as Kai's had been.

A breath of wind and the mist parted, allowing me to see the knight clearly. He wasn't alone. I shivered, and not because of the rising wind. Two outrunners were with him, one on each side of his mount.

Holding fast to the stirrup straps, they were using the momentum of the horse to help them keep pace with the knight. They were barely fifteen meters away, keeping close in by the trees.

The knight reined in, bringing his horse to a stop, then gestured silently toward Senlac Hill. The runners dipped their heads in obedience then sped off through the mist toward the woodland on either side of the ridge, one to the right, one to the left.

I remembered to breathe. These couldn't possibly be our people. During all the years I'd been coming to battle recreations in this area, several times before I'd caught sight of shapes in the darkness, ghosts if you will, especially on the coast at Norman's Bay. When we'd arrived last night, I'd seen the flicker of campfires in the surrounding woodlands, fires that I knew didn't exist—in our time.

The knight looked so real, so unlike the other shapes I'd seen in the past. Transfixed, I stared disbelievingly. I could see every detail clearly; the dark gleam of his long mail hauberk, reaching down to cover his knees, his conical helmet, darkened, probably with soot from a campfire—even the nasal showed dark against his skin. I could hear the muffled jingle of his horse's tack despite the bindings wrapped around it as the horse snorted gently, tossing its head.

Leaning forward, the knight patted his mount's neck, murmuring reassuringly.

At my side, Kai shifted, dropping his small bow. As he bent down to pick it up, the knight sat up and looked sharply, his gaze suddenly meeting mine.

I gasped. He could see me! Whirling around and grabbing Kai, I thrust him through the gap in the fence. "Run to John and Gina's tent and wait for me," I said urgently, pushing him into the field. "Hurry, Kai!" Heart pounding, I blocked the stile entrance with my body, bow gripped tightly in my hand, wishing I had the comforting weight of my sword at my side. Tomorrow—if there was a tomorrow for me—I would wear my sword during the battle.

As if he heard my thoughts, the knight's hand clenched around the pommel of the sword hanging from his right hip as he urged his horse toward me. I could feel his fear, twin to my own, reaching out to touch me as if it was a living thing.

He barked words in a language I didn't understand. I shook my head, too terrified to look up at him.

He moved the horse closer and spoke again, this time more harshly. "What are you doing here?" he demanded. "Scouts and foragers were told to be back in the camp before nightfall."

I understood him this time and understood more: this was no chance meeting. Somehow, this real Norman knight from nine hundred and twenty-four years in the past and I had been brought together for a reason.

"I'm not with your people," I began, raising my face to his, then stopped as, with an exclamation of shock, he recoiled from me in fear. Trusting my instincts, I leapt forward. "I need to tell you about tomorrow," I said.

Duke William's Camp, Wilting
Friday, October 13th, 1066

"God's wounds! Why will you not believe me?" I yelled in exasperation, gripping the pommel of my sword tightly in anger as I looked around the circle of barons seated at the table. "I tell you, he was dressed as one of our archers! It was a true vision of tomorrow I saw!"

"Watch your language, Ranulf!" my father snarled. "We'll have no blasphemy here!"

"Peace, Corbet," said Bishop Odo, the Duke's half-brother, sitting back in his seat, his eyes not leaving my face. "This archer you saw, Ranulf—how did you know he was a Norman?"

"I knew," I muttered, looking away so they'd not see the anger blazing in my eyes.

"You said the archer was clean-shaven, and darker-skinned than the Saxons," my father said forcefully.

"Have the pickets been checked? Could one of them have strayed so far?" murmured Fitz Osber. "Or a forager, returning late?"

"Archers don't do picket duty, and none were sent out foraging alone," said Mortemer. "And certainly none with a child."

"It was a fetch, a sending! Saxon witchcraft—or marsh gas! How, in truth, could one of our archers be there? This godforsaken land with its mists and marshes reeks of the devil—even the heavens are full of it with that hairy burning star earlier this year! No good'll come of this plan, mark my words!" someone muttered darkly.

Anger surged rapidly through me as I peered through the flickering candlelight in the direction of the voice, but I couldn't make the speaker out. How dare these barons — and my father! — doubt my word! I wasn't some virgin boy with an unbloodied blade and a wild imagination on the eve of his first battle! I knew what I'd seen, and it hadn't been marsh gas, or a fetch or a ghost.

"An archer with a child? Hardly an image to strike fear into our hearts, Tesson. And the fiery star we saw in the spring was a sign of God's favor," murmured Bishop Odo. "When the Holy Church is with us, how could it be otherwise? I'm inclined to agree with young Normand here that he was sent a vision of the future."

I looked up to find the bishop eyeing me thoughtfully. "And he said that the side striking the first blow would win?"

I nodded. "And that our archers will run out of arrows. He said there will come a point in the battle, late in the day, when we can safely send them forward to collect their spent arrows. After, they should shoot high in the air, from behind the safety of our infantry, so the arrows fall on the heads of Harold's men. My Lord Duke would know the time to do it, he said, because Harold's men will be pressed so hard together they cannot lift their shields to protect themselves."

"We'll carry the field tomorrow, Odo," said a deep voice from the far end of the tent. "By all that's holy, I'll be crowned king in London by Christmas as I said I would!"

I blanched, having quite forgot in the heat of argument that I was in the Duke's own tent.

"The Lord is indeed showing us the way," the Duke continued, emerging from the shadows. "He's telling us that my archers hold the key to this battle, as I've said all along they would. You've done well, Ranulf," he said. "I'll not forget this. What news have you from your scouts?"

Recovering from my embarrassment, I boldly met his gaze. "They reported that the Saxons have lit many campfires in an attempt to make us think their numbers are larger than they are. Each fire is tended only by some five or so men."

The Duke reached out, pushing the parchment on which he'd drawn the lay of the land toward the center for all to see. "The archers will be in the front line," he said, touching the map with an imperious finger, "acting as an offensive unit as well as supporting us from behind our shields." He stood there, his dark eyes regarding each one of us from under a creased brow, daring us to disagree.

"They'll like as not shoot our own men in the backs," objected the voice I'd heard before. "Just because Le Normand's son saw marsh gas and thought it a fetch isn't a good reason to change our plans at this late stage!"

"I believe him," said a voice I knew well. Taillefer. I turned to look at the bard. He held his cup up to me in salute. "A toast to you, Sir Knight! You are blessed to be singled out for such a vision! If God and the heavens are with us, how can we possibly fail? I, for one, will fight with a lighter heart tomorrow. Sire, a favor if you please," he said to the Duke. "For many a year I've sung of great heroes in your court. Let me be the one to strike the first blow that others may sing of my deeds in years to come."

"Granted, Taillefer," said the Duke.

I quickly lowered my head, lest anyone see the look of shock on my face.

My father signaled me to leave. As I saluted and turned to go, Bishop Odo rose and walked with me to the entrance.

"A vision is rare, indeed, Ranulf," he said quietly as he pulled the tent flap aside and we stepped outside into the damp night air. Seeing the guards, he waved them aside that we might talk privately. "Did this archer tell you anything else?"

I hesitated, not knowing what to say.

"It will go no further, I give you my word."

"He said two more things," I admitted reluctantly. "That we would know he spoke the truth because tomorrow, when the Duke's hauberk is brought to him, it will be offered the wrong way 'round and seen as an ill-omen. But the Duke will say that it means only he'll change his title of Duke for that of King, just as he'll turn his hauberk 'round."

"And the second thing?" Odo asked after a moment's silence.

"That Taillefer will ask to strike the first blow and will be the first to die, your Eminence," I said quietly. I liked Taillefer, who could not? He was a man of good humor and even better songs.

The Bishop said nothing for a moment. Then, "I thought you overly concerned when Taillefer asked his boon of the Duke." He held his hand out to me. Taking it, I knelt to kiss his ring.

"Rest easy, Ranulf. God's will be done tomorrow. It's not your place to worry about what you learned in your vision. You were merely the messenger, and you've discharged that duty with honor." His hand touched my bowed head and he murmured a benediction.

From within the tent, I heard Duke William addressing the barons. "Goodnight, Ranulf," said the Bishop.

As I made my way back through the campsite to my tent, I shivered—not from the cold, but from fear for my very soul. I'd still not told the bishop everything. How could I? How could I possibly tell anyone that it hadn't been a *vision*? That the face of the Norman archer I'd seen before me—a face the very mirror-image of my own—had been that of a real flesh-and-blood woman, one who shared my family name and claimed to live in the future? I could doubt her words no longer because already the things she'd told me would happen were beginning to come to pass. One thing alone kept my spirits up. If she was from the future, then I knew that I'd survive tomorrow. But it was going to be a long night.

By the Book

To the casual observer, Mouse was just a skinny girl in boy's clothing, barely visible as she sat in a dark corner of the inn where no one in their right mind would sit. It was too far back for the tavern wenches to see her, and nowhere near the dice and card games or those who mattered in the Quarters. But it suited Mouse. Here she was safe, ignored unless she chose to be noticed. Not that that had been a problem of late. Since word had gotten out that she'd killed the Mage Kolin in a duel, many gave her an increasingly wide berth. Not least because of the tarnach that accompanied her these days. She could see the small demon with the body of a child of three, but others saw only a young tarnach, the local equivalent of a large ferocious canine-like animal, barely under control.

That night the inn was full to bursting. A caravan had arrived from Ithigil earlier in the day. The goods unloaded into the port warehouses, the drivers and guards were now relaxing, spending their hard-earned cash on ale and games of chance. There were even a few off-worlders. Two exotic-looking U'Churians with their black-furred bodies, narrow pointed ears, and short tails. And a human. It was the human, Kris Russell, whom she was watching.

It was difficult to tell humans apart from her kind, but the differences were there once you knew what to look for. Their skins were different in color, and they moved differently, more stiffly than her kind. This human, though, was well known around the Quarters. Over the last year, he'd become a regular feature around the town outside the spaceport. He was a scholar, always asking questions of anyone who'd sit still long enough, always haggling with the merchants in the market and in the port for items he considered rare. And he had something that Mouse and Zaylar needed.

Beside her on the padded bench seat, the tarnach stirred. It was smaller than was usual for its species, and the eyes that looked up at her glowed red as hot coals in the dim light. But then, Zaylar was not a large demon.

"This third night we sit here," he complained, his voice very quiet. "Zaylar want to do, not watch. Not like being tarnach."

"Shut up, imp. Someone will hear you," she muttered, digging him in the ribs with her elbow. "We can't go till Tallan's been here."

He began to mutter to himself, then stopped abruptly. "Someone coming."

Mouse looked around the room, catching sight of Tallan threading his way through the tables toward her. She sighed. All day she'd been having second thoughts about the night's job. With Tallan's arrival, she had no excuse for putting it off.

He approached her table cautiously, stopping a few feet away. Surreptitiously, Mouse nudged Zaylar with her elbow again. Obligingly, he began to growl and show his teeth.

Tallan began to back off as Mouse put her hand on the tarnach's thick leather collar as if to restrain him. "Enough," she ordered sharply for Tallan's benefit then looked up at him. "You're late," she said. "You were to meet me an hour ago."

The older man frowned. "I've other customers, Mouse. Control that damned beast of yours or I'm not coming any closer."

Mouse yanked on the collar again. Zaylar coughed once but stopped snarling.

Tallan edged toward the chair opposite her and sat down. He drew a small package from his pocket and palmed it across the table to Mouse. "Are you sure that's enough? You don't need glow globes, or an acid tube for the lock?" he asked quietly.

She took the package and slipped him the requisite money. "I got good lockpicks, I don't need acid. Besides, I don't want my mark to know I've been there."

"How you going to see in the dark if you don't have glows?"

"I got my ways," she said, stashing the small packet carefully in her pants pocket.

Tallan looked at her uneasily. "I hear you have, ever since you beat that wizard Kolin."

"Tricks, same as you sell," she said. "Everyone knows girls can't do magic."

"Streets say different."

"Streets know nothing," she said contemptuously. "I thought you knew better than to listen to idle gossip!"

"Didn't say I was sayin' it, said the word on the streets is that you are. Better take care lest that gossip gets to the wrong ears," he warned, getting to his feet.

"I plan on being careful," she said.

Alone again, she went back to studying the human. Sitting with his regular group of cronies, he was deep in conversation with them. To her eyes, he was as unaware of her as anyone else in the taproom. From previous observation, he'd stay just where he was for long enough for her to complete her mission.

Sighing, she got to her feet. She didn't want to do this. Wishing it were anyone but the human's lodgings she had to visit, she made her way cautiously out of the inn and slipped into the darkness outside.

Kris Russell's lodgings were in the area of the port town where the more affluent lived. The Quarters were less safe for scholars like him. What he was studying, she didn't know, as no one she could pump for information could tell her.

The way was mostly dark with a few lit braziers scattered here and there, mostly ringed by the homeless or those down on their luck trying to get warm. One alley she passed even had someone with a skinned dead rodent on a stick trying to cook it. She shuddered. That could have been her not so long ago, before the Wizard Kolin had called her to his house to get her to steal the jewel.

Something deep in her mind stirred and uncoiled like a serpent. *So you plan another heist, do you? You treat your life with scant care. Why are you risking all because of a book? I can teach you more than a book and that runt of a demon ever could!*

"He's not a runt," Mouse muttered as she turned down a dark alleyway to avoid the busy street. "He's had his magic taken from him."

"Lady, what you say?" demanded Zaylar quietly from her side. "Is it the jewel again?" A tinge of panic entered his voice. "You know you cannot trust it. You know it lies about Zaylar to you!" His hand snaked out to grasp her wrist, claws just short of penetrating her flesh.

She shook herself free, stopping to glance down at the small demon, no longer a tarnach, at her side. "I can deal with the jewel myself," she snapped.

"Jewel get stronger every magic you learn, must guard against letting it take over," he warned.

Mouse resumed walking, staying to the shadows where the reflected flickering candlelight from nearby windows didn't cast a yellow glow.

With me, you'd not have to steal, whispered the voice in her mind. *Nor learn magic spells. I could do it all for you. A thought and you'd be without this base demon. You'd be known and feared far and wide, never need to be afraid of the mages coming to fight you or kill you because you are mage-born. See, it is but a whisper away.*

"Your cost is too high." She stepped over a particularly foul puddle, rubbing her right palm against her pants leg, trying to scrub away the jewel. "I would cease to be me! Leave me alone!" she hissed. "Your interference will make me get caught!"

The voice, and the presence in her mind subsided — for now. With the jewel's retreat, she felt the mental presence of her demon, worrying that she'd been seduced by that ancient magic and would turn on him.

"Patience, imp. I'm not going to let the jewel win," she said, patting the tangle of brown curls between the small horns on his head.

"Zaylar will always worry till you have enough magics to defeat the jewel."

"There's a way to defeat the jewel?" she demanded, coming to a stop. "Why didn't you tell me this before now!"

"Right spell not easy to find," he said, looking away and shifting from hoof to hoof under her intense gaze. "I not know which mage has that amulet," he whined.

"Then I suggest you make it a priority to learn the name of the mage! You must have demon contacts who can help you."

"No, Lady. Other demons more powerful, don't talk to me. Need you to have strong spells to impress them, then they talk to me again."

"So you're an outcast as well as having no magics but shape changing! I really lucked out when I inherited you, didn't I?" she said, pushing Zaylar in front of her as she began walking again.

The alleyway had come to an end and Mouse had to step back into the main street which was thankfully less crowded now. It was mid-evening and those going out had reached their destinations. Only a few unfashionable folk were out and about now, none who would pay attention to a mere urchin like her. The demon they couldn't see unless she willed it. In his current form, he only existed in the realm of possibilities.

"Tell me again exactly where this human Kris lives," she whispered as they stuck close to the walls of the houses and stores they passed.

"It's on the street of the bookbinders," he said, keeping close beside her.

"I know *that*, I scoped his address out the other day."

"He's in the attic of the fourth house after the street of bookbinders and printers."

"Thanks," she muttered, dodging around an errand boy with a pile of boxes so tall it almost blocked his view. "The attic. That means we'll need to use the rooftops to get there. I was hoping to avoid them since they'll still be wet from the rain today."

I can dry the path you take… The thought was a mere wisp.

She shook her head, trying to rid herself of the beguiling voice. Her palm, where the jewel had entered her body, pulsed gently, then stopped. "Enough!" she growled quietly, mentally forcing the thoughts back down.

Taking the next side street, they headed down past the paper-makers. Many stores lined the street, all advertising their various services as either papermakers or printers of books or block art prints to go in books. All were closed at this time of night. An alley on her right opened up and she ducked down it, Zaylar trotting to keep up with her. She tried dodging the foul puddles but inevitably she stepped in some. Cursing, she made her way as quickly and quietly as she could until they reached the back of a house with a wall around it. Made of rough bricks, the wall would allow her foot and hand grips. Her soft boots already wet, she worried lest she slip while climbing.

Reaching up to her first handhold, she pulled herself upward, inserting the toe of her boot into a gap. Her grip secure, she reached up again and using her foothold, propelled herself upward, catching at the rough bricks with toes and hands, her fear of slipping now put to rest.

Within moments, she was sitting astride the top of the wall, looking down into the back yard. Old wooden boxes and other debris were scattered around, all rotting away in the general dampness and rain that prevailed in the autumn. If she'd had her druthers, she'd have waited until a dry day but Zaylar had been most insistent that they get the book as soon as possible to avoid catastrophic consequences.

So here they were, surveying the back of the building that she hoped would be easier to climb than the one where Kris lived. This house was one of those with cast-iron piping reaching up from the ground to a gutter on the roof. Cast-iron piping meant the owners were wealthier than average, and was a good way for her to shinny up the side of the house. The relative prosperity of the house was of no interest to her now that she owned all the property of the late, and unlamented, if Zaylar were right, Wizard Kolin. Her only interest was in the book that Kris had gotten from a friendly mage.

A noise from the back door! Instantly Mouse flattened herself against the top of the wall, praying that in the dark she wouldn't be noticed, or at least mistaken for one of the roving cats. The person dumping boxes in the yard called back to someone inside.

"Cat out here, Father." the youth said, standing in the middle of the golden glow from the doorway.

"Then throw a stone at it and get back in here!" The voice was muffled and barely audible.

The figure ducked down and as he stood up, a stone came whistling toward her, hitting the wall just below her foot.

Taking advantage of the opportunity, she let herself roll off the wall to land on the ground some ten feet below, the air knocked out of her lungs. Hastily she swallowed her "oof!" of pain.

Fortunate for her, where she fell wasn't littered by boxes, though there were a good few in front of her. Invisible to anyone but her, Zaylar followed.

"Got it, Father!"

"Good, now get back in here and help with the rest of the clean-up."

She heard the footsteps retreat, followed by the light being shut off, and the closing of the door.

"Falling off wall is dangerous," said Zaylar, brushing her down as she cautiously got to her feet.

"I know that but I didn't have any option. He was going to throw rocks at me until I moved," she said, pushing him aside.

Silently and carefully, Mouse snuck closer to the back door of the store where the drainpipe ran up the wall. Looking up, she saw thick retaining rings around the pipe, fastened to the brick wall by heavy spikes. Good. The rings would provide her with hand and foot holds.

Hoping luck was with her and that there were no rusty spikes, Mouse used the brickwork to pull her up to the first of the rings. Feet on either side of it, she searched above her head for a handhold. Beside her, Zaylar scrambled up the side of the building as if it were a mountain slope, his small hooves and claws easily finding foot- and handholds.

He looked down on her from his vantage point on the roof. "Is easy. You climb quicker," he urged.

"All right for you to say," she muttered as she hauled herself up again, searching with her toes for a foothold. "I'm not half mountain goat like you!"

Slowly she made her way up, her heart only jumping into her mouth once when a ring creaked as it moved under her weight.

Finally, she pulled herself up over the gutter and onto the shingles of the roof. She lay sprawled on the slope, panting for a moment or two, regaining her breath before sitting up.

Pulling a small grappling hook out of her pouch, she began to unwind its rope from around her waist. It wasn't long, just long enough to reach the ridge and give her support when climbing the roofing shingles.

Getting carefully to her knees, she swung the grapple around her head, letting go when she thought it would catch on the ridge. It caught with a slight clatter, and when she pulled it experimentally, it held. Satisfied, as quietly as possible she climbed up the roof slope to the ridge. Once there, she squatted down on her heels and, picking up her grappling hook and rope, wound it around her waist again.

Her perch on the roof gave her a view of the nearby buildings, including the one the human lived in. Three rooftops away, it was the only one with both a skylight and a dormer window.

"How you going to get down when we have the book?" asked Zaylar, squatting down beside her.

That she hadn't yet decided. It depended on the layout of the house when she got there. "I'll decide later," she said, leaning forward onto her hands as she began to creep along the rooftop.

The buildings were so close that there was hardly a gap between them. In fact, the first two shared a common wall, so moving from one to the other was easy. The next roof had a flat platform with a wooden pigeon loft set on it. Balancing with one foot on either side of the ridge, she prepared herself to leap onto the platform. Twice she readied herself, twice she changed her mind at the last minute. The third time she made it, falling with her right foot under her. She slid to the platform, landing heavily onto her side.

"Ow," she said, pushing herself painfully up into a sitting position.

"You hurt, Lady?" asked Zaylar, hopping from one hoof to the other. There was concern in his voice. "Can you go on, or need we go home?"

"Don't worry, I can go on," she said, groaning as she rotated her ankle to ease it. "We'll get your book tonight."

"Book not for Zaylar, for Lady. You learn magics, not him. Must get tonight if we can."

She got to her haunches, ducking behind the pigeon coop, trying to keep as low a profile as possible even though there was no full moon. To her surprise, the pigeons only cooed quietly. She'd expected some at least to take flight.

Faint thoughts drifted through her mind. *I helped you by keeping the birds calm. I can easily do things like that for you, without you even knowing. Can't you see we'd make a great combination?*

Zaylar began chittering. He had an uncanny knack of knowing when the jewel was talking to her.

She pushed against the thoughts, not deigning to answer them as she filled her mind with concerns over the rest of her mission.

The rooftops were still slick with the earlier rain and climbing across them had not been easy. Now she had to clamber across another fifteen feet of slippery roof, then leap over the gap and land on the roof of Kris' building, all without falling off.

Sighing, she stared at the rooftop, waiting for inspiration to hit. When it didn't, she finally said to the demon, "Zaylar, help me."

"The chimney is near," said the small demon, flicking his nub of a tail.

"The chimney?" she echoed, looking at it as it shed its smoke into the damp air. "Yes! It is. If I throw the grapple to fasten round it, then jump, I should be able to land safely. Thanks, Zaylar!" She made her way carefully to the edge of the roof.

"Lady ask for help, Zaylar can help. If she doesn't ask..." He shrugged.

Mouse unwound her rope again and took careful aim on the chimney, her grapple at the ready. Swinging it around, she threw it at the chimney some eight feet distant. This time, she wanted the hook to catch on the rope after wrapping itself around the chimney. It would take all her skill to do this.

Her first try fell short, rattling on the roof shingles. Her second and third tries were no better.

"Think the throw successful," said Zaylar. "It can help."

"Can't hurt," she muttered, thinking hard about the grapple fastening around the chimney.

This time, success! She tugged the rope hard and it still held. Now the worst bit, jumping into nothingness and hoping to land on the roof!

She looked at the six-foot gap between her and where she wanted to be. Taking a deep breath, she tightened her grip on the rope and jumped.

The jump seemed to last forever. The wind blew her short hair back against her head, making her want to close her eyes, but she forced them to remain open. Her legs windmilled under her until at last they touched the shingles — then slipped on the moss growing there. She slid unceremoniously down the roof, still clinging tightly to her rope. Then she fetched up short against the side of the dormer window, hurtling into it with a loud thump that she was sure alerted everyone in the street.

Stunned, she hung there for a moment or two then pulled herself up the rope to the chimney. There, she tried to hold onto to the structure for dear life, but the fire that had been on all day had heated the bricks to the point where they were too hot to touch. Instead, she sat on the top of the ridge of the roof holding on tightly until her heart stopped beating so frantically.

If anyone was in the building, they'd have heard her crashing into the dormer window. Now all she wanted to do was sit here until she was sure the building was empty.

There is no need for this, whispered the siren voice. *You could be worth so much more than the thief you are now.*

"Enough!" growled Mouse, hands clenching on the ridge of the roof. "*Enough!* I've said I want no more of you!" With the final *enough,* she pushed hard mentally against the voice, forcing it into silence in the depths of her mind.

Zaylar chittered unhappily as he danced from hoof to hoof in distress at her conversation with the jewel. He reached out a small, clawed hand and gently laid it on Mouse's leg, leaning in against her. The heat of his touch was strangely comforting as a cold wind sprang up.

"Lady…" he began, but she interrupted him.

"I know you need me free of the jewel, imp, even if your concern is selfish," she said, raising her head and looking into his red eyes.

He looked away from her, taking his hand back. "I need amulet you'll make to be free of my curse. You know this. If jewel takes over, no amulet for Zaylar."

"More importantly, there will be no more me left!" she said, getting to her feet carefully. "Time to break into this room before the human comes back from the inn."

Holding onto the rope for support, slowly she rappelled down the few feet to the skylight. Keeping back so she couldn't be seen, she peered inside. There was no light so no one was home. Not even a human would sit in the dark.

She moved lower, stopping when she was level with the front of the dormer window. Again, she looked inside, making sure the room was empty before getting out her lockpicks.

It was a standard turnbuckle catch, with a lever handle that fitted into a grove in the wooden frame. From her roll of lockpicks, she chose a small piece of flat metal and tried inserting it into the top of the lock, hoping to slip it down and knock the lever open; not the easiest job when trying to hold onto a rope with her other hand and not slip down the wet, mossy, shingles. She prayed the window hadn't been painted shut. If so, her current plan would fail. It took two or three tries, but at last she got the lever to move a little. Persevering, she finally pushed it into the open position. Stowing her tool safely into her pocket, she pushed at the window. Nothing moved. She pushed again, harder, and felt the crackling of ancient paint splitting. Another shove and it sprang open. Using the rope, she swung herself inside, catching hold of the frame.

Easing herself onto the broad window ledge, she squatted there, surveying the room.

"Zaylar, check out the rest of the rooms," she said quietly, watching as the imp squirmed past her and into what was actually a suite of rooms, not just one. Concentrating on the room she was in, she jumped down from the sill to land softly on the carpeted floor. A desk faced the window, piled with papers and books.

Zaylar trotted back. "All empty," he said. "I make light for you?"

"Very faint," she said. "I don't want to alert anyone outside that we're here."

A gentle glow filled the room, letting Mouse see the bookcases that lined it. A table near the door was also covered in leather-bound volumes.

"How am I to find one book among so many?" asked Mouse hopelessly.

"Book is important. Will be on desk or table," said Zaylar. "Small book, not big. Like diary you have."

"Why is this book so important again?" she asked, moving closer to the desk.

"Has one or more of spells you need to learn," said the demon, following her.

"What color is it?"

"Not know. Know just is leather book."

Mouse snorted. "Yeah, like every other book here." She bent down to see the stacks of books from the side, hoping to find one smaller than the rest. "How will I know it when I find it?"

"You will know."

Lifting her head, she looked across to the table. It looked less cluttered than the desk. "You do the desk; I'll take the table. Just don't throw the books on the floor like you did at home the other day," she warned him. "I don't want it to be too obvious why we were here."

She checked each stack of books, touching every volume, moved papers aside to find more, and checked them. Going back to the desk, she went around to the drawers, pushing aside the chair. They were locked. Out came her lock picks and within moments, she had them both open.

"There's nothing, not a sign of the book!" she said, exasperatedly. "We'll never find it!"

"You could always ask me," said a male voice from the doorway.

Mouse froze. Slowly she looked up to the door, seeing the human Kris standing there, backlit by the stairway light.

"If you haven't disturbed my things too much, I usually know where everything is," he said, leaning against the door lintel and folding his arms.

"You," she said as Zaylar scuttled across the room to hide behind her.

"Yes, me," he said. "I was watching you at the inn. I had a feeling I'd get a visit from you tonight."

Mouse said nothing, just stared at him.

"You're in my home, ransacking through my books, the least you can do is tell me your name."

Still, she said nothing.

Kris stood up and uncrossed his arms. "Then perhaps you'll tell me what you're looking for?"

Mouse was thinking furiously. She knew that Kris was a scholar and had been seen in the company of some of the few sociable mages. Whether he was one himself, she didn't know. She did know it behooved her to keep on his good side, if that were possible after being caught red-handed going through his books. She knew telling him her name wasn't wise as knowing the names of one's enemies gave you power over them.

She forced herself to relax her stance and smiled at him. "I was told you found a book I had lost," she said brightly. "I was looking for that."

"Do you make a habit of breaking into people's homes in search of your lost belongings, or am I special?"

"Everyone knows you're a scholar and a mage. Too important for the likes of me to bother."

"But not too important for you to rob."

"Only taking back what I lost," she argued.

He reached in the pocket of his coat and drew out a slim blue volume. "I think this is what you're looking for."

She could feel the magic in the book even from where she stood. Zaylar grabbed at her leg. "Yes, that's it," she said. "Can I have it now?"

Kris shook his head. "I don't think so. This book was given to me by a mage, it's mine and it's rather precious. Do you realize how serious robbing someone is? I should call the port police to deal with you."

"No! Not the police!" she said anxiously, taking a step toward him. Involving the police could lead to her being arrested for having mage-blood. Bad enough that they were already watching her because of her involvement in the death of Wizard Kolin and the inheritance of his property! It wouldn't take much to uncover that she had been the cause of his death and not just his benefactor through a female relative. All it needed was one other thing to come to their attention and she'd be in real trouble, even if it was because of thieving, not suspected magic.

The human seemed to hesitate. "What do you want with it?" he demanded. "A girl like you wouldn't be able to read it. Who are you stealing it for?"

She was stung by the assumption that she was illiterate. "I can read as well as you!"

"Really? Then my question still stands—what do you want with it?" His voice had roughened and she knew he was still prepared to call the port police.

"It's a diary belonging to the Wizard Kolin. I inherited it with all his other belongings when he died."

"So you're the mystery girl everyone's talking about. How did you manage to inherit Kolin's belongings?"

"I'm the daughter of his sister, only survivor," she said shortly. She stepped forward again. "The book is mine by inheritance."

"Except for the fact that it was given to me by a Mage known as Corlas, not Kolin."

"It's mine," she insisted. "What would it take for you to give it to me?"

"You have nothing I want. It was a gift and is helping me with my research," he said.

This interchange was getting her nowhere except deeper into the hole of being caught thieving from him. She had to get the book and get out of here as quickly as possible.

The wisp of thought stirred within her again, very faintly this time. *He may have already called the port police on you and be delaying you with his conversation. Let me deal with him.*

No, she sent back. *I can handle it. You'd kill him and leave me with his death on my hands!* Besides, she rather liked him, despite his intractability. Few Jalnians had hair the color of ripe corn like his.

That's your body talking, not you! snapped the jewel.

Zaylar, get the book, she sent to the small demon.

"Don't tell your satyr to take it," he warned, "or I will raise the alarm."

Shock rendered her speechless. She gestured Zaylar to halt beside her.

"Better," Kris said.

"You can see him?" she finally said.

"And hear you talking to him."

"How? He's sworn only to me. No one else should be able to see him."

"I'm a telepath, I can hear what you think."

But he can't hear me. Let me deal with him and we can be out of here in seconds, with the book, whispered the treacherous voice.

"No," she said, shaking her head in an effort to quieten it.

"Oh, I assure you I can. Zaylar is the name of your satyr."

She had to do something quickly, before the jewel took matters into its own hands. "You don't know the danger you are in," she said softly, reaching into her pocket and pulling out a glass phial. Swiftly she threw it at his feet and as white smoke began to billow between them, she rushed forward to snatch the book from his hand.

Eyes streaming from the smoke, he tightened his hold on the book as he doubled up, coughing in real distress. Her grasp proved stronger.

Mouse kept on running, down the stairs from the attic to the ground floor, then out the front door, Zaylar right behind her. Slamming the door as she went, she forced herself to dart to one side, then walk normally along the almost deserted street. As soon as she reached the alleyway, she sprinted down it, heading for home by as devious a route as she could find.

Once there, she unlocked the door, shutting it and barring it behind her, leaning against it to get her breath back.

"He knows where we live," said Zaylar.

"I know. I'll give him the book back as soon as we've got what we need from it. What do we need from it, by the way?" she asked, pulling it out of her jacket pocket and handing it to the demon. It was a small volume, with a metal motif stamped into the front of it.

"Spells," he said shortly, leafing through the book till he stamped his foot hissing in frustration. "Is only one spell in here," he said, pulling the motif off the front then thrusting the book back at her.

"You mean I went to all that bother just for one spell?"

"This is spell," he said, holding out a small casting of a dragon to her. "Put it on chain round your neck, then hold it when you want to use it."

She looked at it, seeing the small pendant hole at the top of the wings. "What kind of spell is this?" she asked incredulously.

"Fire spell," he said. "Lets you use fire when needed. Same with all other spells—each will be a metal figure of the spell. Different fish for water spells, flying things for air spells. You need to learn what each does so you can hold the right one when needed."

"I've never heard of spells like that," she said, turning it over in her hand. "Nor have I seen necklaces with metal figures on any mages."

"How many mages you know?" scoffed Zaylar. "One! Kolin. He learn spells as words to say, you learn them as things to touch."

"And the book?"

"Useless now, only one spell as I said. You female, different magics than men. Yours does, theirs speaks. Takes them longer to use spell. You faster."

Mouse pushed herself away from the door and headed for the room that had been Kolin's office. She'd seen silver neck chains there, one of them would do to put the dragon on. "I thought I had already used fire magic," she said, "when we went after Cullen."

"Jewel did it, not you. Now you a little bit free of needing jewel."

"Believe me," she said, threading the chain through the hole, "I want to get rid of that jewel as soon as I can!"

"Not sure if that possible," muttered Zaylar, climbing up onto the desk chair so his face was level with her. "Need many magics before that could happen."

"With you to help me find them, that shouldn't be a problem," she said, admiring the dragon suspended from it before fastening the chain around her neck.

"Not a problem," Zaylar echoed.

The Wild Hunt

Old Sarum, Salisbury Plain
Wiltshire, England
September 2051

HE SENSED HER PRESENCE LONG BEFORE HE HEARD HER SOFT FOOTSTEPS. Though it was hard to ignore her, he continued scribbling in his book. This was the second time today she'd disturbed him. Normally he'd have welcomed her intrusions, but not now. He knew why she was here.

Coming round to his side of the desk, she stopped behind him. "It's time, Old One," she said, the gentleness in her husky voice stripping the formal title of its sting. "Time for you to Choose."

The sweet, familiar smell of sun-warmed grass enveloped him, making his hand falter. As he forced himself to carry on, his pen nib spluttered, sending small droplets of ink across the page. She leaned against him, reaching across his shoulder to touch her hand to his cheek in a familiar caress.

Distracted, again his pen spluttered, but this time, conscious of the feel of her soft body pressing against his back, he was unable to continue writing. There had been many such as her during his long life — child-women, their physical development arrested for several years while they learned the old arts of the mind — but none like her.

"I'm not done yet," he whispered, closing his tired eyes as her hand slid from his cheek to rest on his shoulder. "There's still much for me to do before ..." His voice petered out to silence as, triggered by her presence, visions of the past once more flooded through him.

I'd still been sleeping when rough hands took hold of me, flinging me on my face and trussing me up like a chicken. There had been no chance to cry out even when they bundled me up in the folds of my cloak. I tried, the gods know I tried, but the fabric only worked its way into my mouth, threatening to choke me.

I must have passed out because the next I knew, I was lying belly-down across the back of a horse.

The blood was rushing to my head and I felt sick as the motion of the beast jolted me up and down. Feeling myself sliding toward the ground, I started to scream. A hand gripped the neck of my tunic tightly, hauling me back up.

"You'll pay for this!" I yelled, trying to turn my head up and away from the horse's flank. "My father will come after you!"

"Silence, brat! We've your father's permission to take you!"

I knew then who they were. "But not my mother's!"

The warrior laughed raucously. "Queen or not, her wishes are unimportant!"

Through the bobbing curtain of my hair, I could see another rider draw level with us.

"They wait in the clearing up ahead, Niall," he called, the wind whipping his words away almost as soon as they were uttered.

"Remind them it's abduction by consent! The fight isn't for real!" Niall yelled as he began to slow down.

His companion nodded, turning his mount, then froze in mid-maneuver, his hand reaching for the arrow sprouting from his throat. Above me, Niall leaned out, grasping the horse's bridle as the rider coughed once then collapsed across his animal's neck a look of confusion on his face.

"Trap!" Niall yelled, letting go of the bridle as if it burned his hand. "It's a trap!"

Earth spattered up into my face as he pulled his horse up sharply. Moments later, the rest of the College's small war band had formed a living shield around us. The scraping of metal rang in my ears as swords were drawn.

"Take the boy, Niall!" a voice yelled. "We'll hold them off! That's the queen's brothers, not the king's men! I recognize their livery."

He hesitated, the horse snorting and dancing, impatient to be off. "Too dangerous."

"I said my mother wouldn't let you take me."

"She breaks the law and puts your life at risk with ours," was the short reply.

Even as he spoke, the ululating cries of the queen's war band filled the air. Fear filled me then. This was no mock battle with my father's men, this was real, and my life was the prize they fought over.

"Conn, Owain, stay with me!" he said, leaning forward to loop the end of the rope binding my wrists round his waist. He jerked it tight, making the bonds dig deeply into my wrists. I bit my tongue in an effort to still my cry of pain.

"Hold still, boy," Niall warned. "Jeopardize my life and yours will be forfeit too." Then his war cry, echoed lustily by the men around him, deafened me as our horse leaped forward to join the battle.

My head buried against the horse's heaving flank, I could see little but pounding hooves and flying clods of earth, but I heard the screams and yells of the warriors and their mounts as swords clashed on shields and flesh. Suddenly my mind did its leaping trick and I could see it all through the eyes of Niall, my captor.

Hair and beard tangled together by the wind and sweat, what was visible of my opponent's face was covered with the blue swirls of war. Contorted by rage, I scarce recognized him for Dairmid, my mother's oldest brother. His sword arced down at us, blocked by our shield as Niall counterattacked with a blow to his side. I gasped, then forced my mind to stillness. Niall was right, should he fall now, I'd be pulled to the ground with him to be trampled to death beneath the hooves of the horses. I had to remain a passive observer, but it was not easy. Great Goddess, it was not easy!

Dairmid's horse swerved at the last moment, taking my uncle just out of range, but Niall urged us after him. Swords clashed in mid-air as Dairmid's horse turned its head, neck stretching toward us. Mouth gaping, nostrils flaring, it snapped at our mount's haunch, narrowly missing my small body. With a scream of pain, our horse reared up, throwing us against its neck as Dairmid's blow struck home. Pain seared our forearm and I only had a quick glimpse of the blood coursing down Niall's arm before my mind was flung back to my own body.

A scream of agony, quickly cut short, rent the air and I saw my uncle fall to the ground, trampled beneath the horses.

I screamed then, over and over till my throat was raw. A rough hand grasped me by the hair, pulled my head up, and slapped my face hard. Shock made me stop and open my eyes.

"Be silent, Llew! You dishonor your family with this wailing! Untie him," ordered Ywain, letting my head drop.

Ywain! I was safe now.

"Our prince will travel in a more dignified position," he commanded.

"Prince no longer," said Niall's tired voice from above me. "He's been Chosen by the College, you know that."

"I know," my father's war leader snapped. "But till he reaches there, he's our prince. The king ordered us to escort you."

My heart sank again. No rescue this. I was to be handed over to the Druids like a levy of grain.

"What of the queen?" demanded another. "She broke our agreement, set this trap for us. We've lost kin!"

"The king will be told of her treachery. She'll be dealt with, never fear," was the grim reply.

Cold iron touched my wrists briefly as the rope was cut and I was hauled up to sit in front of Niall. Head swimming, face still burning from the blow, I grasped hold of the long mane before me for support. On either side of me were Niall's arms, one bound tightly with a blood-soaked rag.

"The College will hear of this," said Niall.

"I will make our apologies," said Ywain coldly as he turned to re-mount his horse. "Understand this, I would as lief not have any dealings with you or the Druids, but we do our king's will."

"And those who attacked us?" asked Niall.

"Will be returned for the King's Justice. Enough talk! Let's get moving."

"I have that memory, Old One. You gave it to me weeks ago," she said, her lips gently touching his wrinkled cheek. "It belongs to one of the first Chosen, not you."

"Not mine?" Even he heard the slightly querulous tone in his voice. He frowned, locking his thoughts away from her. "But I remember it so clearly…"

"I know. Your mind is wandering in the past because you're tired. Leave your writing for now, you have plenty of time to finish it. You must come up to the courtyard and Choose the one who will follow you. Everyone is waiting."

"Already?" He sighed, letting her reach forward to take the pen from his now slack grasp. She laid it down carefully on the desk beside the inkwell.

Once he left these rooms that had been his home for so long, he'd never return. Though his journal would remain unfinished, it contained enough to guide his successor until he learned to trust the memories.

"It's that time," she agreed, stepping back from him to give him space to stand.

There was no avoiding it—or her—any longer. His chair scraped against the floor as he pushed it back from his desk and slowly got to his feet, turning round to face her.

Reed slim, she barely reached his shoulders. Her white robe, as much her badge of office as his blue one, clung to her boyish figure, accentuating her slight curves. Mid-brown wavy hair cascaded over her shoulders, its color echoed in the calm eyes that watched him solicitously. Sensing her sadness, he reached out to take her hand.

She accepted it, letting him draw it to his lips to kiss. Of all the child-women who'd been sent to him over the years to teach, she, the last, was the only one he'd ever loved, the only one to become his lover.

"I still don't understand why you must choose a successor so soon. You're well and fit, for..." She faltered, a faint rose color flooding her cheeks.

"For my age," he finished with a wry smile. Every day brought him new reminders of just how old he was. "It has nothing to do with my health, child. This day of Choosing was decided by the position of the stars at my moment of birth. I am the Goddess' servant. I must obey Her will."

"They still have to find him and bring him here," she whispered, stroking his cheek when he released her hand.

She linked her arm through his as they began to walk toward the door. His thoughts still guarded from her, he wondered if he should tell her that he had to leave this world. Though she held his memories in trust, the contents of many were hidden from her, meant only to be understood by his successor. She was too young to understand fully what must happen, but he knew. He knew only too well. It was impossible for him to forget it, just as it was impossible for him to forget the way he and all his predecessors had been Chosen and taken from their families. Because of his burden of memories, it was not the first time he'd taken this walk.

As they left his study, he barely saw the black-robed druid on duty bowing to them. He shivered, not from cold, but from prescient fear. Something was different about this succession, something he couldn't yet put his finger on.

Their footsteps echoed down the narrow labyrinth of corridors as they made their way to the staircase leading to the surface. Part college and part research establishment, this place of learning was hidden from those outside their Order. Its history, like himself, went back to the beginnings of their people. But those who had need of their services had always known how to find them.

Holding onto the carved stone handrail, slowly he climbed the stairs. Age had made him stiff lately and it had been some time since he'd last ventured out into the world.

This is not the end, he kept telling himself, *it is another beginning, for her and the one who'll succeed me.*

"Briana tells me you'll remain here till you've chosen your successor," she said quietly as with each step, the courtyard gradually came into view. "Then I must receive your memories of the Choosing so I may pass them on to him."

"You must give him all you've learned from me, child," he said tiredly as he stepped at last onto the stone courtyard. "My memories, everything, including my journal. You will be his teacher, helping him understand the purpose of the College and his mental gifts until he reaches maturity."

"I've told you, I don't want to do that!" she said, her voice deepening with intensity. "I want to be with you, not him!"

"That isn't the way it's done. His first teacher must be a woman so he can understand that side of his nature," he said, his mind drawn back to a similar conversation so many years ago.

"Why must you leave?" I demanded, holding her tightly, ignoring in my pain how stiff and unyielding her body felt.

"Because our time together is done," she said. "You must go on alone now, and I must leave to be married. A husband has been chosen for me—a king, lately widowed. It's a good match, as befits the position I held here."

"What of us? Why can't you marry me?" I buried my face in her long hair lest she saw the tears that filled my eyes.

"Because that's the way it is. You're a man now, you must follow your own path, and I'm not part of it."

"But I can make you part of it! I'm supposed to be in charge, their leader—I can *make* it happen!"

Her hands came up and took hold of my face, lifting it from her shoulder so she could see me. "It isn't the way things are, Merlin. The Goddess calls me elsewhere."

"Don't call me that!" I said angrily, pulling her hands away from my face. "My name's Llew!"

"No. Llew ceased to be the moment you were Chosen," she said. "I was your teacher, here to give you the memories of the ones who came before you, help you understand them. My task is done now."

"We shared the nights from the first," I said, part in anger, part in appeal. "When I was old enough, you were my lover! You're more than just a teacher to me!"

She let me go, turning away from me with a sigh. "No, I was only your teacher. It was what I was trained to do by your predecessor."

"Trained?" I felt suddenly betrayed. "You were with him before me? *I* meant nothing to you?"

She glanced at me as she made her way to our bed where the robes for my investiture lay. "I cared for you, but I never loved you, Merlin, nor led you to believe I did."

"What was I supposed to think?" I demanded, hot tears scalding my face, not caring now if she saw them. "That our nights together were meaningless, just a reward for learning my lessons well? That your heart was as hollow as a maggot-ridden apple?"

"That's not so. I cherished you like kin, just not as a lover."

"I don't want to hear it," I said, dashing my forearm across my eyes. "You could at least have left me an illusion!"

"Life is full of illusions, Merlin. I've told you many times, you must learn to see what is true and what is not."

"Llew! My name is Llew!" Behind me, I heard the door open. I swung round. "What do you want?" I demanded.

The druid inclined his head to me. "The College waits for you, Merlin. It's time for your investiture as Arch Druid."

Impotent anger rushed through me and I clenched my hands at my sides. I was trapped, with no escape, just as surely as I'd been from the moment they'd taken me from my mother's house.

"You may leave us," she said to the druid. "I'll bring him to the courtyard."

"I'm not going," I said with finality as the door closed.

"You must. This is why you were brought here," she said, coming over to me, the embroidered blue robe held open before her. "It is your destiny. You are the Merlin."

"Merlin!" Someone was shaking his arm. He blinked, suddenly back in the present. "You were drifting again," she said, tightening her grip on his arm.

He stopped dead, reaching out to cup his hand round her face. "Did you love me? Even for a brief moment?" he asked softly, searching her child-like features for the truth he hoped he'd find there.

She frowned, brow furrowing in concern. "You need to ask me that?"

"Yes," he said, understanding part of the reason why the memories of the long-dead Llew returned to haunt him. "Tell me our time together wasn't a dream, just an illusion!"

"It's no dream," she whispered, leaning forward to kiss him. "Our love is no mist over the heath, Merlin."

Her kiss was as sweet and tender as always, giving him the reassurance he needed so much right now. He sighed as they parted.

"Everything has been made ready as you asked, Merlin," said a male voice from behind him. "The time of Choosing is here."

Merlin looked around at Euan. "I'm coming," he said testily. "You rush me too much. Let me enjoy these few minutes with her."

The druid turned to look at the girl. "You're distracting him from his purpose. It might be better if you left us until you're needed again."

"I need her now," Merlin said, his voice becoming cold as he reached for her hand. "You forget yourself, Euan. Until I've Chosen, I'm still Lord here."

Euan bowed low. "Your pardon, Merlin. I was only thinking of your own good," he murmured.

Merlin ignored him, well aware his apparent obedience was nothing more than a sham. Drawing her with him, he began walking toward the chair that had been set by the fire pit in the center of the courtyard. Around them, flames burned in the College wall sconces, casting flickering shadows.

"Damned newcomers," he muttered. "Got no sense of the moment! The only thing they believe in is their man-made schedules. Not like in the old days when their protocols and rules waited on the Goddess's will."

"What did you mean you're still Lord till you've Chosen?" she asked. "What haven't you told me about this ritual?" There was concern tinged with fear in her voice as she glanced back over her shoulder at the dark figure of Euan following them.

"Later, child. It can wait till later," Merlin said, patting her hand.

The chair was old and comfortable. It had graced many incumbents before him, but as he took hold of the narrow, padded arms and lowered himself into it, he noticed that the covering of blue velvet was wearing thin now. At his feet, the fire burned in its pit, sending occasional glowing sparks up into the cool night air as the resins in the wood sputtered. Beyond it, set low on the horizon, the full moon hung swollen and ripe, its baleful orange glow matching that of the fire.

"Herne's moon," he murmured, shivering again despite the warmth. "The Wild Hunt rides tonight." His uneasiness was growing now, taking form.

"The Riders of Chaos?" She paled, moving closer to him for comfort. "Surely it's dangerous to be out beside such a fire tonight?"

"No one here has anything to fear," he said, frowning slightly. Something was missing, but what? "My staff. I left it in my room. Would you fetch it for me, please?"

When she'd gone, he gestured Euan over.

As he watched the younger man approaching, the gulf of time separating him and Llew blurred once more making him aware of just how different it all was these days. Where once everyone had gone robed, now robes were worn only on ritual occasions like today, or when greeting petitioners to the College. He was more used to seeing his chief administrator in a suit. He looked out of place clad in a flowing black robe. It only added to the strange feeling of unreality that had possessed him since morning.

"What can I do for you, Old One?" Euan asked, coming to a stop beside him.

"Time for straight-talking between us, Euan." Merlin settled back in his chair, refusing to crane his neck by looking up at him. "I know you've little time for all this," he said, gesturing around the courtyard. "You think it has no place in this age of technology, but it does. It's because we've retained our humanity that people come to us rather than consult some electronic oracle of wisdom. It's why they send their children to be educated here, just remember that."

Euan feigned surprise. "I don't understand what you're inferring, Merlin. Every college and university has its strange traditions. Ours are just a little stranger than most. Surely after all my years of service to the College I've shown where my loyalties lie?"

Merlin grunted. "Soon there will be a new leader—a child—in my place, guided by another not much older. You will make no changes while they are too young to object, Euan. For once, follow your God of Protocol, make sure it's done the way it has been for this past millennium. Let the other druids guide you in this."

"Of course I'll see the traditions are kept, Merlin. I'm shocked you felt you needed to say that," Euan murmured.

"Oh, I know all about your little ways, shaving a penny here and there, cutting back on this and that, but it will stop during the Regency, you hear me? None of your tricks, because I have a feeling that this time, you'll have more on your plate than you can handle."

He frowned. "I don't understand you."

"You will, soon enough. Change is coming, Euan, I can feel it. Have you seen the moon tonight?"

Euan glanced behind him at the night sky. "It's autumn. You often get a moon like that at this time of year," he said. "It's a natural phenomenon."

"Was a time when all the College staff knew what that meant, especially the administrator."

"You're living in the past, Merlin. I don't mean to be unkind, but the College is a place of law and logic. It isn't necessary for us to believe in superstitions and folk tales for it to carry out its main function."

"You think not?" He smiled. "We'll see, Euan. We'll see. Perhaps my legacy couldn't be left in the hands of a better man than you! Just remember, guard him — and her — well. Our world is changing fast these days and much depends on his tenure as Arch Druid."

"Is that all, Merlin? Because if it is, then we should get on with this ritual. The sooner it's done, the better. The nights are getting colder now and I don't want complaints from the staff at having to spend hours standing in this chill air, especially now the wind's getting up."

Merlin hadn't missed Euan's faint sigh, nor failed to pick up the other's feelings of boredom and relief that the Old One's tenure would soon be over. So Euan had discounted her already and was planning how he'd shape the new Merlin to his ways, was he? He realized it was no mistake on the gods' part that the night of his Choosing was the night of the Wild Hunt.

Sensing the girl returning, he smiled gently to himself and waved Euan away. He knew for certain that tonight's ritual would shake the College to its very foundations.

"Your staff, Merlin," she said, holding it out to him.

Nodding his thanks, he took it from her, glad to see she was now wearing a cloak. "Come and sit beside me, child," he said.

He reached into the pocket of his robe, pulling out the small packet of herbs and resins he'd prepared earlier. While she settled at his feet, close to the fire pit, he opened the packet then leaned forward to sprinkle some of the contents onto the fire.

Hissing and spitting, flames of purple and blue roared up into the night, lighting the courtyard around them, illuminating the still figures of the druids he'd asked to stand this last vigil with him. Breathing in the scented smoke, he looked around. Mentally, he touched the mind of each one of them, giving them his protection, knowing that they all understood the importance of what was happening tonight. Those like Euan were rare, but for now they were the ones that held the balance of power and influence both in the College and with the world outside these walls. Tonight would change that too.

As he turned toward the small building that was the College audience chamber, he saw Briana approaching, firelight glinting off the goblet she carried. He'd tried to forget this part of the ritual, the setting free of the child-woman who was his lover. This would allow her to reach the maturity that had been artificially denied her these last six years.

Kneeling beside the girl, Briana presented her with the goblet. "Take this cup, Lady, that you may have the strength to welcome the Chosen One when he arrives."

Startled, she reached out to take it from Briana and looked up at him. He saw the light of understanding come into her eyes, felt it with his mind. She knew that once she'd taken it, her life would never be the same. Before he could stop her, she'd plucked from his mind the knowledge that the drink would also cause her to forget they'd ever loved.

The fumes from the fire had already begun to loosen his bonds to this world. Her face blurred slightly, the features changing, resolving into that of another before changing again, and again, each time letting him see the last love of those who'd gone before him. He shook his head, forcing the memories to stop.

Never taking her eyes from his, she raised the goblet to her lips, then stopped. "Do you wish me to drink it?"

No! his heart cried out. "You must," he whispered, unable to look at her, his heart breaking at the betrayal their roles were forcing on them. "But I swear you will be the last one this happens to!" The knowledge that he spoke the truth didn't help him, didn't stop him from beginning to die inside. "Tonight it changes forever."

"I do this only because you ask me." She drank the bitter contents slowly, then returned the goblet to Briana.

They sat in silence for several minutes. "You must feed the fire," she said finally, passing a piece of wood up to him.

He took it from her, saying nothing, still unable to trust his voice. As the eighth piece was added, he took the packet of herbs from his lap and sprinkled what remained into the flames, letting the scented fumes surround them.

She began to stir, knowing she should leave him to his visions as she usually did, but his hand closed on her shoulder, holding her still.

"Stay. Tonight you need to be with me."

"Is it traditional for me to remain during the Choosing? You've told me very little about it."

"After tonight there will be new traditions. Can't you feel it in the air?" he asked softly, his eyes gleaming in the firelight, feeling the air around them thicken and swirl with potentials and possibilities. "It's the wind of Chaos." In the distance, he could hear the faint baying of hounds. Exhilaration filled him at the thought of riding with the Hunt again.

"I feel only a gentle breeze."

"It will strengthen, then it will come howling through this court-yard, sweeping tradition with it as it's done so many times in the past. Nothing stands still, not man, not time, not Earth Herself, child." He could feel her fear begin to rise as the breeze changed direction, blowing from the east.

"Don't be afraid no matter what you see," he whispered, taking tight hold of her hand and turning his face back to the fire.

He looked deep into the heart of it, where the flames burned the strongest, concentrating on the glow as he let his mind loose from the bonds of his body. It took but a moment's thought to link his mind to hers, then they were swirling upward with the current of hot air into the blackness of the night sky.

The baying of the hounds grew louder with each moment. Then, heart leaping in anticipation, he saw them, the rider in front not quite human, his head crowned with the huge, branching antlers of a stag. Behind him came the rider's four kin, each with the look of human men, each set high on a horse of a different color. Raucous laughter filled the night, voices calling to each other as first one then the other of the four pointed to the ground below them. He felt her fear and tightened his grip on her hand, remembering that this was new to her. Closer and closer the Hunt came until he could see those who followed in its wake. All manner of four-legged beasts were their mounts—horse and deer and wolf—carrying on their backs those not of this world—some horned, some with tails, some furred, some scaled—all laughing and crying out to each other, pointing and searching for their quarry. Hounds bayed, darting this way and that beneath the hooves and paws of the mounts, yet never passing the Horned One that led them.

Lower the Hunt swooped until it drew level with them, its leader nodding briefly in recognition to Merlin as he passed by, his followers reaching out hands toward them in welcome, sweeping them up behind them on their beasts.

Greenwich, London,
the same night.

Sleep refused to come to Khyan. His bed was too warm and had become no more than a pile of tangled sheets and covers. Now his pelt felt itchy and uncomfortable. Getting up, he padded softly to his window, clambering up on the covered seat in front of the bay window where the cool night air could reach him. Squatting there, he leaned his elbows on the window ledge, looking out over the city.

From here he could see over the rooftops of the houses lower down the crescent, right out to the heath and woodland beyond. They'd been here, in the Sholan legation, for a month now, and his promised trip to the heath hadn't yet materialized. The adults might be content to remain penned within the walls, but not him. He felt trapped and homesick for the wide-open spaces of his world.

Sighing, he looked up at the moon. It fascinated him tonight, hanging there just above the distant tree line. Back home they had two, but he'd never seen either of them sit so large and orange in the sky. Reaching up, he put his hand against the pane of glass, imagining he was touching it. Tonight, despite the psychic dampers they'd had fitted throughout the building, the air felt alive and electric with promise as if the woodland and the alien moon above it represented some great adventure about to happen. As he watched, it seemed to grow larger, filling the window till he could see nothing but its hypnotic orange glow.

The wood sputtered and crackled, the leaping flames that fed on it flickering first red, then blue before turning almost white. The night air was chill on his pelt, making the longer guard hairs on his arms and legs lift slightly as the breeze grew stronger, bringing with it strange new smells. Fear lapped at the edges of his mind, but curiosity was strong among his kind and he suppressed it. He couldn't understand what was happening, but he knew this was no dream world he was in, it was too real for that.

Lifting his head, he sniffed the air as he looked around, trying to separate the scents. Ahead of him, dark against the glow from the fire, he saw a chair with a seated figure in it. It was from there the strongest scents came — one male, one female. He reached out with his mind, trying to sense them, but met only an emptiness where he should have found people. That puzzled him.

He felt himself pulled toward the seated figure. Trying to stop, he found it impossible. Now fear began to take hold of him, gripping him with claws of ice. Inexorably, he was drawn onward until, by the light of the fire, he could see them both — the old male in the chair, and at his feet, the young female.

A sudden burst of sound from above startled him. Looking up, he saw figures on strange riding beasts silhouetted against the moon. Transfixed, he watched as they rode toward him, growing larger and larger till suddenly he was surrounded by a confusion of noise and scents and sights.

Around him the beasts pranced, hooves and paws clattering on the stone-paved courtyard as they closed him within a circle. Horses whinnied, their breath so close it was hot on his pelt, while from their backs, the riders called out, drawing each other's attention to him. Faces, more alien than any he'd ever seen, leered and laughed, their mouths widespread and full of teeth. He spun around, crouching low, pelt bushed out, claws extended ready to defend himself as he looked frantically for an escape, but there was none.

A voice louder and more raucous than the rest rang out, then a bearded male, long hair blowing wildly behind him, urged his horse forward and leaned down, holding his hand out to him.

"Come up and ride with us, youngling!" he said. "It's time your kind joined our Hunt!"

"No!" another voice thundered, this time from behind him. "He's not for you!"

Again he spun around, his senses reeling, terrified to the core of his being. Where had these alien beings come from? How could their beasts fly through the sky? What did they want with him? A Human figure slid down from one of the beasts, stepping into the circle to join him. Blue robed, his long greying hair blown back from his face, Khyan recognized the old male from the chair.

Striding forward, the elderly male stood between him and the rider, holding his staff before him in both hands. "He's mine, Herne, not the Hunt's. I called him here. He's the Chosen One, he has my protection."

The rider scowled, sitting up and looking to his leader for guidance.

But it was the female with him who commanded Khyan's attention. In all this terrifying nightmare, she was the one being whose mind had touched his. In the brief instant before the Horned One answered, he had time to form but a few thoughts and receive a single answer. Her name.

We have other balefires to visit, other prey to chase. See they're taught the old ways, Merlin.

The Horned One's voice seemed to echo around and around inside Khyan's head as the beasts began to move, circling them faster and faster until all became a meaningless blur and he collapsed senseless to the ground.

Swept up behind the Hunt, their ride had been terrifying yet exhilarating. This was the Old Magic, from the time when the world of Llew was still young. For Merlin, it held faint echoes of his wild ride with Niall's war band. The Hunt had taken them far across the land before returning them to the courtyard, and the boy who would succeed him.

Merlin had almost been prepared for the sight that met his eyes when he finally opened them, but no one else was.

She gasped, scrambling backward until she was at his other side, far from the brown-furred feline that lay on the paving stones beside them.

"What is he? Is he one of the hunters?" she demanded of him as Euan strode over to them.

Merlin laughed gently. "Hush, child. There's no need to fear him. No, he's not from the Hunt."

"How the hell did he get in here?" demanded Euan.

"He came because he's the Chosen One," said Merlin.

"You can't Choose him!" Euan's tone was an equal mixture of shock and outrage. "Have you any idea who that is?"

She looked up at Merlin, confused. "Didn't he see the Hunt?"

"Of course I know who he is!" Merlin said. "I watch the news and read the newspapers. He's the son of the Sholan Ambassador — and my successor. As for me choosing him, I don't Choose! The gods Choose through me. I told you change was coming, but not even I anticipated quite this great a change."

Merlin regarded the unconscious young male critically for a moment. "He's older than usual, quite a lot older, but then they mature later so I've heard." He looked up again at Euan, standing impotent with anger.

"Nothing to say this time, Euan?" he asked. "That's a first. Don't just stand there, man! You've got work to do! Have him taken downstairs then contact his family." He narrowed his eyes, looking beyond him to the woman approaching them. "Briana, dismiss the others and ask Sean to see our new incumbent is taken downstairs. Euan has a call to make to the Sholan legation. We'll wait for you here."

"You can't leave me to deal with this, Merlin," said Euan as Briana nodded and left.

He smiled up at him, eyes glinting with obvious humor. "Oh yes, I can. My schedule doesn't permit me to have anything further to do with you or the College, Euan. I told you that the new Merlin would be more than capable of handling you!" He pointed to the unconscious youth. "He's no child like I was when I was first brought here. Now go and call his family, explain to them the inexplicable — if you can!"

As Euan stormed off muttering and swearing, Merlin relaxed back into his chair. He was tired. Dealing with the Entities always drained him, and Herne was always unpredictable. A hand touched his knee, reminding him she was still there.

"So your minds met, did they?" he asked.

"I didn't say that."

"Yet you know his name," he said gently. "You can't turn your back on him, child. You saw how scared he was. He will need your gentle hand. He'll be your pupil, yours to guide for the future."

"He was brave too," she said. "But I don't know that I can do what you ask." Cautiously, she leaned around him to take another look at the Sholan.

He felt a wave of sadness wash through him as he sensed how she was already being drawn toward the alien youth. "You must. It's up to you now."

Lifting her head, she looked up at him. "Me? What about you?"

"My work is done. All that remains for me to do is give you the last of my memories." He stopped, sensing Sean approaching.

"I mean no disrespect, Merlin, but are you sure he's the one?" Sean asked as he bent down to examine the Sholan.

"I'm sure. Only Chaos could bring about the changes we need to make in order to survive, Sean. And tonight, we rode with Chaos to find him. He is the Merlin, trust me."

"I do, Old One. We'll guard him well, you needn't fear."

Merlin reached out to grasp Sean's shoulder. "I know you will, and in him you'll find a champion against the likes of Euan. They'll be hard pushed to downgrade the magic of the College when the eyes of two worlds are watching them!"

"That's true. Far hail, Old One," Sean said softly before lifting his burden and heading for the apartments below.

Alone again, he gripped her hand tightly for a moment before releasing her. "Now, child, take those last memories from me then I can rest," he said resolutely, locking his feelings for her and his knowledge of his final journey behind a wall she could not penetrate.

When Briana returned, it was over and Merlin sat alone by the fire.

"I'm sorry it took so long," she said, "but I thought it best I reassured the others first."

He nodded, and leaning on his staff, began to push himself out of his chair. Briana reached out a hand to help him but he brushed it away.

"I'm fine," he said. "Just stiff from sitting out here, that's all."

They walked in silence to the far side of the courtyard. He stopped there, turning around for one last look at the College. The smell of wood smoke drifted toward him from the fire pit. Turning abruptly, he pushed the door open and entered the building.

"She'll be fine, Merlin," Briana said, breaking the silence as they made their way down the stairs to the ground floor. "I mixed the drug exactly as you said. She'll remember you only as a dream."

He said nothing, just gripped his staff more tightly. All they'd shared, all she'd felt for him was ebbing away from her mind now, but it was that or have her grieve for him, unable to give the new Merlin the help he'd need. At the vault door, he stopped, waiting for Briana to push her authorization card through the sensor. The door swung slowly open, allowing them into the bare anteroom. He waited at the second door while she sealed them in.

"You have to put your hand in the DNA scanner," she said, indicating a recessed unit at waist height beside the door. "It will only open for you."

He stuck his hand in the opening, jumping slightly when he felt the sting of the sampler.

"Identity confirmed," intoned the computer. "You are authorized to enter."

The locking mechanism clicked loudly. He pushed the door open and stepped inside, momentarily blinded by the intensity of the lighting. The first thing he noticed was the gentle humming that filled the air. As his eyes adjusted, he looked around. The room was circular, its single wall lined with a dozen tall, narrow doors. Set into the wall beside each was a control panel. All were dark save one. On it, the lights showed green. To one side of the entrance stood a console.

As Briana went to the console, Merlin walked over to the active panel, placing his free hand over the door beside it. This was where his predecessor slept.

"Can you dream in cryo?" he whispered to the one within. "Are we allowed the luxury of reliving precious moments? Or are we consigned to a night without end, a living death against a time when they might need us once more?"

He started as the door adjacent to him slid back exposing a transparent cylinder some six feet tall. Mesmerized, he watched as the empty cylinder was propelled smoothly out of its niche into the room.

Llew had died in his bed. Maybe that was preferable, it was at least an ending. This electronically controlled limbo was not. But then, they'd cut Llew's head from his body and hung it above the fire in the College to dry in the belief that in time of trouble, he would speak to them. Automatically, he put his hand to his neck. No, he didn't fancy that either.

A section of the cylinder wall slid back as Briana left the console to join him. He could feel her sadness engulfing him. Blocking it out, he walked unsteadily toward the cryo unit, waiting for her. Impulsively, she flung her arms around him.

"I shall miss you," she said, her voice rough with emotion. "I wish you didn't have to do this."

He patted her back awkwardly. "There can never be two Merlins, Briana. I can best serve the College and our country by doing this. Khyan will have my memories, including these final ones that you take, but if I should be needed again, then I can be wakened." He pushed her away firmly. "Now, let's get this over with," he said.

She sat on a stool by the bed, waiting for Khyan to awaken. While he'd been unconscious, she'd studied him carefully. There was less of the feline about this purple-clad young male than she'd first thought, despite his strange form. His hands were definitely hands, though different from hers. He had hair, long and light brown in color. She'd spread it out carefully on the pillow so that when he woke, he'd not be lying on it. His face was almost human. His nose felt cool on its unfurred tip, and his mouth was bifurcated, but it was a nice face. And his pelt was soft, pleasant to touch. She reached out to stroke his hand once more only to feel it close around hers.

Crying out in shock, she tried to pull back but he held her firm. As their eyes met, so did their minds, bridging once more the barrier of species.

"Nimue," he said. Her hand relaxed in his as the memories began to flow between them — his to her and hers to him — their minds merging, becoming one, linking them together for life.

About the Author

Lisanne Norman was born in Glasgow, Scotland, and has lived in the USA since 2004.

"Strong-willed, independent, a whirlwind, a dreamer, she lives in another world." These phrases followed her around from her earliest days. They were partly right: she had grander plans than a world, though, she was already creating the universe of the Sholan Alliance, where Magic, Warriors, and Science all co-exist.

She began writing when she was eight because she couldn't find enough of the books she liked to read. How difficult can it be to write them myself, she thought with all the confidence of a child. After all, the libraries were full of books. It must be easy.

Real life took over as she entered college and began to work for the first time, but thanks to the constant nagging of two very good friends, one of whom is the sister of her editor, she finished a novel she'd started back in 1979. It was called Turning Point, and her friend's sister at DAW bought it. The Sholan Alliance Series is now nine novels long. She also has several short stories out in DAW anthologies, and one in Defending the Future series number IV, "No Man's Land" called "Valkyries".

The Feline Alliance

Abigail Reilly
Alex Jay Berman
Andrew Kaplan
Andy Holman Hunter
Anthony R. Cardno
Aysha Rehm
Bailey A Buchanan
Barry Nove
Benjamin Adler
bill
Bill & Kelley & Kyle
Brendan Coffey
Brian D Lambert
Brian Klueter
Brooks Moses
Buddy Deal
Caitlin Rozakis
Candi O'Rourke
Carla Spence
Carol J. Guess
Carol Jones
Caroline Westra
Cheri Kannarr
Christine Lawrence
Christine Norris
Christopher Bennett
Christopher J. Burke
Coats Family
Colleen Feeney
Craig "Stevo" Stephenson
Crysella
Dale A Russell

Danielle Ackley-McPhail
Danny Chamberlin
Denise and Raphael Sutton
Doniki Boderick-Luckey
Donna Hogg
Duane Warnecke
E.M. Middel
Ef Deal
Ellen Montgomery
Emily Weed Baisch
Erin A.
"filkertom" Tom Smith
Frank Michaels
Gary Phillips
Gav I
GhostCat
GraceAnne Andreassi
    DeCandido
Greg Levick
Ian Harvey
J.E. Taylor
Jack Deal
Jakub Narębski
James Aquilone
Jamie René Peddicord
Jennifer Hindle
Jennifer L. Pierce
Jeremy Bottroff
Joe Gillis
John Keegan
John L. French
John Markley

Jonathan Haar
Judy McClain
Karen Palmer
KC Grifant
Kelly Pierce
Ken Seed
kirbsmilieu
krinsky
Lark Cunningham
LCW Allingham
Lee
Lee Thalblum
Lisa Kruse
Liz DeJesus and Amber Davis
Lorraine J Anderson
Louise Lowenspets
Lynn P.
Maria V Arnold
Marie Devey
Matthew Barr
Michael A. Burstein
Michael Barbour
Morgan Hazelwood
Mustela
Niki Curtis
Paul Ryan
pjk
Rachel A Brune
Raja Thiagarajan
Reckless Pantalones
Rich Gonzalez
Rich Walker

Richard Fine
Richard Novak
Richard O'Shea
Rigel Ailur
Robert Greenberger
Robert Ziegler
Ronald H. Miller
Ruth Ann Orlansky
Scott Schaper
Shawnee M
Shervyn
Sheryl R. Hayes
Sonia Koval
Sonya M.
Steph Parker
Stephen Ballentine
Stephen W. Buchanan
Steven Purcell
Subrata Sircar
Susan Simko
The Creative Fund by BackerKit
Thomas Bull
Thomas P. Tiernan
Tim Tucker
Tom B.
Tracy Popey
Tracy 'Rayhne' Fretwell
Will "scifantasy" Frank
'Will It Work' Dansicker
William C Tracy
wmaddie700

www.ingramcontent.com/pod-product-compliance
Lightning Source LLC
LaVergne TN
LVHW090817080525
810575LV00001B/17